Hart Island

.

Hart Island

GARY ZEBRUN

THE UNIVERSITY OF WISCONSIN PRESS

Publication of this book has been made possible, in part,
through support from the Brittingham Trust.

The University of Wisconsin Press
728 State Street, Suite 443
Madison, Wisconsin 53706
uwpress.wisc.edu

Gray's Inn House, 127 Clerkenwell Road
London EC1R 5DB, United Kingdom
eurospanbookstore.com

Printed in the United States of America
This book may be available in a digital edition.

Library of Congress Cataloging-in-Publication Data

Names: Zebrun, Gary, author.
Title: Hart Island / Gary Zebrun.
Description: Madison, Wisconsin : The University of Wisconsin Press, 2024.
Identifiers: LCCN 2023041536 | ISBN 9780299348342 (paperback)
Subjects: BISAC: FICTION / Literary | LCGFT: Fiction. | Novels.
Classification: LCC PS3626.E24 H37 2024 |
DDC 813/.6—dc23/eng/20231016
LC record available at https://lccn.loc.gov/2023041536

This is a work of fiction. Names, characters, places, and incidents either
are the product of the author's imagination or are used fictitiously,
and any resemblance to actual persons living or dead, businesses,
companies, events, or locales is entirely coincidental.

For all the lost souls unclaimed
or unwanted at their deaths

It's a very scary thought to be buried and have nobody
know where you are, or not care where you are.

—Miguel Marrero, a former Rikers inmate, on Hart Island burial detail

Contents

Hart Island

Fat Chance

Not much has changed in the bedroom Sal and Justin began to share twenty-five years ago. The bed is here that replaced Sal's twin, the queen that Ida and Francesco hauled down the steps of Justin's house next door and into Sal's room, so small there is barely space for night tables. Today, *The Lives of the Saints* on one stand, *The Perfect Storm* on the other. A CD player is on the floor beside Justin. No room for homework desks, which back then were in the basement next to Francesco's horse-racing memorabilia. The closet is spacious, though, the length of a wall. Gone are Sal's poster of the fedora-clad Michael Jackson doing the Moonwalk and the *Lord of Illusions* movie bill, which was the only keepsake Justin insisted on bringing with him those many years ago. Still above the bed is the crucifix Ida found at the Salvation Army: Christ nailed to a driftwood cross. Blood is dripping from his palms, his side, and his crossed feet. His hair matted around the crown of thorns. His loincloth barely covering his sex. Sal pauses before it, notices the muscles in Jesus's torso and calves cast in the amber light from the garage, and tries to remember the first time he thought Jesus was sexy (what was he, twelve?).

Justin lies asleep with Christ's head tilted over him. Sal can hear Ida sleep-talking, wrestling with her demons, in the room across the hall. Depleted from another night at Mother Pug's, he strips to his boxers. *Shut the fuck up, Mom*, he thinks. Half-hammered, he doesn't want Justin to wake. He doesn't want to talk about drinking too much. He doesn't want to talk about God or love or the priesthood. Or loss or sorrow or desolation. Or redemption. He doesn't want to talk about his father. In a few hours he and Justin will wake up, if they're lucky, in an embrace, with maybe whispers turning to kisses, and maybe a sunrise fuck, or more likely, miles apart. Then a new day will start, and Sal will take the ferry to South Street, not long after Justin heads off to Our Lady Queen of Peace for morning Mass, and Anna arrives to look after Ida.

Sal walks across the hall, his eyes accustomed now to the nightlight darkness, and stands over his mother. She's been sleep-talking lately about the eyes of a wolf she insisted stood outside her bedroom window in Cinisi when she was young, eyes that could kill and that shone in the moonlight. "Who says the Sicilian wolf is extinct? I *see* him, at night," she started saying, out of the blue, in the weeks after Francesco's murder. Had she been mumbling all night? Reliving the sound of gunfire hitting the stoop out front? He stands watching her for a moment, and then rearranges the blanket her restlessness has disturbed.

When he goes back and climbs into bed, Justin stirs. Sal turns on his side and lays his arm over the only man he's ever loved. His head hurts. The clock on the nightstand shines red: 2:28. A half hour ago he had finished last call at Pug's. The horn of the Staten Island Ferry, docking at St. George, echoes over the neighborhood.

Justin takes his hand and whispers, "Try to sleep, Sal." And that is comfort enough for Sal, before he closes his eyes and, finally, gives himself to the night.

∼

"You shouldn't stay at Pug's so late," Justin tells him the next morning. He's at the stove, scrambling eggs.

"Where were you?" Sal pours himself a cup of coffee.

"I didn't feel like pissing away another night there. You're drinking too much."

Sal ignores him and picks up the *Staten Island Advance*. A story about Carlo Cali donating a million dollars for a wing at the Nalitt Cancer Institute. "Fuck Carlo. He hasn't done anything about the Russians."

Justin nods. "He doesn't want a war with them. We should leave this place."

"You're *not* leaving the Church."

"I could." He dishes out a plate of eggs and toast for Sal. "Or I can get a transfer. Somewhere out West, far away from gangsters."

"Like that's going to happen, Just. What about Ida?"

"What about her. She'll be fine wherever we are."

"She won't be fine."

"Jesus, Sal, you never used to be so hopeless."

"If you haven't noticed, there's not much to cheer about."

Justin turns away and mutters, "Christ."

"You should have been at Pug's. You could have done last rites. Some guy was soaking up tequila—who drinks tequila at Pug's?—shot after

4

shot. He started ranting about immigrants: Mexicans, Africans, Jews. No one ever saw him before. Like there are any Jewish immigrants crossing the border. A few assholes from Ladder 44 invited him over, but on his way the guy passed out. They couldn't revive him."

"He was dead?"

"Maybe, if we're lucky."

"Nice, Sal."

Sal finishes the eggs and gives Justin a kiss. "Don't worry. I'm going to get things together."

"Father Damien from Buffalo is spending the day at the rectory. He's saying morning Mass. I'll stay with Ida today and give Anna a break. Why don't you come straight home tonight? I'll help Ida cook something special, her pasta alla Norma."

"We'll see."

"She didn't sleepwalk last night."

"That's something."

"I'm telling you, leaving this place would do her a lot of good. She won't even look at the front stoop."

"Jesus, Justin, I don't want to go over this again."

Justin runs some water on the dishes in the sink. "It's not like Hart Island is going to cheer you up."

"Why? What's wrong with the island?"

"You're hauling corpses," Justin reminds him.

"Hey, you're a priest, there's life after death, right?"

"Go ahead and mock me. What else is new," Justin says glumly.

Sal, slightly chastened, gives him another kiss and shrugs. "Well, maybe it won't be a bad week."

"Fat chance," Justin says as he watches Sal head off.

Rikers Angels

The five pine coffins stacked in the NYC Department of Corrections refrigerated truck are waiting to be transferred to *Vesuvius*'s main deck, a light load for the week's first haul of the city's discarded dead. Four days a week New York City's deserted are hauled onto the ferry at City Island dock: the indigent or unclaimed, stillborn babies, bodies and their dissected parts that had been donated to medical and mortuary schools under the one condition that cadavers and their remains would not be burned. The pine boxes were tagged in black marker with a name, if one was known, and a number: Today's funereal cargo: Jamaal James 042301, Female Unknown 042302, Sally Winston 042303, Male Unknown 042304, Abraham Eisenberg 042305.

Back at the city's Office of Chief Medical Examiner, each body had been photographed. A clerk also filed physical details reported by police or medical staff at the time of their deaths or when they were discovered cold and rotting—sex, height, hair, eyes, other features such as tattoos or unusual moles, age if known. Personal histories a blank slate, except for the manner and whereabouts of the deaths for victims, or the foredoomed who had met violent or suspicious ends: shot in the head, knifed, drowned in the East and Hudson rivers or a hotel bathtub, run over on the West Side Highway and FDR, discovered naked and stone cold in the thickets of Central Park. Suicides, too. Occasionally a body is exhumed, identified, and claimed by someone who loved and lost a brother, sister, uncle, father, mother, son. Or there could be a rare cold case call for DNA evidence, a break in the history of the city's unsolved homicides.

Sal Cusumano arrives ahead of the Rikers crew. He opens the gate and stops before the coffins in the morgue truck. The guy in the cab waves and opens the window. "Hey, Sal. I'm retiring today. My last run. Just five boxes."

"Retiring?"

"Yeah, thirty years running trucks for the city, ten years to Hart. I'm moving to Florida. We bought a trailer home in Key Largo. Pelican Cay. There's a palm tree right next to it. I'm getting a boat. I'm thinking of naming her *Fuck the Bronx*."

"No shit, George. You never said." He puts down a tray of coffees that he had brought from Clipper's.

"Family secret until today."

"The Sunshine State. Beware of the rising tides." He hands George a coffee.

"I figure Moe and me will be dead before the great flood. And hurricanes, well, we figure it's about time we took risks. I'm sorry about your father, Sal. I meant to tell you that a while ago but, you know, it's awkward."

Sal can't stand others bringing up Francesco. "Well, don't talk about it then."

"Moe tells me every day, no one's a saint."

"Gotta go, George. Just beware, I read somewhere about Florida, you think you've got forever, and it's a mile wide and an inch deep and full of alligators."

George sips his coffee and gives Sal a bewildered look. Sal pats him on the shoulder and turns toward *Vesuvius* and the Sound.

Inside the ferry Sal leans against the handrail at the back of the wheelhouse and sees the DOC bus come through the gate and pull up to the dock. Officer Mary Hemins is driving, her head barely reaching above the steering wheel. James Booker, the DOC sergeant in charge of the burial detail and all matters small and large on Hart Island, is first down the steps. He looks as breezy as his charges, five Rikers inmates. Sal watches as they place their sacks on the deck, all filled with lunch and water, some with paperbacks and magazines, and packs of cigarettes. "Hey, Cappy," Jesús Riboul says, almost singing, waving to Sal, "ain't it a kick-ass mornin', just five in the icebox. There be chillin' on the island today, baby."

Sal nods.

Booker says, "All right guys, get those coffins aboard *Vesuvius*."

"You the man, boss," Jesús says, and the other inmates follow.

The five Potter's Field gravediggers—Class A misdemeanor offenders slapped with nine months with good behavior—were chosen by Booker, who has an eye for ferreting out trouble. Booker is more preacher than enforcer, though he's tough, and if an inmate on burial detail crosses the line, no second chances. Few ever do, because Hart Island is a day pass out of Rikers' hellhole, where everyone is a skell and no one has a name, where some psycho guard, ready to beat the lights out of anyone for no good reason, calls out a number or just yells, "Body, get your fuckin' ass over here." Take Jesús, who got shit-faced at Lucky You dive and crashed his car into a bodega storefront in Queens. Jesús isn't going to give Booker or DOC Officer Mary Hemins a lick of trouble. Neither is Al Sims, whose mistake was to send a twelve-year-old kid on an errand to buy a stash of Georgia Homeboy; not Franklin Watts, who was so stupid in love with his ex-girlfriend that he broke a no-contact order five times and finally drew a judge who had no patience; not Zookie Jones, who year after year tagged buildings along the High Line until a judge said enough is enough; and not Jason Fitzgerald, the only white guy, who bought the purple passion that a frat boy pledge swallowed. He never expected the poor schmuck would jump from an NYU dormitory.

The crew knows they're lucky because Hart Island's dead don't moan and shriek as Rikers' skells do at night, don't awake in the morning with their fists clenched ready to break a nose, don't brandish batons that could crack a rib and land you breathless on the floor in a single blow. New York City's unwanted dead, more than a million strong now, are serene in mass graves where today's sea breeze wafts over them and the sun warms the earth. And when these inmates return to Rikers, these road dogs are the Trusted Five, assigned to assist in quarters reserved mostly for those who need protection—famous or notorious or just filthy rich inmates with pull awaiting transfer or bail or trial, men like Rikers alums Tupac Shakur, Sid Vicious, David Berkowitz, and Mark David Chapman. There, at Stoney Lonesome, the Hart crew delivers chow trays to the solitary cages, and then they hunker down in the same row of cells, their own car. The grave-diggers are close enough to gen pop to hear the incessant barks and shrieks from other cells, but distant enough, too, so they can sleep most nights.

"Two to a box, guys, let's get moving," Booker says.

Jesús and Zookie are the first ones on deck. "Man, this dude's some minivan. How'd he fit inside?" Zookie asks.

"Bet he got mongo FUPA," Jesús says.

"Not for much longer," Zookie says.

At the wheelhouse, Sal hears the men joking and nods as they lug the oversized box, Male Unknown 042304, onto the deck. He knows they aren't being disrespectful to the dead because later, after the coffins are placed in the trench and covered with plywood sheets for the night, the crew will huddle and look down silently until someone says something—a prayer, a goodbye, a last word. Then the inmates will head off to mowing burial fields, cutting overgrowth, and eventually, if there is time as there surely will be today, stretching their tackle until the trip back to Rikers.

Al and Jason haul the last coffin on board, Sally Winston 042303, her weight inconsequential. "She's as light as the shoeboxes," Jason says.

The shoeboxes—the tiny pine boxes—are hard on everyone. Not even as big as a grapefruit crate. Sal calls them the *little people*, babies who die in dumpsters or in the arms of maternity nurses. Their mothers unknown, or impoverished and aggrieved, or so zeroed out on drugs they don't know a city burial means a trench containing a thousand babies. Sal winces when he hears the crew talking about them, remembering it's been a rare string of days since he's ferried a dead baby to the island. Some days, babies outnumber the other dead. Sal nods and thinks, *Fuck, Jason, why'd you have to go and mention a shoebox.*

Mary Hemins joins him on the top deck. "Booker heard the college boy."

They watch the sergeant pivot on his heels and stare Jason down. "Don't test me," he warns.

The infants buried on the island hit Booker the hardest because he remembers his only child, Jasper, who got sepsis and died two days after his birth. Booker's wife, Mary Lou, hooked on heroin, died of AIDS a year after the boy was born. During the epidemic the number of babies buried on Hart Island soared. Booker wasn't in charge of Potter's Field then. He was still a cowboy DOC officer at Rikers, when Jasper, according to a nurse, *expired* in his mother's arms. Booker saw how AIDS ravaged his wife and Rikers inmates, hundreds with unbearable coughs and fevers and sarcoma lesions over their necks, arms, chests, and legs. He couldn't hate his wife—she was only sixteen when another kid from Hunts Point took her to Alphabet City. When Booker met her three years later at Ebenezer Pilgrim Holiness in the Bronx, Mary Lou told him she'd been clean for six months, but the "D," as she called "Downtown," lured her back to the Lower East Side on evenings he was guarding junkies. He couldn't hate her even though he wanted to.

Every year on the day Jasper died, he goes alone to the southern tip of the island where the baby trenches are dug. Sal told him long ago if it's a day *Vesuvius* isn't ferrying coffins the sergeant could count on him for the sail. "A short crossing," he told Booker. "It's easy, you've got a ride." There at the baby burial site on every anniversary of his own son's death, Booker prays before the island's only solitary marker, "SC-B1 1985," for the first AIDS infant buried on Hart Island. Just beyond densely forested poison sumac and shadbush trees that twist and snake their way toward the sun, the unclaimed baby is entombed under fourteen feet of earth, deeper than any pine box in any trench anywhere. The AIDS panic reached even this lonely island. Now these decades later, Booker believes this singular marker for the little lost soul is a memorial to all babies who die suddenly, sons like his own Jasper. Hauling the little ones to their graves is a kind of penance for all that he couldn't do to save his boy. There are days on Hart Island when Booker doesn't want to be reminded of the son he lost before he had the chance to even know him, so he tells Hemins to take the baby detail alone, and she nods, not eager for the assignment to lead the crew to the forlorn southern tip. Sympathetic to the sergeant's loss, she doesn't complain.

Jason doesn't know what he's done wrong and whispers he's sorry. The sergeant, if he heard him, ignores the apology and lumbers up the ramp to *Vesuvius*.

Franklin, who tended ferries at the South Street terminal before he got sent away, prepares the boat to cast off. He grabs Jesús and Zookie while everyone else climbs the ramp to the deck. Sal was surprised he didn't have to train Franklin, who knows boats inside out. Right away he put the inmate in charge of docking and undocking the ferry. Franklin checks to see that Zookie and Jesús have cast off the stern, spring, and bow lines. "We ready," Jesús says, as he unhitches the last line from its cleat and hops onto the deck with Franklin and Zookie. "Clear," shouts Franklin as he fist-bumps the two dock hands. Hemins comes down with the tray of Clipper coffees.

"You the man," Jesús shouts up to Sal. "Worm juice, just like we like 'em."

Sal sends them a thumbs-up and the inmates fill the bench across from the coffins. Hemins sits on a stack of pine boxes near the gunwale and gives the crew a look. She's five foot six, maybe 120 pounds, tops, and no matter the weather, winter or summer, she wears the dark blues of NYC Corrections. She replaces the city-issued DOC cap with a vintage Yankees hat, creamy white with red pinstripes and the NY team logo dead center. She doesn't carry a gun and holds her baton more like a plaything than a weapon. Shaking her head at the inmates, Hemins taps her heavy black shoes against the front of a pine box while the inmates who notice stare back, kind of goofy, like the small-fry offenders they are. Booker walks to the bow, leans forward on the rail, and with his mind's eye, a sailor at heart, he charts a dead reckoning to the island. He listens to the ferry's deep signal horn echoing over the channel where the East River becomes Long

Island Sound. He feels its impressive hull plowing the water, which on this windless morning lazily laps back portside against the boat. He thinks it's good to be alive. There are days, though, when *Vesuvius* seems to want on its own to pull back, tired of hauling so much day after day. But today she's as content as the morning is blue and bright and curiously calm.

~

Sal turns and watches the houses of City Island recede, mostly aging clapboard cottages, the kind you'd find everywhere in old New England fishing villages, so different from his family's Staten Island brick split level. He moved back there after leaving the Coast Guard, the house with its five-hundred-pound rose stone lion next to the front stoop that his father installed the summer before the old man was murdered. When Sal asked, *Why a lion?* Francesco described a museum in Palermo with a room dedicated to the lions of the island's conquerors: Greeks, Romans, Normans, Arab emirs. "The lion," he said, "has courage like no other animal. The lion will guard our home, Sal. You'll see." *So much for myths*, Sal thinks. He turns back to the open water and Hart Island in the distance while everything that nags about life in the boroughs and his father's murder mercifully ebbs into the prospect of docking once more on the mile-long strip of land shaped like a miniature boot of Italy. It's been home to the forgotten since 1869 when Louisa Van Slyke, who died of smallpox in the city's Charity Hospital, was buried in its sandy earth.

Sal surprised everyone when he left the Coast Guard for the NYPD ferry crew. After he graduated from the academy, he trained in intelligence and became a lieutenant assigned to drug enforcement. The Coast Guard believed that Sal's father's connection to the Gambino family presented an advantage. Sal was the good son, according to law enforcement and Mafia folklore. He'd be a dogged enforcer. They figured that his father was just a low-level bookie for the mob. Few knew Francesco was closer to the boss, Carlo Cali, than any ordinary bookmaker. Sal himself didn't know the half of it. In Sicily, Carlo was like a brother to Francesco's father. One evening after having an espresso in La Vucciria, where they teased and wolf-whistled at girls, the boyhood friends walked arm in arm to the Piazza di San Domenic. Nicola Cusumano noticed a rival gangster hiding behind the Column of the Immaculate Conception. Francesco's father, pushing his friend to the ground, took the bullet meant for Carlo. Nicola died in his friend's arms, and a month later when Francesco was born, Carlo, who'd eventually lead the Gambino crew in New York, became Francesco's godfather. He cradled the infant boy while the priest poured holy water over his head at the baptismal font in the Church of Santa Ninfa dei Crocifer. "Sono tuo padre adesso," Carlo whispered in his ear, and then kissed the boy's forehead. Ever since, Carlo has trusted Sal's father more than his own son. Francesco was born to be his godfather's consigliere.

Francesco started out handling the racetracks and bookies. He was smart and charming. He never went to college, but he understood economics. After dapper John Gotti went to prison, Francesco explained that the business had to change. It needed to get off the radar of the feds. It had to go underground. He had an idea: The stack-them-up model. Let's say, he told his godfather, you start an events company. You know, the business that runs parties for the super-rich or conferences for whiz-kid entrepreneurs. You make sure you own the bakery where you get the sweets, the liquor store that supplies the fuel, the catering house that makes the food, the grocery, and fish and meat markets, too. Then you charge whatever you want. You own it all, so you don't just get a take of each part. If someone asks you for a quote because he wants to shop around, then you put a little pressure on him. You tell him something like, *You know, my uncle is John Gotti's brother.* You let some clients go. It's good for business. Shows you're reasonable and weigh all the different circumstances. In a good economy, there's plenty of business to go around. No need to be greedy. The stack-them-up model. Cali loved it. So did the other four family bosses.

Sal's superior in Homeland Security used to joke about his father's mob connection. "You could-a been a contender on Mulberry Street," he'd say in a raspy Brando knockoff. "You could-a been a boss." Sal would smile, even though he'd be cringing inside. When he was too young to know what was really going on, Sal overheard Francesco telling Antony he didn't want his sons to be part of the *family business.* Antony gave his father a look that said, *Like try to stop me.* Sal worshiped his older brother when he was a kid, but even then, unlike Antony, he didn't want anything to do with the "uncles" Francesco met in Little Italy and who sometimes sat around their kitchen table, guys with nicknames like John "No Nose" DiFronzo. Sal would see a gun tucked under the belt at an uncle's back and worry. He was glad he could leave the house to play with Justin. Ida would watch on his way out and smile, relieved this one son would take another path.

If Sal were going to be discharged from the Guard, he always believed it would be because someone thought he was a plant for the Gambino family. He never imagined he'd be given the choice to leave or be forced out because he's gay. He had tried so hard to be careful. "Sal, we've got this information. It isn't good. Jeez, your own brother," his commander said. "Adopted brother," Sal told him. "Justin is my adopted brother." The report detailed a night he and Justin spent at a bar in the Village. It was the only time they'd gone to a gay bar since Sal entered the academy and Justin the seminary. They had seen a reprise of *Jesus Christ Superstar*. Sal had already given up on Jesus, but he wanted to please Justin. After the show, in a dark corner of the bar, Justin, uncharacteristically drunk, his libido supercharged, said, "Judas was a giant gay hot mess, wasn't he? A lot like you." Sal laughed, and, usually more constrained in his public affection, he leaned into an embrace. And then Justin sang, so softly only Sal could hear, and he felt his lover's breaths like silk on his cheeks, as Justin mixed his own words with lyrics from the play: *I never thought I'd come to this. You're a man, you're just a man, I don't know how to love Him like you. I want you so.* They kissed and kissed again and kissed again. Sal thought of denying it to his commander, but he didn't. He thought of lying and saying the report is wrong, that he kissed Justin the way Italian brothers or *paisanos* do. It was 2010, and "Don't Ask, Don't Tell" was still the policy. In some cases, a fabricated story might have flown, even if the brass didn't believe it. But an intelligence officer in Homeland Security? Sal knew he was too compromised to be tolerated.

Days after the interview he left the Guard, *honorably*. No need for a public scandal, his superior had told him. It's rare for an officer to end active duty at twenty-eight years old, long before qualifying for a pension, unless he is hit with something like incurable cancer or commits a major crime. Or, apparently, gets caught kissing his adopted brother in a dark corner of a gay bar. Certainly no one leaves after just six years out of the academy to command a lowly New York Harbor ferry. Sal didn't know until the morning when he arrived for duty assignment that, of all the city boats on the harbor and Long Island Sound, he would be given *Vesuvius*. Justin called him Charon on the River Styx. He gave Sal a packet of coins on the first day he took command of the ferry. "The dead won't make it to the afterlife unless they pay," Justin said. "You're a strange Catholic," Sal told him.

～

Booker climbs the ladder to the wheelhouse and pats Sal on the shoulder. "Thanks for the coffee. You okay? You look like you were lost in something."

"We're all lost, Book, don't you know."

Booker shakes his head. "Another late night, Mr. Philosopher? You gotta get more sleep. I read in the *Daily News* on the drive from Rikers that people once they turn forty who don't find seven, eight hours are three times more likely to get dementia."

Sal gives him a look.

"Jeez, I wasn't thinking. How's your mother?"

"Still lost. She doesn't know what she's doing."

"Who knows why we do what we do sometimes."

"It's not the why, it's the what." Sal doesn't want to think about Ida, not now. He says, "It's George's last day."

"Yeah, he told me. Shithead kept it a secret. We could have gotten him something. Maybe sunglasses or a straw hat."

"Only five on deck. That's strange. We're in for a bad stretch. I got a feeling."

"You worry too much, Sal. I remember the days of AIDS. Corpses were stacked up like cordwood. That was hell."

Sal isn't interested in hearing Booker talk about *the bad old days*. He had charted the course, a straight line east to Hart Island. He engages the autopilot and bends down and fishes the flask of Jameson from his backpack.

"Here you go, Book. Take this, a little Irish." He pours some into the sergeant's coffee and then more than a little in his own.

"It's early, ain't it. Heck, no one's watching. Fuck it." Booker takes a sip.

"The guys are jauntier than usual," Sal says. *Jauntier*, he thinks, *where the hell did that come from?*

"I heard Jesús say they had some prison hooch last night."

Sal raises his coffee like a toast. "You think Fitz is going to fit in?"

"College boy hasn't learned how to suffer yet, but he's on his way, I think."

The sun blasts out of a patch of mountainous clouds.

"It's like a diamond in the sky," Booker says. "Kind of like God's work."

"You believe in God?"

"Does a born-again pray?"

"Tell you the truth, I don't see you as evangelical. You don't seem like any I've known."

Booker rolls his eyes. "Look, Catholic boy. You live, you die, then you live again. It's blues and jazz, the improvisation doesn't end after you die either."

"You should have been a preacher, Book. Me, I've moved from Heaven and Hell to agnostic, north of it now."

"I've seen that string around your neck." Booker reaches under Sal's collar and pulls up a scapular. "Looks religious to me."

Sal smiles, kissing the image of Mary sewn onto it. "On the loop down my back there's another square with the Immaculate Heart of Mary, pierced with a dagger."

"Why'd you kiss it?"

"It's what you do. Believers say it saves them from hell. Me, it's like kissing the dice before rolling them, 'OK, give me a little luck, Mary.'"

"Your brother the priest must not like to hear that. It's like sacrilegious."

"Adopted brother. He was *adopted*, and he knows better than to try to save my soul." Not wanting to talk about Justin, Sal says, "You thought at all about last week?"

Booker massages his forehead between his eyebrows. "First time I ever saw a detective tag along on a burial."

Sal looks out at Hart Island, a little sharper now as *Vesuvius* moves closer.

"All the poor suckers that day unknown, too," Booker goes on.

"The guy wasn't sharing, that's for sure. Maybe there was a corpse he wanted to make sure got buried," Sal says.

Booker, taking off his DOC cap and running his fingers through his curly flattop, says, "Five nameless chumps. I used to think, no rhyme, no reason for these dead. You know, *fate*. But there's gotta be a reason."

"Maybe the reason just is they didn't have anyone who cared."

"Nah, there's always someone somewhere, even broken people find love with broken people." Booker shrugs, pats Sal on the shoulder and returns to the main deck.

∼

Bronx-bound drivers turning the curve of Throgs Neck Bridge can see *Vesuvius* approaching Hart Island; later, people with binoculars walking their dogs on the shore at Orchard Beach would be close enough to watch the crew unloading coffins. The city bought the island for $75,000 in 1868, and the earth's been opened to the dead ever since. The pine boxes and their corpses, none of them embalmed, decompose in thirty or forty years, depending on the vicissitudes of weather, the winds and rains, humidity and heat, the nature of the soil recharged season by season. The oldest trenches can be opened again, providing perpetual burial ground. A mass grave—fifteen feet wide and eight feet deep—holds 150 adult corpses, their coffins stacked one on top of another, three high and three or four across, depending on the number of extra-wide pine boxes that contain the heaviest corpses. A single white stone, or more recently just a three-foot white PVC pipe, marks each mass grave. Because the earliest records are sketchy no one knows exactly how many people are buried on the island but it's certain the remains of more than a million have been entombed.

For centuries Hart Island was uninhabited, until the Union seized it for a prison for Confederate soldiers. Since then, it's been home to yellow fever victims, an old folks' prison for men, tuberculosis hospital for women, reformatory for boys, a Navy barracks for court-martialed servicemen, prison for three German U-boat sailors, a Nike missile base during the Cold War, a Phoenix House for addicts, even a proposed amusement park for "Negro boys." "The Negro Coney Island" was built but never saw a visitor on a Ferris wheel or boardwalk. The city shut it down and razed its buildings because the DOC feared "temptations" like contraband or escape boats. Through all these incarnations, the island has remained the Potter's Field for New Yorkers who take their last breaths alone, without money to pay for a funeral and, for many, without anyone ever knowing they've died.

Sal picks a spider's web strand from his forehead and fishes out the flask from his knapsack. He takes a swig and slips it back in, all the time keeping his eye on the Sound, regaining control from the autopilot, and steering the ferry closer to Hart. He hides the flask from Justin because he's promised as a first step that he wouldn't take the whiskey onboard the ferry anymore. "You're drinking too much" has been Justin's refrain ever since Francesco was slain. Putting the flask back in his sack, Sal thinks, *It's getting easier and easier to lie, even to Justin.*

Any boat, big or small, can run into trouble around Hart Island. Navigation charts warn sailboats and ships of the swirling currents and jagged rocks through Hell Gate Passage. The shoreline is carpeted with dangerous mudflats and other shallows strewn with submerged rocks, some so sharp they can open holes in a small boat's hull. Fluke burrow into the rocky black bottom. Every year the landing path is dredged to allow the DOC ferry to navigate the slip's walls that extend out like enormous arms to embrace *Vesuvius*. Sal doesn't tire of berthing the ferry between the rubber rollers, which guide the boat to the dock. It feels familiar, the way going home from CYO basketball practice used to, walking down the steep driveway, side by side with Justin, standing at the garage entry and hearing Sinatra or Crosby filling the house while his father looked through race cards from Aqueduct. Antony, if he were home, might be nursing some boxing wound, which everyone knew was a knuckle hit in the face or fist in his ribs from a street or bar brawl. His mother always in the kitchen cooking onion-laden sauce or something else Sicilian.

Franklin and his docking mates jump up and tie the ropes to the pilings at the stern and then wrap the others around the starboard and portside cleats. Franklin shouts, "Moored," and Sal cuts the engine, creating for a second, before anyone says another word, a stillness that he imagines must be like the first moment of peace a dead man knows.

Booker checks his watch and says, loud enough the others can hear: "10:30, a half hour off schedule. Let's run a tight ship today."

"You practicing sea terms again, boss? Remember, we've just got five boxes today," Hemins says, unusually cheerful.

She walks over to get the DOC truck parked near a weathered statue of an angel, while Booker and the inmates wait on the landing to unload the coffins from the boat and transfer them to the truck. Everyone looks up at an Air Canada Airbus flying over the island.

"Close," Al says.

"Never been to Canada," Jesús says.

"They speak French in Montreal," Franklin says. "My girlfriend whispered French when she wanted me. She'd say, *Cheri, fuck moi.*"

Booker says, "You're supposed to be forgetting that lady."

"When I was a kid," Zookie says, "I wanted to be a pilot, you know, those Top Gun dudes." He shoots up his arm at a steep angle like a Tomcat lifting off a runway. "Taggin' was second choice."

"Look at youse now," Jesús says.

"Fuck, look at you," Zookie says.

"Yeah," Al says, "look at all our sorry asses."

~

Jason turns away and walks to the visitors' gazebo. The DOC built it not long ago after relatives won the right to graveyard visits. There, during a service, the new Rikers chaplain, a Buddhist, usually reads something from an appropriate scripture—Christian, Jewish, Muslim—maybe a poem if he knows the departed was an unbeliever. His favorite farewell: *Every single moment we're undergoing birth and death. This is the way things are.* The chaplain told Jason that the dead aren't trapped in the earth forever; some migrate to other incarnations until the cycle of birth and death ceases. In that moment, the energy of one's existence achieves Nirvana. It's the end of karma, those moral or immoral actions that drive the consequences of each new life slipping into one after another. Jason told the chaplain that he's imagined the fraternity pledge stepping out of his battered body where he plummeted to the pavement on Ninth Street. His soul wandering the West Village, searching for a new vessel: Another student stumbling out of a bar on Bleecker Street. A cop entering the arch at Washington Square Park. A Labrador lumbering ahead of its owner talking on a cellphone on Christopher Street. He told the chaplain that he wished he had known the pledge better.

Jason walks to a weathered stone memorial beside the gazebo. He looks over to rows of grave markers, and then, squatting down, he reads aloud the last lines of the stone's inscription: *He must have loved them / He made so many of them.*

"Hey, college boy, don't stray too far," Booker shouts.

Jason says so low he can barely hear his own words, "What did I do?" as he heads back to the landing, even more hangdog than usual.

~

Sal is the first to hear the boom. Two quick blasts across the sky bouncing off the water, and in the distance, the Lear jet flying closer. Its two engines flame out and spew black plumes. The jet goes soundless, struggling to hold a glide, nose slightly down.

Sal shouts, "Booker, shit, get the crew aboard."

Hemins steps out of the truck. "What's happening?" Then everyone sees it just before the belly of the fuselage strikes the surface with one gargantuan cannonball splash. The plane stops dead.

Sal blows five rapid blasts on the horn to signal emergency and, with the crew aboard, rushes to the crash site. He radios the Coast Guard and says *Vesuvius* will reach the plane in a few minutes. It's intact and drifting; it's not sinking, he says.

The dispatcher asks, "Do you have a crew?"

"Yes, the Hart Island burial detail from Rikers: five inmates, two DOC officers, and me."

"Burial detail?"

"No joke."

Sal tells Franklin and Jason to ready the lifeboat while Hemins and the other inmates fetch the cradle and drape it over the starboard gunwale. Franklin and Jason, who was a lifeguard in high school, are lowered to the water, while Booker scans the scene with binoculars and reports that there are five people, including two young boys and an old woman, on the wing.

The pilot, who is in the water, swims to the lifeboat. He says they hit birds. Not long after, everyone is safe aboard it.

"It's a miracle," Booker says, watching everything unfold.

"It's a rescue," Sal says.

The brothers, twins, huddle together while the pilot drapes his blanket around the boys. "It's okay," he tells them. "It's okay."

Jason, who was in the water the longest helping the survivors aboard, is shivering next to the twins. One boy takes his hand, while their mother is comforting her husband, who'd cut his leg on the wing. A Coast Guard Jayhawk appears and circles overhead. Approaching the ferry, Franklin shouts that the father has a bad gash in his thigh. He takes a towel and ties it around the wound with his belt. The wife tears up and huddles with her sons. The old woman, covered in blankets, seems catatonic. Sal on the bullhorn tells them to place him in the cradle first, and Booker, Hemins, and the inmates pull the netting up to the rail and lift him onto the deck. Sal radios the Jayhawk, and the Guard lowers a basket onto *Vesuvius*. Hemins removes the towel, wraps gauze around the wound, and tightens a tourniquet before he's lifted off the ferry. The others one by one are hauled aboard. "Where's Dad going?" one boy shouts.

Hemins says, "The helicopter is taking him to the hospital to fix his leg."

"He was bitten by a shark," the other boy says.

"No, he wasn't," his brother cries out.

Their mother pulls them close. "Dad's going to be okay."

"What's happening, Laurie?" her mother-in-law mutters.

Sal radios the Coast Guard that the survivors are aboard the ferry.

"Great job," the dispatcher says. "Making Rikers proud."

Jesús hears this and gives a thumbs-up.

Sal tells the dispatcher he's on his way to City Island. Safe onboard, he says, is the Klock family from Minneapolis and the pilot. The father, though, with an injured leg, is on the helicopter. The grandmother is disoriented. The dispatcher tells him that there will be an EMS bus at the dock to take them to Montefiore Med.

One twin points to the coffins and asks, "What's those?"

Hemins tells them they're boxes. Nodding to their mother, she asks the twins, "So, what are your names, kiddos?"

"Dumb and dumber," the other boy says. "That's what our dad likes to call us sometimes."

Their mother smiles.

"Carey and Daniels, that movie was a blast," Hemins says. The boys give her a look.

The grandmother stands up. She drifts a few feet here and a few feet there like she's forgotten what she's looking for.

"Eleanor, come back here," Laurie says.

"Where's Peter?"

"On his way to the hospital," Hemins says. "He's going to be fine. No worries."

"I don't know where I am," the old woman says.

"Don't you remember? The plane crashed. It was remarkable how these guys appeared," Laurie says.

"Peter's dead." The old woman begins to weep.

"Daddy's dead?" the twins ask. They're crying, too.

"He's not dead," their mother says. "Eleanor, he just hurt his leg."

"Hank is dead?" she asks.

"He's been dead for years."

The old woman is chewing on her lip. "I was never on a plane."

Hemins guides Eleanor to a bench across from the pine boxes and sits beside her. The twins, crouching nearby with their mother, regard their grandmother warily.

In the wheelhouse Sal, who overheard the conversation below, grimaces. "Fuckin' dementia," he says.

Booker and the crew gather around the survivors on the main deck while Sal turns the ferry around to head back to City Island.

"Shit, we is lucky," Jesús says.

The pilot pats him on the back.

Booker goes over to Jason, who's wrapped in a blanket and sitting on the deck by the engine room. "You okay?"

Jason looks up, his eyes wet. His lips still blue from the sea. All that is visible under the blanket is his head.

"You did good, college boy," Booker says.

"After the last person was lifted out of the raft, I looked at the sky and saw the pledge plummeting into the water. It was like he was there."

"No time for that now, Jason. Like I said, you did good. Doing good means something."

College boy shakes his head. "Then why don't I feel so good."

Booker pats him on the shoulder and walks off to the wheelhouse.

"How's Jason?" Sal asks. "He was in the water a long time."

"He's down there crouching by the engine room and blaming himself."

"For what?"

"He's thinking about the pledge."

"I get it."

"You do?"

"When you're *really* sorry about something terrible you did, you never stop blaming yourself. You don't ever feel worthy, no matter what good you end up doing."

Booker mutters, *Guilt-ridden Catholics*, and goes back down to keep Jason company.

On the way to the City Island dock, when *Vesuvius* passes Hart, Jesús turns to the pilot and says, "Good thing we was there."

"All those dilapidated buildings and white markers. You were there? What's the story?"

"That our island, and today we was angels on the water."

Zookie nods. "You don't have to worry. Rikers angels won't let you die, not today. Isn't that right, Jesús?"

"Hundo Po," Jesús says.

The Right Trigger

By the time the 5 train pulls into Bowling Green, it is early evening. Sal had already talked to his mother, to Justin, to newspaper reporters; he'd been interviewed by local TV stations and CNN. Even his brother, Antony, who hasn't called or stopped by the house since December when their father was killed, left him a message: "Fuck, Sal. Never thought you'd be a hero."

On the escalator at the station, his phone breaks into the Beatles' "Blackbird." It's his mother calling for the fourth time. She's having a rare, animated day.

"I saw you on TV. You were with Jesus."

"Jesús, Mom. J-e-s-ú-s. The J is like an H in Spanish. You don't hear it."

"Not like the Son of God?"

"Not really."

"Justin's here."

"Let him explain it to you."

"You're famous."

"Ha."

"A hero."

"I'm still nobody, Mom."

"I like the redhead."

"That was Jason. He did most of the work in the water."

"Justin was there?"

"No, Ma. The kid's name is Jason."

"He let *Hey Zeus* do the talking."

"Jason's the quiet type."

"Ask him over for pasta and sauce."

"That's not happening, Ma. He's in jail."

"A good white boy?"

Justin takes the phone before she can hear Sal say, "Racist, Ma."

"Sorry about the father," Justin says.

"What about him?"

"You don't know? He died."

"That's crazy. He had a leg wound."

Sal's mother takes the phone. "I made pasta e fagioli."

"You made pasta alla Norma, Ida," Justin says.

"Mom. I'm tied up with the boat." Any excuse. It doesn't matter.

"I made manicotti."

Sal shakes his head. "I'll heat it up later."

"Your father's going to set you straight." She starts to cry. *"Fanculo,"* she says, which signals she's spiraling out, just like that, without a warning.

He hears Justin say, "Ida, give me the phone."

"She's gone to the couch. I turned on *Wheel of Fortune.* That'll calm her. You okay?"

"You're kidding, right?"

"That rescue was a miracle."

Sal pauses and wonders if Justin really believes that. "Fuck miracles, Just. Talk to the dead father and his family about miracles."

"Why so angry? You on the way home?"

"I can't deal with Ma tonight."

Annoyed, Justin says, "When is tonight any different."

"You're right. I'm sorry. I miss him."

"We all do, Sal. I'll see you at Mother Pug's after I get Ida in bed and finish the hospital calls. We've got to talk."

"We shouldn't leave her alone anymore."

"Anna's coming over."

"Give her a Lunesta. That'll knock her out," Sal says, thinking about the Sicilian wolf eyes in her head.

Ida has been forgetting things for years: the names of cousins, neighbors, TV shows, actors, singers, and places she and Francesco had been. At first, a single lost memory here and there would, if she gave it time, surface right before she was about to give up on it. For a while she would go in and out of awareness as casually as flipping channels on a remote. Now, most days she's in a fog, with a rare burst of animation, as if she's reclaiming herself. The doctor calls it a "sanity storm." He thinks the depth of her retreat comes from the shock of seeing her husband slaughtered on the front stoop. An emotional-trauma-induced response. He said it might be temporary, maybe weeks, or a month. Or sometimes a trauma in the elderly intensifies old-age dementia, which has been skulking in a brain, waiting for *the right trigger,* those were his words, to unleash it irreversibly.

And then it happens, the memory of the doctor's phrase, *the right trigger*, swamps his thinking, and Sal hears the gunshots. Ida, first out the door, enveloped herself like a swell around Francesco. She was still blanketed over him, rocking and whimpering, when EMTs arrived to carry off his body. Antony was at the Ninth Precinct just starting the second detective shift. Justin was hearing Thursday evening confessions and giving out mercies at Our Lady Queen of Peace. It was the week before Christmas, and there had been a fierce snowstorm the night before, a *bomb cyclone*, TV weatherman Al Roker called it. Home alone with Ida and Francesco that evening, Sal knelt beside his mother and tried to pull her off Francesco, but she shrieked and fought him. Francesco's head was draining blood. Crouched beside his parents, Sal hugged his mother, trying to steady her. He gazed at the stone lion blanketed in snow and splattered in blood, a string of tiny Christmas lights down its mane buried under the snow and blinking gauzy patches of red, green, and yellow light. He picked up a bullet casing from the stoop. It was warm and smelled of charcoal and sulfur.

The right trigger, Sal says aloud, *the right trigger, the right trigger, the right trigger.* "Get out," he says. "Get out of my head, Agnes," the name his mother, even before dementia, has called people and things she can't remember. Or doesn't want to remember.

With this fury in his head, exhausted by living that same day again and again, Sal walks down Whitehall Street to the ferry terminal and enters the men's room. Someone takes the urinal beside him, even though others are free. The guy's wearing the suit of a second-tier young lawyer or rookie Wall Street stockbroker that he pulled off the rack at Men's Wearhouse. He puts his leather briefcase on the floor and tucks it between his legs, as if he's worried someone will snatch it before he can zip up. He doesn't seem to mind the sticky accumulation of urine where the case sits or whatever dribble his own piss might trickle on it. Sal stares at the thick hard cock that the handsome suit is stroking. "Do you want it," he hears a voice say. And Sal, without thinking, without a quiver of desire, reaches over and takes it in his hand. When the young man sighs, Sal lets it go. He zips his pants and starts to walk out. The good-looking suit turns his head to Sal's back and mutters, derisively, "Nice." The sting of shame seizes Sal. "What the fuck," he says to himself. The only other time he had touched someone else's cock besides Justin's happened at the Academy's Swab Summer. He was nineteen. Justin was spending the break at the seminary in South

Bend, the only summer they hadn't been together since they were eight. The captain of the tall ship *Eagle* invited Sal into his cabin during their sail from Halifax to Portland. "Swab Cusumano," the captain said. "I admire the way you work together with the other cadets, showing leadership and camaraderie at the same time. There's no room for showboating on the ship." He latched the cabin door and poured Sal a shot of "congratulatory" Bushmills. He was Irish, Captain John O'Leary, youngest commanding officer of the *Eagle* in the history of the Coast Guard. He explained how the tall ship is a perfected piece of naval ship craft. You, he told Sal, are lucky to experience it. The night was cloudless on the Atlantic, with barely a sliver of moon and an explosion of stars spreading out everywhere over the water. Sal could see the ocean and the darkness sparkle from the port-hole of the captain's quarters. He didn't flinch when he felt the buttons of his deck pants open, nor when the captain pulled down to his ankles Sal's Guard-issued white skivvies. He remembers being nearly breathless by the time he filled the young captain's throat. Until now in the ferry termi-nal's men's room, it was the only time he'd betrayed Justin, and when years later he confessed, Justin said, "Oh, Sal, you didn't really have a choice, did you?" The reaction irritated Sal. *How can Justin be so goddamn forgiving?* he thought. He didn't tell Justin that he did have a choice; maybe Sal wanted the captain to have him. And now, he worries, *Why the fuck did I take this suit's hard cock in my hand? What was I thinking? Will I tell Justin? Not tonight,* he thinks. *Someday. And what about Justin? Does he have his own secrets? Dalli-ances back in the seminary in Indiana? Is it really like Justin always says: "You and Christ, Sal. I don't need or want anyone else." How fucking stupid is that?* Then a stall door bangs, and the echoes of the gun rampage inside his head return. He finds one of the last empty seats in the vast hall and sits beside an old nun worrying rosary beads on her lap. He buries his face in his hands, while he waits the twenty minutes for the next boat to St. George Terminal.

Sal looks up and almost no one is left sitting in seats. He realizes he's nearly missed the *Spirit of America*—the 4,400-passenger powerhouse whose keel was built with steel from the ruins of the World Trade Center towers. He heads to the gate but turns around, remembering he left his backpack under the seat, and sees an NYPD officer and bomb-sniffing dog are heading there too. He knows the cop.

"Hey, Jack. That's mine, I left it there less than a minute ago. I've got to run and catch the ferry."

The cop shakes his head. "You should know better, Sal. Not much is safe here. And you don't leave a sack in the station."

"You're right, Jack. Sorry to set you and Jake on the call."

The dog is sniffing the backpack and then turns away, disappointed that there was nothing to go apeshit over.

"Hey, the gate's about to close," the cop says.

Sal rushes to join the stragglers at the end of the crush of commuters heading home to Staten Island—young Wall Street pikers priced out of the villages and Soho; Italian and Irish cops and firefighters, some of them the sons and daughters of cops and firefighters who died in 9/11; kids on sports or academic scholarships at Catholic preps like Regis and Marymount; doormen of Upper West Side and East Side apartment buildings; teachers and coaches at public schools no rich kid would set foot in; lunch shift bartenders and servers at restaurants charging twenty-five bucks for a BLT; out-of-work actors and musicians back from an audition that, if they killed it, might get them to new digs in Chelsea or Hell's Kitchen, or at least Inwood; and tourists, too, who want a free sunset ride past the Statue of Liberty. The Staten Island Ferry, a city itself, sailing twenty minutes between two islands.

The main deck is filled. That doesn't matter because Sal prefers being alone when he watches Manhattan recede as the *Spirit of America* crosses the bay. He heads to the stern of the double-ended ferry and climbs over the chains on the cordoned-off tip of the deck. The crew doesn't shoo away the former Coast Guard intelligence officer, and if a passenger tries to lift a leg over the chain to share his solitary perch, Sal flashes his NYPD badge and says, "Sorry, guy, off limits." He loves this sail out of Manhattan almost as much as he loves docking *Vesuvius* on Hart Island, and he's grateful that the routine recurs, day after day, week after week, month after month, and if he's lucky, year after year for as long as he can foresee, or at least until the earth on Potter's Field no longer opens itself to New York City's unwanted.

He stands facing the harbor at the tip of Manhattan, the 10,000-horsepower engine reverberating in his chest as the ferry accelerates and leaves the dock, unveiling the Lower Manhattan skyline, which Sal could, if he had the talent, sketch with his eyes closed. Diesel fumes draw through his lungs and mix with whiffs of fried fast food from McDonald's and KFC, Chinese beef and pork stir-fries, Mexican rice and beans, greasy pizza slices, drifting out from the main deck. Once the ferry enters the Upper

New York Bay all he breathes in is the salt air kissing his face. He catches sight of airliners in a holding pattern circling over the bay and imagines them one by one dropping into the water. His mind's a mess.

~

Sal doesn't remember when exactly his once insistent drive for meaning began to diminish. He's doubted God's benevolence and mercy ever since he left high school at Our Lady Queen of Peace. *Big deal*, he used to think, *Justin still loves me, and isn't that enough?* Justin tells him to be patient with God, to remember this from the book of Isaiah: "Whether you turn to the right or to the left, your ears will hear a voice behind you, saying, 'This is the way; walk in it.'" "You're kidding, right?" Sal usually says, and Justin smiles and says, "You'll see." But Sal doesn't see, and he worries that the day will come when Justin tires of Sal's failure to accept how beautifully uncomplicated love can be. That's Justin's phrase, *beautifully uncomplicated*.

And what about this search for meaning apart from the love he and Justin share? Sal knows he's mattered to his parents; he knows he's not a menace like Antony; he knows he's luckier than all the dead whom he hauls, day after day, to Hart Island's trenches: men, women and babies without a single person caring enough to claim their bodies. So why, he asks himself, does all his abundance mean so little? Why has he felt, even before Francesco's death, as lost as he suspects the Potter's Field dead were before they died? Why does he awaken and see threats outside the window instead of trees? Why does he believe sometimes the eyes of the Sicilian wolf that Ida sees are searching for him, too? People lose faith in God all the time and still believe in one another. Parents grow old and sick and dotty, and they die. He can't identify his regrets, point to a failure that haunts him. Not even being forced out of the Guard. So, why so much drifting? *What the fuck is wrong with me*, he thinks. Once his father said, "Remember when you doubt yourself, Sal, your name means salvation." *How fucking stupid is this*, he thinks. And maybe that's it. How stupid is a father's impossible faith in a son? A gangster father, no less, who's been gunned down. Try to find a word for a father's death. *Abandonment? Release?* If you're a child when your father dies, you become an oddity. You feel deserted but somehow special. And imagine losing your mother at the same time, as Justin did those many years ago. "Poor boy," the neighbors said. "Thank God the Cusumanos took him in." Even the children of murdered mobsters receive the sympathy of fellow gangsters: envelopes bulging with cash in a bowl on a table in a home where goombahs gather for a last goodbye. Sal was knocking on middle age when Francesco was murdered, and what he's left with is the loss of someone who believed in him, left with what he believes are only a father's wishful words. *Salvation,* he thinks, *like that's possible.*

The sun is setting southwest of the ferry, close to Newark Liberty. It is so low on the horizon that molecules in the air create orange, yellow, and red ribbons everywhere behind the Statue of Liberty while the harbor skyline bathes in shimmering cobalt blue. The building everyone recognizes first is Freedom Tower. Tonight, lit by a hundred searchlights and a blue LED extravaganza, the icon of New York's defiance casts its reflection across the harbor, reaching the ferry's stern. Sal thinks of the day he and Justin watched the Twin Towers fall. He leans over the metal gate separating the deck from the water, close enough, he thinks, that he could leap and disappear into the blue light.

On the morning of 9/11 Sal and Justin skipped classes at Our Lady Queen of Peace and boarded the 8:15 ferry to Manhattan. It was Sal's birthday. They were both seventeen, old enough, they believed, to do whatever they wanted. Old enough to skip school and go crazy in the city. The Cusumanos adopted Justin a few months after the boy's mother and father were killed in a car crash. Barbara and Tommy Flynn were driving back from the Veterans Hospital where Justin's father was being treated for opioid addiction. He had done six tours in the Army Special Forces and fought in Kuwait during Desert Storm. He hardly knew his son when he ended his service and returned home to Staten Island. Most of the time Justin's father sat before a mute television, watching the news crawl on Fox. There seemed to be so many casualties during the country's endless wars. He repeated names of the missions he'd been on: Bright Star, Urgent Fury, El Dorado Canyon, Praying Mantis, and the last two, Desert Shield and Desert Storm. A barrage of U.S. depleted-uranium rounds hit the Bradley tank he was commanding. With him were two other crew members and a squad of six soldiers. The dart-like missiles, two-and-a-half times denser than steel, blasted perfectly round holes in the tank, igniting white phosphorous and spewing shrapnel and radioactive dust inside the hull. The gunner in the turret, the driver, and two of the troops in the rear were killed in the explosions, while pieces of metal tore into his shoulder and hip. Everyone was bathed in uranium dust, 1,500 times less than the amount, the Army said, needed to cause radiation sickness. Still, Justin's father believed his bleeding gums, migraines, and grating joints were all uranium induced. "Fucking military cover-up," he told the doctor treating him for pain medicine addiction. His wife tried to boost his spirits, reminding him of the good days ahead that he could spend with his son. That morning, before they left for the hospital, was the last time Justin saw his parents alive.

Justin and Sal were already like brothers by then. The boys spent almost every day together since the Flynns had moved in next door. They skateboarded up and down the boardwalks at Midland and New Dorp beaches, traded Mets cards, watched *Empire Strikes Back* and *ET* so many times the wear and tear shredded the tapes. Not long after the Flynns' funeral, Sal's father and mother moved Justin's parents' bed into Sal's room. "There, now you don't have to sleep on the floor, honey," Ida told Justin.

Honey, Sal thought. She never called her sons *honey*.

"But it's my parents'," Justin said.

"It's yours and Sal's now," she said, matter-of-factly. "No need to spend money on another bed when there's a perfectly good one the two of you can share."

"It's big," Sal said. "There's no room for anything else."

"You've got the whole basement to mess around in. We'll put desks down there." Francesco said.

After he thought a while, Justin said, "It's okay."

Even then he had the knack for turning the page on things he couldn't control, just like the prayer recovering alcoholics and addicts repeat over and over. Sal can't understand how he does it. *Give me the serenity to accept the things I cannot change.* It's laughable, Sal thinks.

"They gave it to us," Justin said.

"Who?" Sal asked.

"My mom and dad. I heard them say so."

Sal's parents looked at each other. "Well, that's it then," Ida said.

Not long after, the Cusumanos adopted Justin, who didn't have a relative in the world who wanted him. No grandparent, no aunt or uncle, no one. At the time Antony, already eighteen, said the family didn't need another son, especially an Irish kid. Francesco said that he'd known some good Paddies. Ida struck the table with her open hand and said that Justin was family now. He was upstairs in bed, wondering where his parents had gone, to heaven or hell, or to some black hole in the sky that sucks souls into it. He prayed the Our Father and Hail Mary. He hoped they were blessed and not tormented. He thanked God that he was with Sal in the

Cusumano home. It was the beginning of what Justin would later always tell Sal was "God's plan."

~

On the September morning the two boys played hooky, the sky was a blue bowl, not a wisp of cloud anywhere over the five boroughs. Sal doesn't remember exactly when their attraction became so intense that they knew something unavoidable was happening. He doesn't remember the first day he let his eyes linger on Justin undressing. He was surprised but relieved, too, the morning his adopted brother stepped into the shower and held his sex and kissed him. Their romance remained their secret, until Antony, back home because his wife had kicked him out of the house for the second time in a month, saw them naked in bed, Justin's arm around Sal, spooning. It was about a month before September 11, and Antony didn't say anything to Ida and Francesco. He shook his head, and days later told Sal and Justin, "Really? Who would have thought? Two queers. Don't worry, I admire people with secrets. Shows you got balls."

Sal packed sandwiches and chips, a Thermos of vodka and cranberry juice, a beach blanket, and two copies of *Huckleberry Finn*, which they were reading in their English class. As soon as the ferry landed, they had planned to head to Central Park and The Ramble, where gay men cruise and lounge naked on a gigantic slumbering rock. They went there once before, too shy to take off their shirts and pants, but the day before Sal's birthday Justin dared Sal. "Bet you wouldn't take everything off on the rock if I ask you." A little hesitant, Sal said, "Bet I would." After a morning in the park, Justin said he wanted to go to the Metropolitan Museum of Art. He loved wandering through the ancient and medieval galleries; he wanted to see the great altar canopy from the twelfth century and Caravaggio's *Entombment of Christ*. Back then, art didn't interest Sal the way it did Justin, though he liked the antiquities, Greek and Roman statues of naked gods and warriors. He thought Caravaggio's Christ was sexy, too, and when he said so, Justin smiled. "See, you are kind of religious, Sal."

He wasn't then and isn't now, certainly not like Justin, who that fall was applying to Notre Dame. Justin is devout but complicated, more amorous than Sal. One night, after Sal had slid out of him, Justin pulled him close and told Sal that he would never love another person, not even God, more than he loved Sal. Those words were as worrisome as comforting. *How could that ever be true?* Sal thought. Justin told Sal that while he was in the seminary, he wondered whether unbelievers aren't really like Doubting Thomas, and there's no assurance God will give them all the proof they seek. So, what to do with insistent doubters? he asked himself. After months of debate with seminarians and his spiritual adviser, Justin decided that unbelief really is a form of doubting, and what matters is the life one lives, the kindness or cruelty at the heart of one's being, and Sal, he knows, is kind. That's all God needs. The first time he explained this, Sal said, "I want to believe you, but how am I supposed to compete with Christ?"

"Why can't you listen?" Justin told him. "You worry about everything." He leaned in and took off Sal's shirt, undid his belt, and unzipped his pants. "Consider this, you're allowing me to have a lover, someone invisible who might even be watching us now, and smiling."

Sal sighed at the thought of voyeur Christ in the room and whispered, "You're crazy," until he surrendered to Justin's kiss and the inescapable tenderness he knew was as real and consuming as the air he breathed. And at that moment at least he wanted to believe no one else in the world existed, certainly not Christ hovering over them. Only Justin, always only Justin.

~

The ferry on the cloudless September 11 morning docked at South Street Station. It was 8:45. They were on their way to catch the uptown train at Bowling Green. Sal said he wanted to stop at Trinity Graveyard. Even as a boy, long before he knew Hart Island existed, he felt at home in a cemetery. He told Justin it was good luck to knock on the gravestone of Alexander Hamilton. "It's your birthday," Justin laughed. "Whatever you want. But don't forget." He tugged on Sal's shirt and pants. "These are coming off." In the Trinity courtyard, they heard the roar of a jet and looked up. The American Airlines Boeing 767 was flying low, teetering until it got closer to the World Trade Center, when it gained some power and crashed into the North Tower. The explosion was deafening. The two boys felt what seemed like a sonic boom course through their tendons. Flames and black smoke, thick as billowing storm clouds, shot out the enormous gash in the glass and steel tower. They smelled burning jet fuel in the air. Windows shattered and debris hit the ground everywhere. They saw people burned by showering fuel. Pieces of glass and steel and concrete rained down on the church courtyard. They rushed into Saint Paul's Chapel with others, somehow escaping falling debris. By the time the second airliner struck the

South Tower, there were others, running from the street into the chapel. People were crying, others were calling friends and relatives on flip phones until cell networks were overwhelmed and failed. A man at the organ, an immense wooden pipe instrument on the balcony, played a hymn that Justin learned years later in the seminary was "Lo, He Comes with Clouds Descending." The organ music stopped when the rushing sound of a freight train–the South Tower imploding—filled the nave of the chapel. Within minutes, people covered in white silica dust, more specters than human, entered the church.

Sal grabbed Justin's arm and said, "Let's get out of here and take the ferry back to Staten Island."

"The church is safe, Sal."

"Fuck it is. What if the other tower collapses and buries us?"

Justin nodded.

Outside the air was thick and white in endless waves of acrid powder. They took off their T-shirts and wrapped them around their mouths and noses. The streets were filled with others heading south to the harbor. They ran with the exodus down Broadway to Whitehall and back to the South Street Ferry Terminal. The harbor was filling up with boats—the Staten Island ferries, tours, tugs, fishing vessels big and small, even pleasure craft—all boarding people fleeing southern Manhattan in what, they would learn later, was the largest boatlift ever, bigger than Dunkirk in World War II. The chalky dust covered their torsos and heads, as if the antiquities in the Met they had planned to see had come to life. Sal and Justin weaved their way through the stunned panic. They slipped onto the deck of the Staten Island ferry just before the gate closed, and as it cast off, others at the dock screamed for the boat not to leave. Some jumped into the water and swam to the armada heading their way. Others simply stood at the tip of the landing, relieved, it seemed, to be so close to the island's edge with the prospect of escaping. Sal and Justin heard the second distant rushing swoosh and held each other as they watched the North Tower collapse into billowing clouds of horrifying dust.

"The church," Justin said. "It's standing."

"How do you know?"

"I know," he said. "It's a miracle, you'll see."

Sal just gave him a look.

~

A crew member of the *Spirit of America* climbs over the chain and pats Sal on the shoulder. "I saw you on TV today. That must have been some rescue. Ten minutes before we dock. I've got a nipper and a Thermos of coffee."

"Why not," Sal says.

"This way, hero."

I'm No Rosemary

Anna walks into the kitchen. Justin is wearing a custom printed T-shirt: *Hospital chaplain because BAD ASS miracle worker is not my official title.*

"Really?" she says.

"You'd be surprised, patients appreciate the humor."

Ida is watching a rerun of *The Price Is Right* on the Game Show Channel and shouts out, "I knew it was Door Number 3!"

"She's lively," Anna says.

"For now. I think seeing Sal on CNN gave her a lift."

"Sal was on CNN?"

"You didn't hear?" Justin gives Anna the rundown of the rescue on the Sound, while he's checking that what he needs is in his chaplain bag: consecrated hosts, crucifix, stole, Bible, and prayer book.

Ida registers that they're talking about Sal, and she asks, "Will Sal be home for pasta?"

"We already ate, Ida, and he's working late, like usual."

"No," Ida goes. "It's Door Number 1, *Stupida!*"

"If this rescue doesn't move Sal, I don't know what can," Anna says.

"You'd think so, but on the phone, he seemed the same as he's been."

"He's drinking too much."

Justin nods and says he's got to run.

"Wait, put these in your bag." She hands him a bunch of Perle di Sole lemon drops that she picked up at Alfonso's. "They're like an elixir for the old Italian ladies."

"Anna's cure-all, I'll tell them."

"Don't let him stay till last call. Drag him out if you have to."

"I try," he says, half-heartedly. "I try."

~

The cross still remains over the entry to the hospital from the time it was St. Vincent's, founded by the Sisters of Charity. The nuns are long gone. Decades ago, Mount Sinai took it over and transformed it into Richmond

34

University Medical Center. A rescue helicopter whirls above the roof. Justin looks up and makes the Sign of the Cross on his way to the chaplains' office to pick up the list of patients who have requested a visit. A nurse's aide he likes hands him a folder with about a dozen names and some helpful information: medical treatments, ages, family histories, religious denominations.

"Check out this one, Father." She points to Dorothea Malicone, 53, advanced breast cancer, divorced, atheist. "We don't get many atheists who want to see a chaplain, hardly ever an Italian atheist. She was pretty insistent on seeing you. Maybe she's reassessing."

Justin nods. "I don't believe in unbelievers, Abby. We're all hovering around doubt."

Abby, a graduate student of biology at NYU, says, "Tell that to Richard Dawkins, Father."

He smiles, and then nods. "The blind watchmaker. Theory of random complexity. I think Dawkins is enjoying that debate with God. Doubters rule, remember that, Abby."

Abby's got long black hair with neon green streaks across it. She raises her eyes. "Ah, priests, you're so hopeful."

He pauses, as if he were hearing Sal saying it, and unexpectedly serious, even a bit harsh, Justin says, "So, you prefer the alternative?"

She gives him a look and a placating nod as he heads out. "Wait, you left the list, Father."

Disappointed in himself for snapping at her, he says, "See, I'm hopeless without you, Abby."

"That's right, Father."

Justin decides to save Dorothea Malicone for last. Among those seeking comfort is someone he knows, Tommaso Salamone, a young associate of Carlo Cali. Justin stops there first. He's twenty-five, and his father was killed in a robbery in Brooklyn when he was three. For months his mother's been taking confession Thursday evenings, explaining how worried she is that her son is going down the same path as his father, how she knows in her heart he's going to be killed, too, if he doesn't leave the *family* soon. *La maledizione del Salamone.* Justin at first counseled her that this isn't her fault, not her sin, and she told him she didn't believe God would forgive a mother who can't save her son. She's inconsolable. Justin looks at Tommaso's record: *Radical bilateral orchiectomy.* Testicular cancer. Both testicles removed.

"Salut, Tommaso." Justin thinks of joking, *So, how they hangin'*, but instead he pats the young man's shoulder and says, "You hangin' in there, kid?"

"Both of them, Father. I'm shit out of luck. They offered me some sperm banking, but I said, Christ, I never wanted kids anyway."

"Your mother's worried, Tommy."

"Shit, she's not the one who's lost balls."

"You know, wise guy, it's things like getting cancer that can help you reassess your life."

"My woman's got a surprise ahead of her. No more tea-bagging." Tommy laughs, obviously hopped-up post-anesthesia. "Who the fuck is Walt Whitman?"

"A dead poet."

"Did he have a big beard?"

"He did."

Tommy starts rapping. "Doc goin' to shoot me up with testosterone, said I gonna get a beard like the poet."

"You're liking those painkillers, Tommy."

He ignores Justin. "I'll be shooting blanks but don't go all celibate like," and he points to Justin, "like *Father.*"

Justin pauses, thinking of Sal entering him in bed. Tommaso reaches for water, and it spills over an I LOVE NAPOLI postcard with a picture of a masked jester carrying a pizza before a backdrop of the sea and smoking volcano. Tommaso's mother must have put it there. He thinks about the Russians mowing down Francesco, and Antony's allegiance to them and the five families, and the mess he wants to flee with Sal and Ida. "Maybe you should think about leaving Carlo Cali. Your mother told me she wants to go back to Naples. You could go, too. Meet a nice Italian girl."

"Fuck Italy," he says. "I'm staying in Shaolin." Then rapping Wu-Tang, he goes: "You're brainwashed, watch starships, I can make cars flip, Deck bomb atomic."

"We're going to talk when you get home, Tommy. We're going to talk, you hear me."

"Kiss the comet, this time, he's gone, I grip the don, rip arms out the socket." He pauses, "Father?"

"Yes."

"I'm fucked."

Justin takes Tommaso's hand. "Do you want Holy Communion?"

"Can't hurt."

"First, I want to know if you believe in kindness."

Tommy, for the moment, seems jolted out of his high. "She says I'm kind."

"Who?"

"Ma."

"Do you believe her?"

"She's usually right."

"Then, I'll give you Communion." Justin opens his bag and removes the pyx. He takes a host, holds it between his fingers, and makes the Sign of the Cross over Tommy, "In the name of the Father, and of the Son, and of the Holy Ghost." He places the host on Tommy's tongue, and in almost a whisper, says, "Close your eyes, Tommaso, and sleep."

It takes a couple hours ministering to the others on his rounds before he gets to Dorothea. She's sitting upright against the raised hospital bed, reading a book about dogs.

"You saved me for last," she says, not accusingly.

"How did you know?"

"There's a lot I know that you wouldn't think I know. I saw you the other day. You were talking to that handsome doctor; he looked like he wanted to pull off your shirt and ravish you right there in the hall."

Justin gives her a look. Dr. Jeremy Gottlieb is closeted and resembles Jason Bateman. They haven't confided in each other, but in his own closeted experience Justin has learned that gaydar is a real thing, and the flirtation with Jeremy, to his embarrassment and guilt, hasn't been unwelcome. A few days ago, Justin didn't flinch when the doctor brushed his hand across Justin's crotch.

Dorothea notices the crucifix sticking out of the chaplain bag. "Expecting an exorcism tonight?"

"Never know."

"I'm no Rosemary, and I'm not having a baby."

Justin smiles.

She touches his T-shirt and says, "*Bad ass*, that's a nice touch. Unexpected."

"It's good for a first laugh."

"I noticed you smiling when lover boy, well, how should I put this, *copped a feel* in the hallway. Don't look so surprised. I'm an intuitive therapist and picking up on high-energy vibes is how I connect. The two of you were charged."

Justin pulls a chair over to the bed and sits. "Are you sure you're not just a busybody?"

"You don't have to worry. I didn't ask for you to blackmail you."

"That's reassuring."

"The Catholic celibacy thing is for the birds. I was just thinking, 'Here's someone not afraid to test the boundaries of risk management. I've got to meet him.'"

"Risk management?"

"I told you I'm an intuitive therapist. Don't you priests study psychology somewhere along the way? They're all the rage these days, we're like clairvoyants practicing snake-oil therapy. I figure a hot-blooded priest like you must be tuned in to his unconscious communication and wouldn't dismiss me out of hand."

"You're making a lot of assumptions, Dorothea?"

"See, that word *assumptions*, it was flat when you said it. But *Dorothea*, it had a ring of curiosity. I like that."

Justin, without thinking, says, "You're right about the doctor."

"You don't have to *tell* me."

He laughs. "I've got a secret, but he's not it."

"I know."

"So, what am I thinking?"

"It doesn't work that way. It's not what you're thinking, it's how the secret is making you feel. And I got a sense you want something more from someone you love."

He doesn't respond. Moments turn into more moments. He's thinking about Sal, how Justin's never cared that the Church tells him he can't love Christ and Sal, too; what do these bishops, cardinals, and popes know about love? But what worries him is this: Sal, after all these many years, remains afraid that Justin will abandon him and beg Jesus's forgiveness for going astray. And then Justin thinks of the doctor's advance. Was this a test of his faith in Sal? He cups his hands around his neck and slides them off in a stretch.

Seemingly accustomed to the silences she can engender, Dorothea waits and then goes, "See, I'm hitting a nerve. A fellow intuitionist told me that Freud believed intuition is the red-headed stepchild of psychotherapy. But in the company of friends, he confessed that he sometimes felt a kind of telepathy when he was with a patient. I can sense your secret runs deeper than Mr. Sexy Scrubs."

Justin stands and stretches his leg.

Dorothea looks suddenly tired, the beginning of a lethargy that, without notice, cancer induces. A little plaintively she says, "Don't go."

"A charley horse," he says, massaging his calf and then sitting and taking her hand. "*Intuition.* In my line of work, we call it grace: *I know the thoughts that I think toward you, thoughts of peace, and not of evil.* Jesus said this."

"I'm dying, Father."

"I know. I can feel it, too. Is that why you asked to see me? You want to be accepted into the afterlife? You really don't need me for that."

He was going to share his theory that faith and eternal life are all about kindness, but before he could, she mustered the strength to raise her voice. "Ha. *Hell, no!* I just wanted to tell you, before I die, I *saw* you, and you made me happy."

She coughs like the dying do sometimes, raspy and deep. Justin fishes out a lemon drop from the bag, unwraps it, and says, "Here, this will soothe your throat."

She opens her mouth, and he places it on her tongue. She sucks on it and squeezes Justin's hand. "Now, get out of here, Father, and fix that anxiety inside you."

Justin leans in, smiles, and kisses her forehead, while in his head he's saying, "In the name of the Father, and of the Son, and of the Holy Ghost. Grace be with you, Dorothea."

I Fuck, You Pay

Mother Pug's Saloon is nearly empty by the time Sal gets off the bus from Saint George. He steps over a hotdog roll splayed on the rubber welcome mat that proclaims in scuffed letters: BEGGARS, BEWARE. It's soaked in ketchup and mustard. Neon beer and whiskey signs—Blue Moon, Brooklyn Lager, Jack Daniels, and Jameson—cast nervous reflections in recesses of the bar. Tuesday night karaoke doesn't start until 8. A couple auto mechanics from the shop around the corner are shooting darts. Two EMTs are racking spots and stripes at the pool table. Next to it there's a plaque on the wall for fallen cops and firefighters. No room for all the names of local rescuers who died on 9/11 and are still dying from the toxic dust and fumes they breathed in that day, and day after day. The wooden plaque, with an NYPD badge and NYFD helmet carved at the top, says: IN MEMORY OF STATEN ISLAND HEROES: SEPTEMBER 11, 2001, TO ETERNITY

Sal notices Aidan O'Shea's empty stool at the other end of the bar and thinks, *He's never not there.* Aidan works in the public library six mornings a week, restacking books. When he's done, he hunkers into a seat in a corner and reads until five, when he catches the bus to Mother Pug's. People who know him say he's probably read ten thousand books, and not just popular mysteries and thrillers but histories about ancient Rome and Greece, the Civil War, the Spanish Flu. You name a historical event and he's a human encyclopedia. He reads the poets from A to Z, and he can talk about Chaucer, Shakespeare, Joyce, and Pynchon as if he were an English professor. His brick-red beard is specked with gray. His blue eyes are all bloodhound. Like a lot of Irish drinkers Aidan can be mercurial, blowing hot one hour and cold another, one moment a storyteller and another a recluse. His sister, Sherry, back from the Midwest where she's lived ever since leaving the island for college, is a big shot in the FBI. Like a lot of Staten Island kids, once she fled to college, she became a ghost. But unlike most escapees, Sherry is back, and she's been living with Aidan in the house they grew up in. She pops in Pug's once in a while, orders a whiskey, and speaks in a hushed tone mostly while Aidan listens without saying much. But he seems happy to see her and she leaves before boozing sends O'Shea into his lonelier places, as if he's in a time warp, or fallen into one of his books, where he's probably more at home than anywhere else. When Sherry first got back, she wore bug-eye sunglasses day and night that covered half her face and wrapped a light scarf over her head. She looked comically undercover. Turns out she had a bad case of pinkeye.

Back then, Nina Salvagio, the bartender, asked O'Shea, "So, what's Miss Sunshine doing back here?" He gave her a look and made a slow zipping gesture across his lips.

Only a small coterie of confidants knows anything about the case she's working. And until Francesco was dead, Sal didn't know the deepest secret of all: Sherry is Francesco's daughter and the sister Sal had never dreamed he had. She's mostly kept her distance from Sal, but ever since he discovered she was his sister, Sal's gotten closer to Aidan. Last week, they went to an AA meeting together, the only time Sal set foot in one. Aidan had been trying on and off forever to earn his next chip, but he's never gotten past an initiate's twenty-four-hour silver. The night Sal tagged along, Aidan's testimony was brief. He stood up and said that even when he isn't drinking, he divides humanity along two lines: the lonely and not so lonely. "Fuck it," he abruptly told everyone in his Irish baritone. "Fuck it." Some of the recovering drunks turned to watch him walk out and others shook their heads more in sympathy than disapproval while a guy in a Buffalo Bills cap stood and recounted an unremarkable sad-sack story that sobriety had helped him escape. In that moment, Sal decided that he wouldn't ever make another foray into AA.

"Fuck it," he says to himself as he watches O'Shea walk out of the bathroom to his seat at the other end of the bar. "You are here," and he thinks, *Lonely, or not so lonely; isn't that the truth, Aidan O'Shea.*

It's what Ida says now, too, *funculo*, whenever she surrenders to whatever blur she enters as the world she's known slips away. A slow insistent dissolution is what age does. If you live long enough, Sal has come to realize, one day you'll awaken into a place where past and present and future no longer have borders. Time and place and people become more and more indistinct every day. Even the people you've known and loved forever. And after death, well, what's there to say about that.

Aidan still hasn't noticed Sal, who decides to wait awhile before taking a seat next to him. There's a string of American flags hanging across the bar mirror. Nina is clipping a piece of gray cardboard bordered with black bunting to the string. She's pasted a photograph of Bobby Avallone and a Mass card from his wake in the center of the makeshift memorial. The NYPD detective was killed in Queens a few days before. He had just gotten off duty, on his way home to Staten Island and his wife and daughter, when he stopped at a bodega for a pack of Winstons. A thirteen-year-old kid, armed with a .45 Colt semiautomatic, triple the size of his skinny hand, was robbing the clerk. Bobby was shot in the heart as he reached to take the gun. He had grown up a few streets from the Cusumanos and graduated from the police academy the same year Antony did. He was a relative of Frankie Avalon, whose cousin, Bobby's dad, owned a pool hall on Staten Island. Most everyone on Staten Island believed that Bobby had a better voice than Frankie, and when Bobby came to Tuesday karaoke, he'd pack the bar. Old Italian ladies made pizza strips for everyone. Their daughters came wearing leopard-spotted and tiger-striped blouses, silk or polyester, depending on how far up the money ladder these *belladonnas* and *donnas de casa* had climbed. They ordered whiskey sours and smelled like they'd spent the day on the assembly line in an Aqua Net factory. Most of the time the men stayed home and those who did come to hear Bobby sing stepped outside to puff cigars after every other song or so. When Bobby sang "Venus," the women swooned.

Sal's brother, Antony, never liked Bobby, not when they were kids and even less years later, on the force together. He told Sal that Bobby once reported some *minor* infraction that he'd committed but Sal's brother wouldn't say what it was. "Stick up his ass," Antony told Sal. "*Pezzo di merda.* It was a nothin' burger, but Avallone reported it anyway."

Two months ago, sitting next to Sal and Aidan at Pug's after buying them shots of Jameson, Bobby asked Sal how he could be so different from his brother. "Christ, you and Justin are like saints, and Antony, well . . ." Bobby said that he had seen Antony leaving a cathouse, a girl, a teenager not much older than Bobby's daughter, chasing him, yelling, *I fuck, you pay; I fuck, you pay; I fuck, you pay.* Antony walked back to the girl, slapped her face, and knocked her onto a pile of garbage bags. As he walked away, he shouted at her in Italian: *Vai a farti fottere, puttana!* "Imagine *that*," Avallone told Sal. "*Go fuck yourself, whore.* Jesus, she was a kid." Bobby told Sal that he phoned in an anonymous complaint and knew the desk sergeant would tell Antony about the call and it would die there. "It was a message, like, *now you know someone is watching*," Bobby said.

"That's Antony," Aidan said.

Sal wasn't surprised either. He was about to say that he knew that his brother could be an asshole. But then Bobby said this: "I can't see how he's your brother. Guess he takes after Francesco. Look what happened to your dad."

Without thinking, Sal punched him in the chest, knocked the wind out of him as he fell off the barstool. "Fuck you, don't shit on my father," Sal said.

Aidan, worried, called out, "Bar brawl."

Justin arrived before all hell could break loose and calmed them down. Even now, seeing Bobby Avallone's face hanging in memoriam behind the bar, Sal doesn't feel sorry.

Finishing up the memorial, Nina says, "Poor guy had a fourteen-year-old daughter."

"Yeah," Sal says, in no mood to talk about Bobby.

One of the guys shooting darts calls over. "Hey, nice job, Sal. You were all over television."

Sal sends a thumbs-up, hoping the gesture will end any conversation.

"What?" Nina asks.

The guy goes, "You livin' in a cave? His boat and crew saved a family that ditched its jet in the water."

"No shit," Nina says.

"Yeah," he goes. "There were twin kids, and an old woman on it. Good thing your boat was there, Sal."

"How'd I miss it?" Nina asks.

The other guy laughs. "You work at night, Nina. You gotta get those afternoon delights."

She flips him the bird. "A hero, hey. Sal, I guess this round is on Mother Pug's."

Leo, the karaoke DJ—a sixty-something who decades ago played bass in a Bowery heavy metal band—comes in and pats Sal on the back. "Saw you on TV today. Shit, that was crazy."

Sal ignores him.

The Tuesday night singers trickle in. A waiter from Umberto's Clam House in Little Italy, a couple of retired cops, an old lady who's always pickled by the time she gets to the mic, two wiseguys who've spent seventy years upstate between them and a black college kid and his white girlfriend. Nina had told Sal that she worried there'd be trouble when the pair showed up around a month ago. Integration moves at a snail's pace at

43

Mother Pug's, like at a lot of other neighborhood island bars. You aren't in Manhattan anymore. But the kid's got a voice like an angel, and perfect pitch goes a long way at Tuesday night karaoke.

Some of the regulars come over to Sal to talk about the rescue. One of the wiseguys tells him that his father would have been proud. "Fuck you," he says, turning away. He stands up. "Hey, it was nothing. I'm just a guy with a boat. So, everyone, fuck off."

The other wiseguy mutters, "Let him be."

"Easy, Sal," Nina says. "They're just happy for you."

He kills the shot and asks her for another. Embarrassed and calming down, Sal gestures toward Aidan. "He looks half seas over already."

"Yep, library boy got an early start. He's been here since three. He seems kind of off today, even for him."

Sal walks over and sits. Aidan doesn't acknowledge Sal right away, and in a kind of whiskey reverie, his head hung low, he's talking to himself. "Seamus Heaney knew what's up: *All I know is a door into the dark.* Fuck it." After what seems like a long time but is just really a minute or so, Aidan says, "Reluctant hero, hey. I get it."

Sal ignores him and asks, "You okay?"

O'Shea signals to Nina. He knocks the bar top with his knuckles and says, "Two Jamesons. Doubles. Frodo looks thirsty."

"Frodo?" Sal asks.

"You should read the *Ring* someday."

Nina, back with the whiskies, says, "Good to see you back among the living, O'Shea."

He smiles and gives her a mock evil eye.

Nina pours the whiskeys and lingers nearby, while Sal and Aidan look cheerlessly at each other and down the shots.

"Jeez, big surprise, another boo-hoo moment, guys," she says, turning as Aidan calls for another round, this time two on ice.

Aidan goes, "Your father was a good guy, Sal."

Sal is surprised. Aidan hasn't talked much about Francesco since Sal discovered Sherry was his sister. Sal palms the back of his neck. "You know squat about him."

"Like I said, he was a good guy, and I know he never made any bones. He was closer to Carlo Cali than most people think. Everyone thought he just ran horses for the Gambino family. Sure, he could pick winners. Still, he wasn't just a fixer. He was complicated."

Nina sets down the two whiskies.

Aidan pauses until she leaves and then leans in. "I know that Francesco worked in the Cali family stable in Palermo before he came to New York. Your grandfather was shot there in a city square, right next to Carlo. They were buddies. At least that's what Francesco told my mother. A man tells things to the woman he loves that he doesn't tell everyone."

Sal tries to imagine Francesco and Aidan's mother sharing a life that Sal knew nothing about. Before he can ask Aidan about it, Sherry walks in. She sits on the other side of Aidan. Nina's ignoring her, and she says, "What did I do to that bitch?"

"Don't start, Sherry. This is my territory." He gestures to Nina, and raising his whiskey, he points to his sister.

"So, you two are really chums now?" Sherry asks.

"Brothers," Aidan says, and Sal gives him a slightly puzzled look. "We're talking about Francesco. I told Sal we knew a lot about his father."

Sherry reaches across her brother and grabs some peanuts from a bowl in front of Sal. "My brother's a drunk and he makes up a lot of stories. Don't believe everything he says."

"The file on Francesco is a hundred pages long," Aidan says.

Sherry kicks her brother in the ankle. "Sure, we know a lot about Francesco, that's obvious. He was a gangster."

"Do you know why the Russians killed him?" Sal asks.

She gives him her don't-ask look. She says she saw Sal on CNN earlier and toasts him. "That was something."

"Leave it, Sherry. He thinks he's no hero."

"Tell me more about what the FBI had on Francesco," Sal says.

"Sorry, that's confidential, and if Francesco kept you in the dark, what you don't know isn't going to make you any happier." She finishes the whiskey and gets up. She presses her hand against Aidan's cheek. "I thought I'd try to get you to come home for Chinese."

Aidan draws back. "I'm not hungry."

"Figured so, you're some piece of work." She turns to Sal and tells him again not to listen to Aidan. She says she wants to get together this week, the three of them, and wants Sal to bring his handsome "man of the cloth." A family affair. She starts walking out and stops when she meets Justin at the door. It looks like they are talking like they have something important to share.

Sal goes to join them, but Sherry's gone before he gets halfway there.

45

"What was that?" Sal asks.

"What?"

"What did she want?"

"She told me that you and Aidan are hopeless drunks."

When they get back to Aidan, he nudges Sal. "What we were saying, well, *fugetaboutit*. Like Donnie Brasco said, just *fugetaboutit*." He orders a drink for Justin, who gestures to Nina that he doesn't want it.

"I'm taking your buddy home. You could use an early night, too," he says, patting Aidan on the back.

"What has night got to do with sleep," Aidan says.

"You know there's more to life than books and booze." Justin turns to Sal. "Come on, we're going home."

"Fuck it," Aidan whispers, too softly for Justin and Sal to hear.

It's raining, and Sal, thinking about Sherry, steps in an oily puddle. "Fuck."

"What?"

Sal's looking at his wet shoes. "Sherry knows more about the Russians, and she's talked about it with Aidan. She wants to meet with us."

"Give it up, Sal."

As they walk to the car, the door to Pug's opens. The break in karaoke has ended, and they can hear the kid singing as if he were channeling Sam Cooke: *It's been a long time coming / But I know, but I know a change is gonna come.*

Sal takes his backpack from Justin and fishes out the flask, finishing what's left. "Jesus, Sal. You said you wouldn't take it to the boat again."

Sal looks at him. "Fuck Sherry, fuck the Russians."

Gi-gi-li gi-gi-li

When Sal and Justin get home, Ida's sleepwalking around the dining room table. Her eyes wide open, she marches, muttering in a language that might as well be Sanskrit. Ida's a small woman, and she's wearing an *I'm Sicilian* T-shirt that could fit a boxcar. Her face is caked with almost an entire jar of Noxzema that she plastered on after Justin had left. The T-shirt ends just before her knotty knees. Her white hair is short and boyish. Her arms sway stiffly. The doctor told Sal that science can't explain why some sleepwalkers move in circles. He described an experiment in Norway: subjects, wide awake, were blindfolded and, sure enough, most of them veered off course and ended up chasing their tails even though they believed they were holding a straight line. In psych hospitals, it's not unusual, he said, for patients to get caught in a holding pattern, wending around a room on their feet as their minds meander in a loop of memories and inventions. Maybe circumambulation is more natural than we think. Hindus and Buddhists do it all the time, he said. The doctor told Sal sleepwalking and talking gibberish in the elderly can manifest itself in daytime behavior, too. And when it does, it can be a sign of dementia's escalation. "Ida's mind is at war with itself," he said. "And there's no winner."

"Jesus, I told you we shouldn't leave her alone anymore. Where's Anna?" Sal asks.

Justin, nervous too, says, "She's probably walking Lola."

When Sal and Justin found Ida like this a week ago, they discovered that a chair pulled out and placed around a turn provides an exit ramp, and then the looping breaks. They wait a minute more before putting it in place. She's babbling "gi-gi-li gi-gi-li," to the rhythm of her steps.

Sal says, "She looks like a mime."

"I think she's trying to say *giugiuleni*," Justin says. He pulls out one of the burgundy velvet dining chairs and places it on her path. Sal takes her arm and says, "*Bellamamma*, rest a bit."

Ida halts, as if she's been given a hypnotist's signal jolting her from a trance. She opens her eyes and stares at Sal. He guides her onto the chair. "It's okay," he says. "You're awake. Let me take you back to bed, Ma."

"I'm not your mother," she says.

He laughs. "Sure you are."

"Sal?"

"That's right."

He pulls her up and Ida kisses him on the chest. "Okay, enough circling for the night, Ma."

She doesn't say anything and lets him lead her to the bedroom. Her head is resting against his arm. Justin smiles.

"Why so happy?" Sal asks.

"It's sweet to see you both together like this."

"The priest thinks love conquers all. What does he know? Right, Ma?"

Ida isn't listening anymore. Sal warms a towel in hot water and wipes the Noxzema from her face. After he helps Ida into bed, he leans in and kisses her forehead, raising the blanket to her neck. He stays beside her until she closes her eyes and considers asking if walking in circles pleases her; instead, he shares their silence and thinks of what she and Aidan O'Shea say when they've had enough, *fuck it.*

Anna returns from her walk with Lola, who rushes to look for Ida. Justin says, "You missed the circus act."

"What?"

"Ida was sleepwalking."

"God, she was sleeping like a sloth fifteen minutes ago."

"This isn't the first time. It happened last week. I should have warned you. Sal's with her."

Anna gathers her purse and phone and finds Lola lying outside Ida's door. "You two are inseparable," she tells the dog. "But you're stuck with me. Let's go." She kisses Justin. "It's because she saw Francesco slaughtered. That sent her over the cliff." At the door, Anna adds, "We'll manage, honey."

Justin is heating up the pasta that he and Ida cooked for dinner when Sal walks into the kitchen. "I bet you haven't eaten all day."

Sal ignores him. "We're losing her."

"Maybe it's the Lunesta."

"It's not the pills. The pills are supposed to make her sleep."

"Let's see what tomorrow brings."

Justin's optimism grates Sal. He goes to the cupboard and pours himself a Jameson.

"Really, Sal?"

"*Really*, Just." He sits at the table and downs the whiskey.

Justin pushes the plate of pasta in front of him. "Here, eat this and make Ida's day."

Sal swirls the pasta around the plate and touches Justin's hand. He thinks of kissing Justin but pulls back. He puts down the fork. "She wasn't this bad before Francesco was killed. I can't stop reliving the night either. Even on a day like today when so much happened."

Justin takes a sip of Sal's Jameson. "PTSD. You need to see a therapist."

"You seem okay."

"I wasn't there."

"My brother's a detective and he isn't doing anything, or if he is, how would we know. He's been a ghost ever since. And Francesco's godfather. What's Carlo done? So much for *family*."

Justin notices Sal's right hand abuzz with tremors and tries to settle it. "Your hand's shaking."

"Fuck it."

Justin holds on until the tremors stop. "Sal, we've got to leave."

Sal gets up, ignoring him. "O'Shea knows everything about Francesco, maybe more than Dad shared with me. I think he's seen the FBI file. Before Sherry left, she told me that she wants to meet with us. Ha, she called it a *family* get together. I'm surprised she didn't tell you on the way out of Pug's."

"She's *your* sister."

"Half sister. I don't trust her."

"Why can't the FBI do what they're going to do and not involve us?" Justin asks.

"O'Shea told me that Francesco was closer to Carlo than anyone suspects, as if he were more involved in the five families than just being Carlo's numbers guy."

Justin fidgets with the salt and pepper shakers.

"The Russians' hit on him would make more sense if they thought he was a big threat. O'Shea made it sound like Francesco was Carlo's consigliere."

Justin gets up and wipes down the counter.

"We always sensed Francesco was deeper in than he pretended but we didn't want to face it," Sal says, more agitated than he's been.

"He wasn't a killer; I know that for sure."

"You're naive."

Justin gives him a look.

"Maybe he wasn't a killer, but he wasn't *just* a bookie either. Francesco must have been up to something."

In the months before he was murdered, Francesco shared confidences with Justin that he had never told Sal. He felt freer, knowing his adopted son's love was less fragile. They would sit on the porch, waiting for Sal to return home from Hart Island. Ida would be watching a game show, or struggling to read magazines, which had become harder to focus on, the words slippery in her diminishing memory. At first, Francesco would reminisce about Sicily, then venture into stories about being a bookie, stories about his closeness to Carlo Cali. In their last conversation, he sighed and said, "Justin, I have a lot to be sorry for, a lot God would not want to forgive me for." Justin told him, "You'd be surprised what God forgives." Francesco, like Sal, wasn't a believer, and Justin didn't press Francesco about the burdens on his conscience; when Francesco shared secrets, Justin knew Francesco expected his confidence; the priest believed the revelations were as sacrosanct as the confessions he heard in church.

Pushing the plate of pasta aside and trying to deflect any more talk about Francesco, Justin leans in and kisses Sal. "Tell me about the rescue yesterday."

And it works, Sal becomes more relaxed. Justin can do this sometimes. The blessing of a priest, the bestowing of grace. Sal doesn't think it's a gift from God, but he concedes it's a gift. "What was it like?" Justin asks again.

Sal describes how the morning started out, how at ease the Rikers inmates were with just five coffins to bury. He admits that he had an early nip, a bit of Irish coffee with Booker to celebrate. But just one. Yet another lie among so many these days. Then, when the Lear jet crashed, no one panicked. Everyone dove into action. Sal had given the orders and sat back. He doesn't tell Justin that it really was like he and Booker say, a little like a miracle. "These Rikers inmates," Sal says, "each one stepped up."

"Well, that's good, right?"

Sal shrugs and describes how the survivors watched the father of the family waving to them as he was being airlifted in the chopper, unaware that he'd end up dead. "That's fucked up," Sal says. He describes how the family cried and laughed; they were so thankful everyone was safe. The crew, too. All of us so engaged, except the college kid. Jason squatted on the deck outside the engine room all the way to City Island. "You'd think, with all he did to save that family, in that moment the kid would be able to shake what had happened to the pledge," Sal tells Justin. "I get it, though, there are things a person does that he can never recover from."

"That's not true. Everyone is wired to handle suffering with the help of others and God."

Sal gives him a look, thinking, *Does he really not understand?*

They don't say a word for what seems like a long time, until Sal takes Justin's hand, and says, "On the way home tonight I stood alone at the back of the ferry and watched a blue reflection of the Freedom Tower dissolve on the water as the boat sailed from the harbor. It was shaped like one of the trenches on Hart Island, and it was shimmering. I thought, *I could leap into it and disappear.*"

"Sal, you're scaring me."

"You never thought of disappearing?"

Justin puts his arms around Sal's shoulders and whispers, "Why do you think you're so alone?" He leads Sal into the bedroom and lifts Sal's NYPD sweatshirt over his head. Sal unzips his pants and steps out of them. He slips off his boxers and lies on top of the comforter, turning on his side to watch Justin undress. His hand strikes the headboard, and the crucifix rattles above him. Sal notices a piece of Christ's feet chipped away. Justin kisses his finger and rests it on Christ's chest before climbing over Sal, running the finger along Sal's neck and back, as much a blessing as a familiar tenderness. He reaches over Sal to hold his sex and says he couldn't bear losing Sal, who isn't listening but shivers when his lover enters him, and in those moments as Justin slides back and forth so effortlessly, Sal feels like he is sailing on the blue reflection of Freedom Tower.

They Shoot Horses

Justin is in the kitchen making pancakes when Sal awakens. It's six in the morning. Ida, spent from a night of circling like an airliner over JFK, is out cold. Sal can hear her snoring, a distinctive wheeze with occasional trumpeting that reminds him of a sound one recent night on the National Geographic Channel. Before Francesco was killed, Ida slept as if she were in hibernation; now her room periodically erupts into a cacophony of moans.

Sal gets out of bed and walks to the kitchen in his boxers.

"Hey, sexy," Justin says, pointing to the plate of untouched pasta from last night still on the table. "You can't live on Jameson." He takes it to the sink and slides a couple of pancakes onto another plate.

Sal pours himself a cup of coffee. "Did you hear Ma? I don't know how she can sleep through her own clamor."

"At least she's out in the morning. She hasn't started sleepwalking in the daytime. So, that's a good sign."

"You know, last night, I'm sure O'Shea was right; Francesco was in deep. He was probably doing something dangerous for Carlo. That's why the Russians killed him."

"Not again. Let's not go there, Sal. You're playing with fire with the Bratva." Justin starts wiping down the pancake griddle. "Let Francesco's secret die with him, and let's get the hell out of Staten Island."

"That's what I'm talking about: Francesco's secrets. He didn't even tell me I had a sister. All those weekend trips to racetracks: Saratoga, Freehold, Fort Erie—and others far away, Churchill Downs, Santa Anita, and even Ascot in England. Ida never went along, even though the horses were the bread and butter of the house." Milk curdles in his coffee, and Sal spits it back into the cup. "Nice way to start the day."

"I'll pour you another."

"Save it. I'll get one on the ferry. I think Ida knew about Sherry. You remember what she told Francesco whenever he asked her to go to the track with him. She said, 'They shoot horses, don't they?'"

"Yeah, from the movie about a horrifying dance marathon. Man, that was dark. We couldn't understand why she was so fixed on it."

"Ida sensed there was another woman, betrayal like in the film. Michael Sarrazin dumping Jane Fonda for Susannah York and then taking Fonda back, and in the end shooting her in the head."

"What are you talking about?"

"Think about it. Ida was hinting that she knew about the affair, and still, she wasn't going to leave Francesco. She wasn't going anywhere."

"Jesus, Sal, that's some analysis. So, you're saying Francesco could shoot Ida in the head, like in the movie. You're not making any sense. I don't think she was talking about infidelity." And unusually adamant, he says, "I think she didn't like the movie, she didn't like the races, she didn't like horses."

Sal smiles. "Who are you, her confessor?" He finishes the last pancake. "I bet O'Shea can tell me what Ida knew and didn't."

Justin tenses up. "Why do you care what Ida knows about Francesco's affair? She's in no shape to revisit that past. Anyway, O'Shea doesn't know what he's talking about."

"I'm not going to ask Ida. But I told you last night O'Shea probably read Francesco's FBI file, or his sister told him everything. They're close. What do you think about Francesco being Carlo's consigliere?"

"O'Shea's Irish, a storyteller. That's what I think."

"He knows a lot."

"Well, *fugetaboutit*. Wasn't that what he told you at Pug's? He's right. Some secrets are better left buried."

"Says the priest. What about *ours*?" he asks, immediately regretting that he's given Justin an opening to talk about leaving the priesthood.

"Well, we didn't have much of a choice, back then. But like I've been telling you, we do now."

Sal's unwilling to be derailed. "We're not going there now, Justin. I want to know why you're so reluctant to learn that Francesco was hiding so much?" Pausing, as if he senses Justin is keeping a secret, too, he says, "You'd tell me if he were confessing to you."

"No, that would be a sin."

The thought of Francesco entering a confessional seems so remote that Sal dismisses it as quickly as it occurred. "Ha, my father baring his soul in confession, what was I thinking?"

"Nothing you do is going to bring him back. So, yes, let it lie."

"I'm his son . . ." Sal's voice trails off, not knowing what to say.

"So, what do you want to do? Massacre the Russians?"

"Fuck it," he says. "I can't talk to you."

Justin gives Sal a look and goes back to cleaning the griddle.

Francesco used to tell Justin that he was proud he had kept Sal away from the Cali side of the family. "It's the one thing that I did right," he said. "But there's so much else I regret." Justin remembers, not long before Francesco was killed, they were waiting for Sal to come home from Hart Island. Sinatra was singing "That's Life," on the stereo. Ida was watching Ellen DeGeneres with Anna. Francesco reminisced that before Justin moved in, whenever he took Antony to Aqueduct, Sal stayed home and cooked with Ida. Sal read about dinosaurs and watched Disney movies, while Antony did unspeakable things through his adolescence. Later, until he went to the police academy, Antony hung out at the Mulberry Street Bar in Little Italy with the sons of tough guys. Back then, before the yuppies moved in, there were no parents pushing baby carriages there, with corgis and dachshunds in tow. Back then in Little Italy, you could get killed for a pair of Nikes. Francesco didn't want Sal anywhere near wannabe wiseguys. Justin remembers Francesco leaning close to him and saying: "Antony will always be a street kid, but Sal has a soul like you. I'm glad Sal didn't turn out like Antony. You have a lot to do with this, Justin." He had never seen Francesco so troubled and reminded his adopted father that as in the parable of Cain and Abel, two sons can be as different as north and south; a man chooses what his heart and mind drive him to do. He told Francesco that according to Saint Augustine, the soul is not moved to abandon higher things and love inferior things unless a man wills it. Francesco said, "You don't know the half of it. I'm not who you think I am." And when Justin asked what he meant, Francesco said there was something he had to do that, despite his still believing his life in the mob was irredeemable, could remove the family from the Cali shadow. "No matter what," though, he said, "promise me you'll watch over Sal."

Justin clears the table and puts the dishes in the washer. He walks over to Sal and wraps his arms around Sal's shoulders. He whispers, "It's better to let sleeping dogs lie."

Sal, lost in his own memories of his father, doesn't respond. He remembers how the breakfast table was covered with racing magazines: *Equus*, *The Blood Horse*, *Practical Punting*. Beside a plate of scrambled eggs was a stack of daily racing forms from tracks around the country. Every morning Francesco pored over the fundamentals of horse betting and handicapping: Speed, class, form, pace, track condition, post position, appearance, weight, and, of course, jockey. Billy "The Limp" Baldoni, one of Carlo Cali's nephews, whose riding career ended when a horse fell on top of him, delivered the daily forms to the doorstep. Sal from his bedroom window would sometimes see the little man limp off. He always wore the racing cap that José Lodero had over his helmet the day his mount, Make a Buck, won the Kentucky Derby. It was a gift Francesco had given Baldoni from the racing memorabilia that he had amassed over his career in reading horses. Francesco would tell stories about Lodero, who acted as if Diogenes had shined his lantern into the rider's eyes and ditched it right there in front of Lodero, the search for an honest man over. But before José climbed atop a horse and became the King of Saratoga, he had been a bettor. That should have raised red flags. If someone wants to fix a race, easiest way is to pay riders to lose. And when the mob is running the sheets, if a jockey doesn't take the bribe, an enforcer threatens to break both his legs. Once a dirty rider starts betting on his own fix, you have him indebted to you. He's yours forever. Sal should have known back then that his father was a gangster, but when he was a boy around that table, it was easier to believe his father was more magician than enforcer. "The horses," Francesco would say, "they're majestic."

If only this table could talk, Sal thinks, remembering his father studying the forms and magazines, reading the names of horses—Bojangles, Cleopatra, Pinkie Pie, Butter Milk, Real Quiet—as if they were pals, and Sal unaware, then as now, of the secrets that Francesco had kept.

~

Justin lightly slaps Sal's shoulder. "Where are you?"

"What?"

"I'm saying you've got to forget about what O'Shea is telling you. We have to stay clear of Francesco's murder. Like your father would say, listen, Sal, *capisci*." And suddenly losing his patience, he says, "Jesus, Sal, *enough!*" He turns away and grabs his collar from the counter and snaps it on. He fetches his clergy jacket.

"Where are you going? I thought you said Father Damien was here."

"I need some air. I'll tell Anna to come by for a while."

"You're pissed."

"I'm worried, Sal. We've got a lot to work out."

A neighbor waves to Justin in the driveway, thinking there's nothing unusual about the parish priest staying so many nights in his childhood home.

"You're up early, Joanne."

"Sunrise shift like you, Father. How's Ida?"

"She's had better days."

"All things considered, she's lucky you and Sal are around."

Justin, tired of pretending he's simply the faithful adopted son in the eyes of everyone who knows him, forces a smile, and heads off.

~

Sal checks on Ida before he leaves. She's surprisingly quiet. He wonders how much of love and loss her addled brain reveals during somnolent hours of dementia. There's so much Sal doesn't know about her.

He doesn't know that in her dreams, she visits her childhood in Sicily and eats Christmas cookies piled high surrounded by mandarins. She relives the evening she met Francesco at a neighbor's house, Connie Francis on the radio singing her hit "Mama" from America. There's the night Francesco returns from Santa Anita when she finally says, "Enough. The whore and bastard kid are dead to you." At night, snippets of memories flicker past like celluloid on a runaway movie reel. But sometimes a recollection plays out slowly enough that she can place herself in it and remember who she once was. Eventually, her dementia chokes her off from everything definable, as if she were swimming through algae bloom.

Sal leans over and kisses his mother's forehead. She looks so alone, and he whispers, "I miss Francesco, too." Ida's eyes open briefly, and Sal sees what he imagines are nascent tears before her lids close again. He finds her housedress and slippers and places them on the chair by her bed. He goes to the kitchen and puts out boxes of Raisin Bran and Cocoa Puffs. He turns on the television and the morning NY1 news is showing yesterday's images of the downed Lear jet in the Sound. A reporter is talking about Peter Klock's heart attack as the video shifts to the clip of the Klock family disembarking from *Vesuvius* on City Island. Unaware that their father is dead, the twins are smiling and waving beside their mother.

"Christ," Sal says.

He switches to NBC, where the *Today Show* is about to begin. Ida's depended on Al Roker to get her through the seasons. Now, any other channel to start her day throws her for a loop. With the weatherman nearby, she'll be content to sit at the table waiting for every update—blizzards in Buffalo, floods along the Mississippi, fires raging in Southern California, twisters in Nashville, or today's gray morning. No matter the weather or breaking news—school shootings, earthquakes, Trump bullshit—she's content to pour a cup of coffee from the pot that Justin has left for her, if Al Roker comes and goes across the screen. Whoever she sees that morning, she'll greet them with something she's heard from the weatherman. "It's cold out there." "Head to the beach today if you can." "No school today, boys and girls. It's snowing!"

Anna is on her way, and before she arrives, Sal organizes what's on the table: finger puppets of Dean Martin, Frank Sinatra, and Sammy Davis Jr. that Francesco gave Ida when she started forgetting the music she loved; the *You bet your bocce balls* coffee mug that she picked up at a yard sale decades ago and that still somehow makes her smile; and a picture book of Sicilian villages, including her own Cinisi, that a goombah gave her not long after Francesco was killed. *What joy, what sadness*, he wonders, *does any of this bring her as she sits in her dementia with Al Roker laughing on the television?*

It's Japanese, Stupid

Sherry is usually awake when Aidan shambles into the house after last call at Mother Pug's. But yesterday, even though she had wanted to talk to him about Sal, she went out like a narcoleptic. This morning, up early, she pauses at the window to watch the sun struggle to rise in the gray sky. The kitchen table is strewn with papers about the Bratva mob. The scope of its criminal enterprises in Brooklyn is colossal: from its beginning of extorting bakeries and defrauding jewelry stores to human, drug, and arms trafficking; gambling; fencing and money laundering. None of its successes would have happened without an alliance with New York's Italian mob families, and until he was gunned down, Francesco was the Gambino emissary.

There's a half-empty cup of black cherry Yoplait left from the day before next to a coffee mug that Chicago agents gave her; printed on the front is *You Are Dead to Us*, and written across the back: *Sherry, kick ass in New York*. An alley cat that had leapt into her Dodge Charger Pursuit outside a Chicago trap house is purring on her lap. All that time prowling the streets and now all he wants to do is stay inside, as close to Sherry and Aidan as he can get. Go figure. She named him Elliot, after the legendary FBI Untouchable.

Sherry packs the papers into her briefcase, leaving the yogurt and mug for Aidan to clean up. Elliot follows her into his bedroom and jumps onto the bed. "Get the fuck up," she says, "before he claws out your eyes."

"Fuck it," Aidan goes, barely opening his lids.

Sherry pokes him in the side like he's a kid needing prodding. Elliot settles on the pillow beside him. "I don't want you talking to Sal about Francesco."

Aidan's too tired to focus on what she's saying but nods anyway.

"We're all going to meet soon. So, button it until then."

He drags himself up and sits back against the headboard. "What did you say?"

"Jesus, Aidan. I said no more talking to Sal about Francesco." And more forcefully than usual, she adds, "Understand!"

Sherry opens the blinds, and the gray morning light and her unusually strident tone jolt him. "Jesus," he says, "what I do?"

"There's coffee in the kitchen, shithead." Pausing, recalling a time when Aidan was more a comfort than a worry, she sits on the bed. "Remember how we'd recite lines from *Peanuts*? You switched from Charlie Brown to Linus to Woodstock; I was Snoopy, Lucy, and Peppermint Patty."

Aidan, his head aching, channels Linus, "Sometimes I lie awake at night, and I say, *No problem is so big or so complicated that it can't be run away from!*"

"Jesus, Aidan, that would be the first line to come to you." In her best Lucy imitation, holding out her palm, she says, *"Snap out of it! Five cents, please!"*

They laugh. Still in *Peanuts* mode, she says, *"I oughta slug you!"* Then, getting back to what she came in to tell him, she goes, "I'm serious, no more talk about Francesco with Sal. I need you to help me convince Sal to play, but we're going to do it together. Can you get that into your boozed brain?"

"Yeah, count on me, sis." Elliot crawls up his chest.

"See how comforting companionship is? You've lived alone too long."

He stretches his arms and says, "You gotta love Snoopy: *To live is to dance, to dance is to live.*"

"If only you believed it, big lug." She pats his knee, and the cat jumps off, following Sherry to the kitchen. Aidan slides back down on his side and closes his eyes. "Fuck it," he says.

"We'll do this, Elliot," she tells the cat watching her pick up the brief-case on her way out of the house.

∼

Aidan's got an hour before he clocks in at the library. He steps into the shower, and when Elliot pokes himself in at the side of the curtain, he douses the cat. "Got you," he says as Elliott runs off. While Aidan is drying off, he catches a glimpse of himself in the mirror, the bloated stomach of a heavy drinker, someone who swills Guinness and slams shots and eats a diet of peanuts and pizza strips. He grimaces and says aloud, "Fuck it, I never was a looker anyway." Dressed in the same jeans he's worn all week and a rumpled grandfather shirt one of the librarians brought back from Ireland last summer, he walks barefoot into the kitchen, his toes yeast-encrusted from so much alcohol.

He's taken to talking to himself some mornings, or on others addressing Elliot, who tags along more like a dog than a cat. He likes to go over aloud what he might say if he ever decided to tell a sad-sack sobriety testimony. But what he always ends up doing is reminiscing about some moment he was happy. And he thinks of them as moments, no matter how long they might have lasted. He pours a mug of the coffee Sherry left for him and considers fueling it with a little Bushmills that she had brought in a few days ago. He told her, "You would desecrate a house with that Belfast swill." Then he thinks, well, a nip is a nip after all, but decides to make it a cold-turkey morning. And then he goes:

"I remember Marianne. She was only eight, though she wore pierced dolphin earrings and carried a lunch box with Gamera vs. Jiger on it. He looked more like a monster turtle than Godzilla. There were red, blue, and green kana and hiragana ideograms everywhere. If anyone asked her what it was, she'd just say, *It's Japanese, stupid.*" Even the nuns didn't know what to do with her. Her father ran The House of Paradise, an "art cinema" in Times Square. And this morning, the taste of coffee like rust in his mouth, not knowing where this story is going, the memory of Marianne and her turtle monster is enough to make Aidan smile, and so he goes, "Ah, fuck it, that's my story for today."

BB and the Mother of God

It's cold and drizzling when Sal boards the ferry to Manhattan, as if the day had entered another latitude where the weather is more like November than yesterday's summer tease. Riders are grumpy. Sal finds a seat next to a window where he rests his head against the glass and watches the rain, a little heavier now, slide down the pane. The whole way to Whitehall Terminal he looks out at the turbid Upper Bay and imagines pine boxes in Hart Island trenches being buried in the sandy earth. *Jesus*, he thinks when the ferry docks, *my mind's not right*.

He has another hour and a half commute before he gets to City Island. He walks to Bowling Green Station and catches the 4 train to 125th Street, then the 6 to Pelham Bay Park, where he picks up the bus to City Island and hoofs it five minutes to the DOC dock and *Vesuvius*. He could buy a car and cut, if he's lucky, fifteen minutes from the commute, but he hates sitting in traffic on the Verrazzano Narrows and Brooklyn Queens Expressway, the Bruckner and Triboro Bridge. He can't get used to calling it the Robert F. Kennedy. Sal hates the rutted feel of a car on the road, the stops and starts. He hates drivers, angry or oblivious, weaving in and out of lanes exchanging withering expressions. He hates the sight of asphalt and apartment high-rises and warehouses, spiritless office buildings and shopping plazas everywhere along the way. He hates driving. He's content to cross the Upper Bay and accept the ferry's surrender to the protean nature of the sea. He respects the underground trains plowing through the tunnels of New York's boroughs. When he surfaces, he feels lucky to be back above ground.

Sal stops at Clipper Coffee for a jumbo Americano and java for the crew. He hunts for the flask in his backpack. "Shit," he says, remembering that he'd left it empty behind the rolls of paper towels in the pantry.

"What's wrong, Sal?" asks Cookie, who owns the shop. "You should be feeling pretty good after yesterday's rescue."

Sal ignores the comment. "I've been wondering. How'd you get the name *Cookie*?"

"Cookie Gilchrist."

"Who?"

"Come on, you know who he is."

"Not a clue."

"The Buffalo Bills star fullback from the sixties. My grandfather was his best friend in high school."

"I'm not a football fan, but I remember a crazy movie where this family tries to kill the Bills kicker Scott Norwood. Guess I identify with failure."

"Anjelica Houston and Ben Gazzaro."

"That's it."

"My grandfather loved Cookie. When he was dying of throat cancer in a nursing home in Pittsburgh, Gramp visited him almost every day, sneaked in a cigar, which Cookie just chewed on. You should read his book, *The Cookie That Did Not Crumble*. Tough life. An activist. Tough guy to get along with."

"Like you." Sal laughs.

"Ha, I'm the cookie that crumbled. Hey, really, Sal, good work yesterday."

He pays Cookie and gives him a nod.

"So, do you think the city is going to shut Hart, turn it into a memorial park?"

"I don't think about it," Sal says, unwilling to go there, not on a morning when he's got an empty flask, not on a day when he already feels like shit and it's not even nine o'clock. He doesn't want to think about losing Hart.

Before he leaves, Sal stops before "Pussy the Fish," a talking large-mouth bass mounted on a wooden plaque that Cookie had just put up. It's motion-activated, and when you pass it, the rubber fish head pops out. In the voice of Sal "Big Pussy" Bonpensiero from *The Sopranos*, the fish, its mouth gumming up and down, says: "Hey, Tone, how's it going. Anyway, four dollars a pound. You know I've been working with the government, right, Tone."

"Really, a *Sopranos* fish?"

"Yeah, and one Sal to another."

Sal grimaces and heads to the dock. He pulls up the hood on his parka and sips his coffee. Too early to stop at the liquor store for a pint. "Cold turkey today," he mutters.

A homeless guy is pushing a cart on the sidewalk, heading toward him. It's filled with garbage bags and other sacks piled up to his chin. There's a square weather warning flag—blue for rain—driven into the bags and flapping in his face. His name is BB, for "Big Beard." In his cart he's stashed a sea flag for every kind of weather. His beard, a deep brown, cascades like a mini-avalanche down his chest. He's tall, maybe six foot three, and more bull-chested than overstuffed. There are days he walks all over town singing the same three or four sea shanties. Some kids when they see him shout out, "Hey, Professor Hagrid, another bad night?" He's never sure if they're mocking him or trying to make a friendly overture.

Everyone on City Island knows BB. Sal has talked to him a few times on his way to the dock. He used to be a big-boat fisherman and bottom-trawled along the Atlantic from Long Island to Maine, hauling in enormous loads of cod, halibut, and rockfish. One afternoon he pulled up a body. The corpse was missing its feet but still had what he told the reporters were "cement ankle bracelets." On its back was a gigantic tattoo of the Virgin Mary holding a rose. A *New York Post* photographer got a bull's-eye shot of it, an artist's handiwork that some Catholics believed was a sign of a miracle. Discovering the body was BB's moment of fame. While it's not rare for bodies to be pulled out of the waters around New York City, an unidentified footless, cement-ankle-braceleted corpse with the Mother of God on its back became a media sensation. Not long after finding the body, he sold his boat and disappeared from City Island. No one knew what happened to him, but a year later he was back. Now BB spends most of the time on the street. In harsh weather and freezing cold, the parish priest lets him hunker down in the basement of Saint Mary Star of the Sea Church. No one claimed the body he trawled out of the Atlantic. Its brief notoriety faded, and the corpse was buried, Mother of God and all, with the other unknown or unwanted corpses on Hart Island, not far from where BB had fished it out.

As he passes by, BB doesn't look up. Watching him lumber behind his cart, Sal thinks of something that the Coast Guard taught him, a quote from Aristotle: "There are three kinds of human beings. The living, the dead and those who go out to sea." He thinks about the Beatitudes that Jason recites at the pulpit and sometimes around the house when he feels the family needs a dose of Catholic comfort. "Well, here's one of mine," Sal says to himself as he sees BB dissolve into fog crawling in from the harbor: *"Woe to you who love. / For everyone you love dies."* Sal imagines his father adrift in the afterlife, shunned or invisible among the masses of imponderable dead. He remembers the morning's turbid crossing, remembers imagining corpses roiling like the sea, as if, in a momentary spasm of awareness, the dead are mutinous in their graves.

He sips his coffee and says, "Why the fuck did I forget the flask?" When Sal gets to the dock, the DOC bus and refrigerated truck are already there. *A half-hour early*, he thinks. *That's unusual.*

Booker, Hemins, and the Rikers burial crew are waiting inside, the bus engine spewing exhaust that hangs in the wet air. Jesús and Zookie are asleep, their shoulders slumped against windows. The other three inmates sit expressionless. Hemins leans on the steering wheel, her head propped up by a hand on her chin. She sees Sal and gives him her tired fuck-this-day look. Booker stands up and heads to the door.

The new guy driving the truck carrying the pine boxes is reading the *New York Post*. When Sal passes the cab, he sees the cover. It's an old copy from months ago: the mayor holding up his hands shooting the infamous Nixon victory fingers and the headline, I'M NOT A CROOK. On the seat beside him is another old one: "BEZOS EXPOSES PECKER." The driver looks like a gigantic bobblehead at the wheel, shimmying to Pink Floyd's "Money," so loud the cab barely contains the sound.

Booker steps out of the bus and says, "What a difference a day makes."

"Hey, you're almost never early."

"I got the word there's a lockdown happening this morning. They let us out before Rikers goes dark."

"The whole complex?"

"Warden called me last night. He didn't tell me anything else. Just that he wanted us out of the gate early. Maybe it's a drill. There's been bad shit happening. Two suicides in solitary in a week. City can't close it down soon enough."

"How's the crew?"

"They act like their asses are in slings. They weren't celebrities once they got back to the house last night."

"Fifteen minutes of fame." Sal, sulky, asks, "How many bodies on ice?"

"Don't know, Sal. I've been on the bus keeping dry." Booker walks over to the truck and knocks on the window.

The driver doesn't hear him. He takes his baton and bangs the hood of the cab. The guy bolts up and turns down the music, the Pink Floyd sound of clinking coins and a ringing cash register barely audible now. He pulls down the window.

"Hey, young Republican, hand me the sheets," Booker says.

Sasha Kalchick is twenty-six and speaks with a thick Slavic accent. He's a certified Rush Limbaugh Dittohead. He loves classic rock, but his politics, if that is what you call a vigilante state of hyper-grievance, is bent on railing against the Four Corners of Deceit: Government, Universities, Science, and State Media. Booker tells Sal that he thinks the kid got a lucky get-out-of-jail card and is in witness protection. Maybe he's a canary grandson of a West Coast Russian mob boss? Who knows, maybe he turned on some Russian oligarch? To protect himself from getting dusted with polonium, he's assumed a right-wing lunatic fringe identity, working in, of all places, the New York City morgue. Who'd think to look for him there? The only Russian turning up there would be a dead one. Booker shakes his head. "I hate to think he's just another ordinary asshole. I like to look for explanations."

Sal nods. "Even when there's none."

Booker checks the sheets. There are eight new corpses on the truck, two of them shoeboxes. "Christ, unlucky thirteen when you add the five on ice that we couldn't bury yesterday. In the rain, too. No mercy."

"And two babies. The maternity wards are getting back into the mortuary business."

Booker doesn't appreciate Sal's flippant remark and gives him a look.

Franklin in the bus hears Booker and says, "Fuck. Unlucky thirteen."

Hemins turns around. "Hey, who said you should expect a day in the park."

He groans. "Ball buster."

"What did you say?"

"Not you, Officer Hemins. The boxes."

Jason mutters, "Two shoeboxes."

Hemins gets up and pokes Jesús and Zookie with her baton.

"OK, sleeping beauties, it's time."

No one sees BB, who's hidden his shopping cart behind a boarded-up shack next to the dock. He's carrying one of the sacks, only a third full, over his shoulder, and it bounces off his butt at every step. In his other hand is the blue weather flag brushing his face. He passes Sal and Booker, who are out of view while Kalchick pulls the truck closer to the pier. BB walks nonchalantly down the dock and boards *Vesuvius*; he's planning to hide at the stern behind a chest filled with life vests and ropes, though he knows it's likely someone will find him there before reaching Hart Island. By then, he hopes they won't turn back; if he explains that he needs to visit the grave of the corpse he pulled out of the water; if he explains it's what the Virgin Mary told him he must do. BB's surprised. Just before he reaches the stern, he finds that the engine room door is open. *Even better place to hole up*, he thinks, *if there's a spot to hunker in unseen.*

BB believes you can tell how much a captain loves his boat by the way he keeps the engine room. But leaving it unlocked? Not a good sign. As soon as he walks in, he looks for a key item of protective gear he'll need, earmuffs. Sure enough, hanging on a hook beside him is a 3M Peltor, the exact set he had on his trawler *Mary Lee*. BB renamed his boat after the great white that was tagged off Cape Cod in 2012; she sent out her last ping off Long Beach in New Jersey on June 17, 2017. *Go figure*, he thinks, *the exact earmuffs*. There are mishaps in an engine room just waiting to happen. Switch panels, fuel distribution valves, battery switches—these need to be at a hand's reach. *Just right*, BB thinks as he makes a mental inspection of the main propulsion engine and all its auxiliary parts and machinery: generator, cooling exchangers, and, surprisingly, thrusters that *Mary Lee* never had. "A piece of work," BB says. "This guy loves his boat." Who knows? Maybe he didn't leave the engine room unlocked. Maybe the Mother of God is looking after BB. He knows that to have a chance of escaping notice, he needs to make sure he doesn't set off an alarm and bring the captain running. So, he finds a place out of harm's way behind the engine, clear of blistering hot metal surfaces or swirling gears that could catch his weather flag or cascading beard. He settles in, and if he's lucky, Captain Sal might not see him. "Good as it gets," he says, and hums in his head, so no one can hear him: *Where the sharks have his body / And the devil takes his soul! / O, poor old man.*

BB has unfinished business with the corpse he pulled out of the water. He gave up everything when he thought the Virgin Mary on the stiff's back was sending him a message: "Go out and find Jesus, my son, or you will end up in cement shoes, too." He remembered what Father Aloysius taught him at Brooklyn Jesuit Prep. Jesus believed what Socrates understood centuries before the Son of God was born to sacrifice Himself for mankind: "The unexamined life is not worth living." Father Aloysius pulled him aside on the last day of classes and said, "Go out in the world and never stop examining who you are. Know thyself, as Jesus did in the desert before he died for us. Know thyself, and you will find the reason you were placed on this earth. I have faith in you, Danny boy."

So, that summer BB set out on the Atlantic, a fisherman. Thirty-five years he hauled a ton of fish from the sea to the dock, never discovering why God had given him life, never finding a woman to love and marry, never engendering a family to care for, never finding a cause. And poor Mary Lee was probably dead. No, until the day he fished out the Virgin

Mary off Long Island, all he had done was haul in cod after cod, rockfish after rockfish, as if he were Sisyphus.

Now, after a year of searching, after pilgrimages to Jerusalem and Gethsemane, Fatima and Lourdes, the Vatican and Assisi, and even after walking the Camino to Santiago de Compostela, he has no clearer purpose than he did as the worn-out sailor in the sea ballad. BB was losing faith that he'd find a way out of his worthlessness until last night, when once again there came a sign. He was sitting, feeling sorry for himself, in the pagoda behind the nautical museum on Fordham Street, musing on decades of regrets and failures, when he watched wispy clouds drift across the sky, slowly curtaining the moon in a sheet of fine gauze. A forked lightning bolt tore a fissure in the horizon from the surface of the Sound to the zenith of the sky. It split the moon in half, and there in the lunar crevasse, the Virgin Mary holding a rose looked down at him and pointed to Hart Island. *Your answer, dear fisherman*, she said, *is there on Potter's Field.*

Decapitation

The burial crew gathers aimlessly at the back of the refrigerated truck. Jesús and Zookie are sharing a Marlboro, the last one in a pack that a guy in protective custody had given Jesús. With white hoods pulled over their Day-Glo orange parkas, the five inmates look like hazmat workers. Kalchick flips the switch on the door of the morgue truck. While the other inmates turn toward the shore and grouse about the cold and the rain, Jason watches the pine boxes creep into view. Michael Borowick 042401 is butted against Male Unknown 042402 as if they were pals; the two baby-filled shoeboxes on top have shifted around like an afterthought during the ride from the morgue. BABY 671 and BABY 672, no names, the latest in the running count of the number of dead infants so far this year. Jason leaps into the cargo bed and reaches high to lift one of the shoeboxes from the stack. He carefully sets down the little coffin at the edge of the truck floor and returns to the stack to retrieve the second, which he places deferentially next to BABY 671. He jumps off the truck, picks up the coffins, and says, heading to the dock and *Vesuvius*, "I've got the little ones."

Sal turns to Booker. "What's up with college boy?"

"Who knows? It's going to be that kind of day." Booker shouts to the inmates loitering around the truck: "Hey, follow Jason's lead and load the boxes on the ferry."

Sal goes to the wheelhouse and watches the murk evaporate over the Sound, losing its immense gray heft. Still, in the dull light, Hart Island remains wrapped in haze.

The crew hauls the coffins onto the deck, and after the last pine box is loaded, the inmates take their seats on benches under the bimini top.

Jason looks at the stack of coffins. "That's weird."

"What?" Zookie asks.

"That last box. The clown is dead."

"Man, wha clown?" Jesús asks.

"Ronald McDonald 042406, there, didn't anyone else see it?"

Everyone looks over at the stack.

"Bad juju," Jesús says. "Gold Arches dude dead is bad juju."

Even Hemins and Booker shake their heads. "What kind of parent does that?" Hemins asks.

"Stupid or perverted," Booker says.

Franklin and Al untie the ropes and shout up to Sal that all the lines are unhitched. Booker remains under the canvas cover with Hemins and the crew. BB is hunkered into his spot in the engine room. *So far, so good*, he thinks, the earmuffs snug over his head, as he feels the engine power up. In the wheelhouse, Sal switches on the navigation to help him through the haze. He's thinking about Justin, wondering why he isn't interested in what O'Shea knows. It's not like him to be dismissive. Sal pictures Ida wrapped around Francesco on the stoop. He thinks, *O'Shea knows something*.

Zookie turns to Jesús. "Did you hear about the tsunami?"

"Wha that, Japanese fish? I don't eat it raw."

"Shit, Jesús. You ain't that dumb. It's the big one. A tidal wave," Franklin says.

"Somewhere in the South Pacific. It swept away a whole island," Al says.

Jason says, "It could happen here."

"Wha?" Jesús asks.

"A lot of death," Jason says.

"Shit, we don't need mo boxes," Jesús says.

A hard rain starts, striking the tarp so insistently that the crew is quiet the rest of the way. When they dock at Hart Island, the downpour has eased to a drizzle and the fog has pretty much lifted. A cold easterly pinprick spray off the Sound strafes their faces.

"Not going to get much better than this," Booker shouts up to Sal. "Supposed to come down hard off and on all day." Turning to Hemins and the crew, he says, "Let's get these coffins in the ground."

"You the boss," Jesús says, trying to put a hint of mojo back in his voice.

Jesús and Zookie carry a coffin, Beatrice Shepard 022407. "What kind of name is Beatrice?" Zookie asks.

"A beauty," Jesús says. "She light. I bet she black, she sings like Summer Walker."

"Who's she?"

"Ain't sayin'. She on Spotify. When you get out, you find Summer. Man, she all sugar."

Al hears them talking and says, "Shit, Shepard isn't a black name."

"You think there wasn't a slave owner named Shepard. Williams, Johnson, Smith, Jones, Brown. Why not a white name like Shepard?" Franklin says.

"He know right," Jesús says.

Al says, "I still bet you Beatrice is white as blow. She's a kid from Kansas no one ever wanted and bit it on the floor in some Bronx bando. Maybe she was with a scum baghead, who just left her there."

"Ain't so," Jesús says.

Al shrugs.

Jason is the first off *Vesuvius*. He's taken the shoeboxes, one at a time, and placed them on the island truck. He just stands there, looking at the boxes, his pants pockets turned out like busted balloons, appearing as lost as he was hyped on adrenaline during yesterday's rescue.

Hemins gives him a look. "You just going to stand there, college boy."

He shakes his head and goes back to the ferry and helps Franklin with Ronald McDonald 042406.

"You the man, college boy," Jesús says.

"What?"

"Takin' the clown."

"Everyone deserves a pallbearer in the end," Franklin says.

"Pallbearer?" Jesús asks.

"Don't you know anything?" Zookie says.

"The guy who carries the coffin to the church and the grave," Jason says.

"So, we all pallbearers," Jesús says.

"Bet your sorry ass we are," Zookie says.

Hemins gets in the truck and warms up the cab before heading to the north end of the island where the latest open trench—twenty feet wide, seventy feet long and six feet deep—was excavated two weeks ago. Booker takes the wheel of the bus—a converted school bus painted white with CORRECTIONS stenciled in blue along each side. Before climbing onto it, Sal stops at a stone memorial and reads aloud: "Blessed are the poor in spirit, for theirs is the kingdom of Heaven." He reads another inscription: "Cry not for us, for we are with the Father," and he pictures Francesco bleeding in the snow. "Fuck that," he says.

"Wha that, Cappy?" Jesús asks.

"You heard me," Sal says, uncharacteristically brusque, taking a seat, signaling to everyone it's a shut-the-fuck-up kind of day.

On the way to the trench the bus passes the ruins of buildings that over the decades until the 1970s housed outcast New Yorkers: the sick with yellow fever and tuberculosis; psychiatric patients; poor men sent to the workhouse to pay off debts. These brick ruins pocking the roadside look even more ruinous under the somber sky: the laundry of the boys' workhouse, the butcher shop and mess hall, a chapel with its stained-glass windows busted out, and remnants of bleachers from Ebbets Field donated to the Hart Island Wildcats when there were inmates who'd committed nonviolent crimes bunking on the island. They fielded a team against the Nike Missile Base players, worked the burial crew, and made the pine boxes for corpses in Potter's Fields all over the Northeast.

When the bus reaches the trench, the crew gets ready to haul out the coffins and bury the day's dead.

"All we do is load and unload these boxes," Zookie says.

"What do you want, a medal? You're in jail," Booker says.

Jason surprises everyone. "What about yesterday?"

"Say so," Jesús says. "We the angels yesterday."

Jason nods, while Al and Franklin give them a look.

Booker turns to Sal. "About half full already. Christ, look at all that mud."

Sal, not listening to him, says. "I'm going to take a hike around."

"In this shit?"

"Yeah, in this shit."

Hemins in the truck with the coffins passes him on the road. She stops and backs up. "You okay?"

"Just walkin'."

"In the rain?"

He waves her on.

~

At the statue of the Virgin Mary and her Child, Sal squats so that he's inches from her stone face. The top of her crown has broken off, leaving a rough patch where once there were stars and diamonds. The statue is spotted with lichen, pocked, scuffed, and chipped. Still, Mary's gown folds gracefully in the weathered illusion of sculpted stone. The rosary around her neck isn't missing a bead and its cross sits perfectly at her knees. She's cradling her son, his arm broken off below the elbow.

Sal thinks of Justin, who long ago stopped asking Sal if he could visit Potter's Field. Sal had decided, soon after he docked the ferry for the first time, that Hart Island was his refuge, his secret place, not unlike what Justin found in the church. At first Sal told him it was impossible; no one except inmates and DOC officers are permitted, and when the island was opened to memorial visits for relatives of the interred, Sal told Justin it was still off limits for him. But I'm a priest, Justin argued. Surely, they'd let a priest, your brother, tag along one day. Not a chance, Sal lied. For a while, until Booker sensed it was never going to happen, he would ask Sal: "Why don't you bring your brother Justin on a run? We can use a priest around here." All Sal would say: "Adopted brother, he's my *adopted* brother."

Sal, after all these years, needs to make sure people know that Justin is adopted. Years ago, before Justin stopped being bothered by it, he had asked Sal, "What are you, afraid of people thinking we're incestuous once they find out we're lovers?" "Nice, Justin," Sal said. "Why can't you understand it's easier this way. I'm not letting anyone *out* us." The closeted life is all Sal's known or wanted since they were kids, and he's been keeping the secret for so long that the well-practiced deception comforts him, or so he tells himself. The lie, he thinks, ensures that Justin will never be forced to choose between him and the priesthood. It didn't matter that Justin has explained that he knows priests who have longtime lovers. A bishop in Ireland has a kid. It's possible to share their lives with others they trust. Secrets don't have to be absolute. Sal wouldn't have any of it.

Sal never revealed that long before Francesco was killed, he'd been visiting the statue of Mary and her Son. He surprised himself when he started to bring offerings: a plastic rose, one of the scapulars Ida had strewn around the house, a pear she'd put in his lunch bag, a copy of the book *Imitating Mary*. All gone, except for the rose and a remnant of one of the wool cloth squares of the scapular of Our Lady of Mt. Carmel that Ida had encased in plastic. The words barely visible: *Whosoever dies wearing this scapular shall not suffer eternal fire.*

The statue opened a door to a faith that he had believed was closed for good, not a faith in God, or Heaven and Hell, but in goodness, kindness, and love like Justin had been preaching. "Do you think he's right, Mary," he asked, the first time he visited the statue. "Is Justin on to something?" Sal would ask Mary for indulgences, seldom for himself, but for his father, who needs forgiveness for the sins of his bookmaking. For his mother, who is forgetting more things than anyone could count. For Antony, who whores around and doesn't give a shit about his own family. For Justin, who is so kind to everyone, who deserves more happiness than Sal gives him. Yes, for Justin, who, after all these years, makes him still see faraway starlight when they make love, and afterward, leaves Sal fearing he gives so little back. He asked for indulgences for the Rikers burial crew, because he knows, as Booker had told him, these men are better than their bad actions. He prayed, too, for the dead he hauls week after week to Hart Island, the junkies and alcoholics, the lost and lonesome, the impoverished, the haunted by regrets, the anguished driven by demons of mental illness, and the innocent infants in shoeboxes who never found the first breath in their inchoate lungs that would let them cry. Sometimes he'd choke up when he'd look at the Virgin and see in her chipped stone eyes a glint of gritty light, the sun reflecting. He imagined Mary, too, was tearing up.

Now, back before the statue, for the first time since his father was killed, Sal squints and stares and tries to find words that express the shame he feels when he doubts the goodness in humanity and his own capacity to love. He looks to the white stone markers on the trenches, which from far away resemble signals of surrender rising from the mass graves. *So much abandonment*, he thinks. He imagines his father watching him, his father broken and shunned in a dark sky. He feels so suddenly desperate and ferocious. So much unexpected rage. When he gets up, he's shaking. He kicks the statue and the head of Jesus tumbles to the ground. He surprises himself and makes the Sign of the Cross. "Fuck," he says, "what's wrong with me?"

～

BB is watching from the window of the workhouse. He had his eyes on Mary and the Baby Jesus ever since he'd found a corner of the roofless building that was protected from the rain. With a pair of binoculars that he's kept from the *Mary Lee* he could see the red plastic rose on the ground around the statue. Proof, he thought, that his vision the night before was no hallucination. The statue of the Mother of God is a sign that the answers he's been seeking are on Hart Island. It's no coincidence that the footless corpse with Mary on its back holding a rose is buried here. BB sees Sal squat before the statue and is surprised that the captain is shouting, and when Sal rises and kicks the head of Baby Jesus to the ground, BB gasps and says, "DESECRATION."

～

On his way back to the trench, the sky opens and drenches Sal. By the time he returns, the downpour has stopped and Booker, Hemins, and the crew are putting on muck boots, getting ready to bury the pine boxes. Water is spilling down his face. He stands before the gully, its floor covered in mud sludge.

Booker walks over and says, "You're soaked."

Sal looks at him and nods.

"You okay?"

"I just knocked off Jesus's head. I went over to the statue of Mary. I was angry. I kicked it and the head broke off."

"Angry about what?"

"I don't know. Ex-Catholics do crazy shit, Book. Railing against the universe, I guess. I didn't mean to decapitate Him."

Booker, incredulous, says, "There are some dry Rikers sweats on the bus."

"Captain Jailbird today," Sal says, sheepishly.

"Don't want to guess what the punishment for knocking the block off Jesus is going to be when your time comes."

"Ha. You know, not a minute after it fell to the ground the sky opened up."

Booker shakes his head and walks over to the truck.

"Hey, Cappy, wha happened?" Jesús asks.

Sal points to the sky. "So, tell me, why did your mother name you Jesús."

"She a church lady."

"It's a tough act to follow."

"Say so," Jesús says. "Cap?"

"What?"

"Yo crib is Staten Island?"

"Born there, live there still."

"You know Wu-Tang Clan?"

"Rappers, that's about all I know. Justin knows a lot more."

"Who's Justin?"

"Never mind."

"My auntie was Inspectah Deck's shawty."

"Who?"

"Inspectah Deck is chill dude. He rap her: *Cut the check and your boy digress. / At my age it's all about the broad / Tryna be nice at 40, you can have it all shawty.*"

"Guess I'm musically stunted."

"Wha that?"

"*Fugetaboutit*, Jesús."

"That's white gangster talk, Cappy. You listen to Sinatra?"

Sal laughs, surprised Jesús knows Ol' Blue Eyes.

"You hang with gangsters?" Jesús asks.

"Everyone on Staten Island knows a wiseguy."

"Wu-Tang rap gangsters ain't like white mobsters."

"You know gang bangers, Jesús?"

"Who don't in Edenwald."

"Tough life."

"Ain't so bad. I got legs."

Sal smiles.

"You know what Shaolin means?"

"Yeah, Staten Island."

"Shaolin is Kung-Fu Temple, too. Nobody touch you there. So, wha about white gangsters?" Jesús asks again.

Sal considers telling him that Carlo Cali is like an uncle. Billy "The Limp" Baldoni used to drop off race cards every morning. His father was gunned down outside his house by Russian bastards. Instead, he pats Jesús on the shoulder and says, "Somebody is always going to know somebody who knows somebody who knows somebody."

"Say so." Jesús understands that Sal doesn't want to talk about the mob. "You better dry up, Cappy." Then pointing to the trench, he says, "They stinkin' bad in the hole today."

∼

The single thing the burial crew never gets used to is the stench of decomposing corpses. None are embalmed. The same day's haul isn't so bad; the boxes are kept on ice until they get onto the ferry. Usually not more than a couple hours in the open air. But the corpses they put in the trench days before, they ripen fast inside the boxes, giving off gases and fluids that smell like Fresh Kills in August. And there are the insects that sometimes mistake the crew's flesh for the dead when they crawl up a pant leg or inside a T-shirt. Insects and worms are adept at breaching the pine coffins. It isn't hard. Coffin flies are the first to wend their way in. They look like fruit flies and easily finger the scent of death; they burrow deep in the decomposition, feast, and lay eggs undisturbed by other visitors that follow. Some of the creatures are so delicate that when they feed, they skim across pale skin leaving only microscopic traces. Eventually, orange and black burying beetles work their way in. They do more to break down what's under skin than any bug. You name it, they eat it. There've been surprises. A rare spider species. Jewel beetle. Redback salamander. Once, so goes a story, an inmate discovered an Arizona scorpion, far from home. The crew sometimes jokes of tossing in *the stiffs*, especially on a wet day like today, but they never do. They're blowing off steam. When the last coffin is carefully entombed, they always stand above the newly dead, and as if they can see themselves in the earth someday, the Rikers angels are for a moment silent as death.

Sal watches Franklin and Al pass a coffin over the trench ledge to inmates standing in pools of rainwater and mud. The pine box, at an angle as if it were about to slip down the ledge, looks like a packing crate. They set it down on the sludge next to a coffin they buried yesterday. Mud obscures part of the identification marked on a box: ale Unknown 042409.

Franklin wipes off the mud.

"Shit," Al says.

"What's wrong?" Booker asks.

"It's leaking."

"What?"

"There's a hole on the side. Gunk's oozing out. Stinks worse than Rikers shithole," Franklin says.

"Just wedge the new box against it," Booker says.

"Bad juju," Jesús says. "Don't touch tha shit."

"You've got those heavy gloves. Don't be a pussy," Hemins yells down.

"Ain't she a fuckin' twat today," Zookie tells Jason.

College boy looks like he's going to hurl.

They push the new coffin against the leaking one.

Sal stares at the men sloshing in the grave. He's dizzy, worried that he could fall into the trench; he turns away and heads to the bus. He puts on the dry Rikers sweats and wishes he had a whiskey. "Go away, Agnes," he says. "Get the fuck out." He's talking to the shit in his head as he curls up against the bus window and sleeps.

Batshit Crazy

Antony is on the couch in his boxers watching *The Deuce*, wishing he and Sal could have been more like the brothers Vincent and Frankie Martino. He's talking to the television, "You've got to get your hands dirty, really dirty, Vincent," when Bruno knocks on the door. It's not unusual for him to stop by without calling, which is why Antony and Bruno's wife, Rosa, always fuck in a hotel. That's how Antony sees it, a fuck, even though Rosa told him that she doesn't think she can be happy without him. It's a position he never expected to be in, involved with the wife of his boyhood friend (what was he thinking?), the one friend he's ever had, who has told him more than once, "You know I'd take a bullet for you, right?" And Antony believes him when he says it, and always goes, "Bruno, you're a fuckin' idiot. I wouldn't die for my own mother."

Bruno, a royal fuckup of a gangster, is usually deferential because Antony is the only friend he can trust, too, the one person who's covered him whenever he's gotten deep into shit that even his father, Don Cali, might not tolerate.

When he walks in, you can almost see his heart racing as he brushes past Antony and sits on the couch. Antony takes the chair across from him. "What the fuck, Bruno. You came in here like some fuckin' honey badger."

Bruno picks up what's left of the beer that Antony was drinking, guzzles it, and smashes the bottle against the table. "You've got a lot of explaining to do."

"What the fuck." Antony's looking at the mess on the table and doesn't notice that Bruno's pointing the jagged edge of the bottle at him. "What's wrong with you?"

"Fuckin' asshole." Bruno throws what's left of the broken bottle against the wall and goes into the kitchen for another beer.

Antony follows and grabs his arm. "You're shit-faced, but what the fuck, you're cleaning that shit up, now."

Bruno bats his arm away. He stares at Antony, the rage momentarily gone from his voice. "Why'd you have to go and fuck Rosa?"

Not surprised, Antony says, "Who said I did?"

Bruno laughs. "She wouldn't fuck for months and now she's fuckin' pregnant. But I beat her so bad maybe I took care of the little bastard in her belly."

"Pregnant? And you think I'm the father. She's a fuckin' whore, Bruno."

Bruno reaches behind him and pulls out a gun from his waist band. "Don't lie to me," he says, sticking the barrel in Antony's stomach.

"Woah, Bruno. You want to kill me? I don't think so."

He presses it harder into Antony's gut. "You back-stabbing bastard."

Bruno's unpredictable even when he's sober. But now, drunk and convinced he's been betrayed, there's no time to talk him down. Antony knows that Bruno can pull the trigger at any moment, and the next regret what he's done. When he's fraught, there's no telling how batshit crazy he really is. Antony grabs the barrel of the Glock, pushes it to the side, and tries to wrest it away. In the struggle, he touches Bruno's trigger finger and the gun goes off, one shot that explodes Bruno's stomach. Bruno folds back against the refrigerator as Antony reaches around him to keep him from sliding down. If you didn't know Bruno's been shot, it would look like they were frozen in a moment of slow dancing. Bruno's looking at him like *what the fuck happened*, as if he'd forgotten he believed Antony had betrayed him. Antony lays Bruno on the kitchen floor, grabs a dish towel, and tries to compress the wound. "You're a dumb bastard," he says.

Bruno groans, his breathing noisy and then sputtering. "Look at me," he says. "You didn't fuck her, right."

"That's right, Bruno."

"The fucking whore."

Antony can't stop the bleeding and feels blood soaking through his boxers.

"Fuckin' bitch." Bruno groans.

Antony thinks he's got to call 911, but how would he explain this?

He says that Bruno's more a brother to him than Sal. He couldn't betray him, and Bruno relaxes. He's losing consciousness, slowly but irretrievably. His breathing is sputtering more and more. "I'm sorry," Bruno says, barely audible.

Antony stays on the floor cradling Bruno. It doesn't take long; maybe ten minutes before his eyes turn milky blue and his sputtering breaths cease. And all that time Antony keeps Bruno in his arms. "What the fuck?" Antony says aloud, lifting Bruno's head and kissing it. "What have you done?" he whispers, not about himself, not wanting to admit that if he hadn't been so reckless with Rosa, he wouldn't be soaked in Bruno's blood. And then he remembers that Bruno said Rosa is pregnant, and, unmoved by the revelation, Antony hopes that Bruno was right, and that he took care of the problem.

Stuck in a Moment

By the time Sal gets off the *Spirit of America*, the sun is emerging from fractious clouds, and he doesn't notice the slight hint of color wisping through. He looks back at the pier and sees gulls pecking at a dead fish. He's feeling like shit since he hasn't had a drink all day. Outside the terminal the S48 is waiting to take him to Mother Pug's.

"Hey, Sal," the bus driver says. "I saw you on the news yesterday. Hell of a thing you did."

He doesn't answer, and the guy gives him a bewildered look. His phone plays "Blackbird." It's Justin. "You back?"

"I'm not coming straight home."

"Ida made pasta fagioli, believe it or not. She just got up from the TV and started cooking it. I didn't help her with a thing. First time in months. Anna's just walked in. Eat with us and save Pug's for later."

"Last time she made it Dad was gunned down. She was in the kitchen dishing it out when it happened. I dream about it sometimes."

"What?"

"In my mind, she's serving pasta fagioli and Francesco is getting massacred."

"Jesus, Sal."

"How is she, really?"

"Call it a *sanity storm* day. She tagged along with Anna at the church. She's been almost like her old self, messing up words the way she used to before things got worse. Like Francesco used to say, she gets things in the right order most of the time, but it's getting the right word that's the problem. She told Anna she liked her so much that she'd give her the skin off her back."

"Classic."

"Come on home, Sal."

He hears Ida in the background. "Tell Francesco to stop and get some octopus, and make sure it has its testicles."

"Hear that, Sal?"

"Yeah." He hangs up before hearing Justin say, "We're not eating for an hour."

By the time Sal gets to his seat at the bar, Nina has a baby Jameson set out. Sal kills it.

"You look beat," she says.

"Hit me again."

The same two EMTs from the night before are shooting darts. One of them gives Sal a thumbs-up, which he ignores. The only other person in the bar is a woman he's never seen before. She's cracking open peanuts and flicking the nuts and shells on the floor as if they were ashes.

Nina notices Sal watching the woman and says, "Don't ask. A few minutes ago, she was crying her eyes out. Screwdrivers. Who drinks screwdrivers these days? I had to go next door for orange juice."

"You getting my whiskey? Make it a double."

"Whoa. Impatient tonight, aren't we."

Sal walks past the woman and kicks away some peanut shells. At the jukebox he puts on U2's "Stuck in a Moment You Can't Get Out Of." The woman looks up and starts to sway to the music. She mouths the lyrics with all the wrong words and smiles at Sal. He just shakes his head.

"Bastard," she whispers, but he doesn't hear her.

"You play that a lot," Nina says.

"Kind of settles me, a little like Mr. Jameson here."

"Nothing ditched in the water today?"

Sal ignores the question and looks up at the memorial photo of Bobby Avallone dangling on the string. He can see himself staring at it in the mirror. "You're right."

"About what?"

"Avallone didn't deserve to die. Not that way, not any way."

"For sure."

"Fucker didn't have to slur my father. I forgive him."

"That's big of you now that Bobby's dead."

Sal gives Nina a look. "No Irish buddha tonight?" Visibly disappointed, he points to the empty spot where Aidan O'Shea is usually ensconced.

"I was wondering that, too."

"Maybe he's sick, maybe he's dead."

"Jeez, Sal, what's wrong with you tonight?"

O'Shea walks in, and when he passes by, Nina says, "Sal was worried you were dead."

"Call me Lazarus," he said, more relaxed than usual. "Bet I know who put on these Irish bastards."

Sal nods.

"Where you been?" Nina asks.

"My sis, she took me out to early bird."

"You ate something besides pizza strips? I don't believe it."

"Surf and turf, she splurged."

Looking over to Sal, he says, "Pour my friend one on me, Nina."

Sal raises his glass and takes the stool next to O'Shea; instead of saying something, he just stares expectantly.

"What?" O'Shea asks.

"Fuck it," he says. "That's what you said at the AA meeting we went to. Surf and turf. I don't believe it. Did you go back to AA this evening?"

"I said Sis took me out. She was celebrating."

"Celebrating what?"

"I don't know. She wouldn't tell me."

"That doesn't make any sense."

O'Shea clinks whiskeys. "Sis can be enigmatic."

"So, what did you talk about?"

"Donald Trump, Mets prospects, the guy who set himself on fire outside the White House, and family shit."

"What family shit?"

"Our family shit."

"Mine, too."

"No, just full-blooded brother-sister shit."

"I don't believe you. You were talking about Francesco's murder, and that's why she said she wants to meet."

"Fuck it, you're getting on my nerves."

Sal pauses. "Maybe you don't know anything about his murder but all these months at the bar together, we hardly talk about the times Francesco spent with you and your mother. Don't you think that's strange?"

Aidan, slipping into full reminiscence mode, goes: "Your dad and my mother used to play 'Sherry Baby' and dance to it sometimes like they were the only two people in the world. That's how Sis got her name."

"Was he with her when Sherry was born?"

"In the waiting room at Brooklyn Birthing. We both were. Nurses wouldn't let him into the birthing room. I remember Antony called, and Francesco told him she was having the baby. I don't know what Antony said but Francesco told him, 'Fuck off.'"

"My brother knew about Sherry?"

"Antony knows a lot. Did he tell you he despises me."

"Christ."

"The feeling's mutual."

"Why?"

"He's a fuckin' dirty cop. A killer. Don't tell me you don't know."

Sal doesn't want to talk about Antony. "Fuck him, Aidan. Growing up, did Sherry know Francesco was her father?"

"She was two years old when he stopped coming around the house. She doesn't remember anything about him back then. I've always thought that Antony told your mother about Sherry. After that, Francesco was a ghost and just sent checks all those years. But I'll tell you, my mother never stopped loving him."

Sal runs his hands up his forehead and across his skull.

"You know, I wouldn't be surprised if Antony had something to do with Francesco's murder," Aidan says.

"Jesus, that's impossible."

"You think?" They don't say anything for a while until Aidan switches to his annoying bookish demeanor. "You look like you've crossed some kind of invisible line. As if you've come to a place you never thought you'd have to come to. It's a strange place."

Sal, not really listening, inches his Jameson back and forth on the bar. He's wondering if Antony really could be involved in Francesco's murder.

"You know who said that? Something like that anyway. Raymond Carver."

Sal gives him a who-the-fuck-is-he look.

"I thought you were educated. I bet Justin knows him. He's in the stacks all the time picking up books. You know, he reads fiction, and maybe you should, too. Good for your soul."

"Don't worry about my soul."

"I know you and Justin like to fuck."

"Christ, Aidan. Where did this come from?"

"Too crass? Call it love, then."

Sal's leg twitches. "No one knows about us, O'Shea."

"You think so? Or you hope so? Don't worry, secret lives are safe with me. Straight. Gay. Going both ways. Trans. It's no big deal. Live and let live. I came across a line in a book today that made me think of you and Justin. *The best way of keeping a secret is to pretend there isn't one.* You've been pretty good at that."

Sal's got to piss but he's afraid that when he gets back, O'Shea won't be so talkative. Still thinking about his brother, he asks, "Why the fuck do you think Antony was involved in the hit on my father?"

"Because he's bad, and sometimes being bad is reason enough."

"You don't know shit about Antony."

"If you say so," Aidan says.

"So, fuck Antony, and tell me more about your mother."

"She read a lot, too, listened to all kinds of music. She wanted to be an actress, but she got knocked up by my father, and my sorry-ass life was born. And until the bastard went away, she never left the house except for grocery shopping. My piece-of-shit father had kept her locked up. He died in Attica a year ago. Felt like Christmas and Fourth of July wrapped into one. When my mother met Francesco, she was at Rego's farm stand picking out tomatoes for sauce. I was with her. He was holding some potted petunias and walked right up. 'These are for you,' he said, and before he turned away, he took out his wallet and gave me a ten-dollar bill. They met again at Rego's, and again and again; you'd think that fruit and vegetable stand was some friggin' courting haven, until she took him home one afternoon. I remember hearing them that first day in the bedroom. I was twelve. Sounds I hadn't heard since my father was locked up. Sometimes my mother went to the track with your father. He let me tag along once in a while. My mother, her name was Caterina, liked to listen to Nina Simone. Francesco preferred the old standards and pop. He didn't have the patience to see past the pain in the blues. When your father wasn't around, my mother seemed, well, melancholy. And she didn't have a drop of Irish blood in her. Rare Italian melancholy, a little like you, Sal. She'd sing, *For my love is like the wind / And wild is the wind*. I remember asking her, 'Where's Francesco?' She'd go to Simone: *Doncha know / That no one alive can always be an angel? / When everything goes wrong. / You see some bad.* Then she said, 'Francesco is a good man, but you've got to be a better one.' I disappointed her."

Sal can see that these recollections have moved O'Shea, and after a long silence that a memory can wander into, Aidan says, "Francesco broke her heart."

The "Blackbird" ringtone sounds but Sal ignores it.

"Beatles calling. You going to answer that?"

It's Antony. "What the fuck, twice in two days after you've been MIA for months."

O'Shea leans in as if he wants to eavesdrop. Sal pushes him away.

"Where are you?" Antony asks.

"Mother Pug's."

"Alone."

"No, I'm talking to Aidan O'Shea."

"What the fuck for? Don't let that asshole know you're talking to me."

Antony says he's in a lot of trouble. He says he's never asked Sal for a *fuckin' thing* in his life, which is no pint-sized lie. That's what he always says when he's royally fucked. He tells Sal to get an Uber and meet him on City Island. He'll explain everything when Sal gets there.

"What the fuck for?" Sal asks.

Antony tells him to hurry. No one can know where he's going. Not O'Shea, Nina, Justin, Ma. His brother says this is life-and-death trouble. "Do you love me, Sal?"

"That's a stupid question."

"Well, answer it by getting your fuckin' ass over there." He says he'll be waiting at the DOC dock gate and taps off the phone.

"Was that your fuck-face brother? Why don't you ask him what he knows about Francesco?"

Sal gives O'Shea a look. "Christ, Aidan, maybe Justin's right."

"About what?"

"You're a drunken storyteller who can't be trusted."

O'Shea laughs. "You think?"

Sal pays his tab and heads out of Pug's to catch a ride to City Island.

Indian Poke

BB's tried countless times to place the infant's head back on the torso, but no matter how he pegs away at it, the head keeps falling off. All he has managed to do is chafe the stone so that Jesus's eyes have lost even more contour than time and wind and weather have consumed. Finally, he clears as much mud and moss as he can with his fingers and places the head inside his sack. He picks up some of the offerings and stashes them inside. He thinks, *Mother Mary has a plan for me.* BB hoists the bag over his shoulder and notices a raccoon not far away staring at him and then running off into a thicket of switchgrass. A raccoon out before nightfall is probably mad with rabies. No stranger to paranoia, he wonders if an army of dark invisible spirits is atomizing from the mass graves like spectral pathogens leading him into a trap. A doe and three fawns appear across the road. The fawns' coats are pig-belly pink and speckled white in the low sun emerging from the last of the day's storm clouds. He doesn't move as the doe and her fawns look back as if to signal: *Follow us out of the raccoon's trap.* The deer bolt, zigzagging across an expanse of graves, as if agility trained. He picks up his sack and ends up at the shore, where he sits on a bed of mussel shells that shimmer blue under the setting sun. The deer are nowhere to be seen. Around him are skeletal remains that have been washed out of eroded trenches nearby: a tibia, humerus, mandible, and an entire clavicle. *Relics*, he thinks. He crosses his legs and looks out at Long Island Sound to the faraway peninsulas and inlets, which, he imagines, resemble prehistoric sea creatures surfacing in the dying light. He closes his eyes and asks Mary to send him the sign he's been waiting for. He waits but nothing appears, so he fetches the head from his sack and places it among the bones in the mussel shells. He's hungry, too tired to think straight.

On the way back to the workhouse, BB mistakes a patch of poisonous Indian Poke for Swiss chard. He thanks the Holy Mother, packs the weed, which he thinks would make a good dinner, into his bag, and walks off. At the workhouse, he hunkers into his corner by the window, and with his binoculars BB watches the evening light disappear across the Virgin and her headless son. He lies down and picks off a few Indian Poke leaves and eats them. He tells Mary he is weary and imagines that the Mother of God talks to him from her perch across the field: "Your time, dear fisherman, is in God's hands. One day you will be sitting beside me. You will find peace and purpose. You will live happily until your death."

Tremors

Sherry O'Shea can't get back to sleep. She woke from a recurring dream about her father. Francesco takes her by the hand to the stables at Saratoga Racetrack. He introduces her to the horses by name: Lem Me Have It, Choose Happiness, Snap Decision, Violent Delights. He says, "Who names a horse Violent Delights, when you've got all these other possibilities like, look, over here, it's Pure Wow." A week before Francesco was gunned down, she had told him the dream. "It wasn't a dream, honey. July 23, 1994. You were almost three. It was the last time I saw you."

"I don't remember it. I don't remember you."

"Sure you do. We went to one of the High Rock spigots at the springs. I carried you on my shoulders and dipped you like a duck so that you could drink the mineral water. It smelled like rotten eggs but tasted like salt. You didn't spit it out."

"You're shittin' me."

"Ha, why would I do that?"

"Because you're a gangster."

Francesco ignored the sarcasm. "I tell you, I remember. That day was also the longest baseball rain delay in history, three hours and thirty-nine minutes, Giants at the Mets. I don't lie to family."

"Who won?"

Stumped, he says, "I don't remember."

"Giants, 4–2. I'm a Mets fan."

"You're your father's daughter."

She laughed. "In your dreams."

Sherry left Staten Island for good when she started at Northwestern. Her mother had died the year before, while she was at the New Dorp Drive-In with Marco DeLuca. She remembers they had a choice of movies during throwback-to-the-'90s film week: *Goodfellas*, *Godfather Part III*, *Pretty Woman* or *Tremors*. Marco's father was killed outside the Mulberry Street Bar when Marco was eight, and his mother remarried a Polish dentist. Marco didn't want anything to do with gangsters, not even a Mafia movie.

He said he was going to be a paleontologist. Sherry said that *Pretty Woman* sounded good. He picked *Tremors* because it was at the drive-in, and it would be easier to make out. Besides, he said an earthquake on that huge screen would be cool. Neither of them knew it was a horror film about monster worms. Turns out, they didn't feel like making out. When Sherry got home, Caterina O'Shea was dead.

Sherry lived the next year before college with Aidan, in the same red-shingled ranch she's moved back to a few miles up the road from the Cusumano family. All those years and so close, not once had she run into Francesco. She didn't know it, but Francesco was at the burial for her mother. He hid behind a statue of Archangel Michael. At funerals of wiseguys in the Moravian Cemetery it's common to see a detective behind the angel's pedestal just close enough to snap photographs. At Caterina's burial, it was a gangster on stakeout. Francesco had paid for everything—wake, primrose white and pink casket lined with pink velvet, flowers, holy cards, obit in the *Staten Island Advance*, and a sizeable donation to Father Giamatti at Our Lady Queen of Peace. He even bought two more plots so that Aidan and Sherry could someday be buried next to their mother. Ida didn't know any of this, and she, without a doubt, would have put a stop to it. There were only half a dozen mourners at the church and fewer—Aidan, Sherry, and Father Giamatti—at the graveyard. And there was Francesco, tearing up as he watched from afar her coffin being lowered into the ground. Father Giamatti gave a remembrance, which suggested he had known Caterina all her life, even though she had never stepped foot in Our Lady Queen of Peace. After the funeral Aidan told Sherry that Francesco was her father. He explained how their mother seemed reborn when Francesco started "visiting." He tried to convince Sherry to let Francesco into her life. She wouldn't have any of it. "This discussion is *anathema*," she said. When she was certain, she chose words deliberately. The depth of her renunciation of her father seemed to have no floor. Still, a month didn't go by that Francesco missed depositing a check for them, as he'd done when Caterina was alive, a couple thousand dollars, more as time went on and things got more expensive. Francesco asked Aidan to tell Sherry that the money came from a trust set up after a medical malpractice settlement. The doctor had read someone else's mammogram and failed to diagnose Caterina's breast cancer. It was a lie.

Years later when Sherry graduated from Northwestern, Aidan decided to tell her that there was no malpractice insurance settlement, no trust fund. They'd been living on money from Francesco. Her brother told her that Francesco wanted to fly in to see her, take her to a steakhouse along Lake Michigan and maybe, if she'd let him, get to know her. "Fuck him," she told Aidan. She'd do to him what he had done to her. She'd shatter any illusion that he was her father, any hope he'd had that she needed one. Francesco flew to Chicago anyway to see her graduate; Sherry never knew he was in the audience.

When the summer ended, she went straight to the FBI Academy in Quantico. The CIA had recruited her, too, but she didn't have a hankering for traveling to remote places like Kyrgyzstan and Sudan. Besides, the only language Sherry knows besides English is Spanish, and she thought it would serve her better to be fighting crime at home. She might have been a Rhodes Scholar, but she told the dean, who wanted to nominate her, that she'd rather track down gangsters and psychopaths than talk about Nietzsche and Freud in a roomful of future politicians.

After the academy, until moving back to Staten Island, Sherry spent her career at the FBI Field Office back in Chicago, investigating the LAFA street gang, notorious for murdering rivals and viciously protecting its drug territories on the South Side. A year before returning to New York, she'd been elevated to Special Agent heading the LAFA probe, which led to dozens of arrests for murder, arms and drug trafficking, and racketeering across Illinois, Wisconsin, Indiana, and Minnesota. Her favorite word back then was RICO. On the front page of the *Chicago Tribune* there was a picture of her over a table covered with handguns and automatic rifles, bags of cocaine and opioids, bricks of marijuana, mounds of cash.

And here she is now, back on Staten Island, living with her brother, her gangster father dead, just as she was getting to know him, offering him the chance of his lifetime.

Capisci

Antony calls again and tells Sal to have the driver drop him in Inwood outside their Uncle Guido's apartment building, and from there to take the bus to City Island. Sal wants to know what all this secrecy is about, and Antony shouts, "Just do the fuck what I tell you."

Sal understands that whatever Antony wants him to do, he'll be stepping into a mound of shit. His brother has a history of leaving behind a lot of damage, and yet Sal has always stuck by him. Their father told him repeatedly when he was a boy never to betray Antony. "Sal, no matter what, you help your big brother. He's not easy like you. You don't abandon family, *la famiglia, la famiglia é tutto*."

By the time he was six, not long before Justin moved in next door, Sal learned how hard it would be to love Antony. Until then, he'd felt like he was the luckiest kid on the street to be looked after by an older brother like Antony, who promised he'd be his little brother's *protector* if Sal remained his *accomplice*, which Sal thought then meant something like a pal. But Cannoli changed everything. Antony hated old lady Salvano. She used to curse him when he cut through her yard. *Ti uccidero io stesso!* she'd scream from an open window. Antony would yell back, "I'll cut *your* throat, you piece of Napolitano shit." One day Antony said, "You know old lady Salvano's cat? Come with me, Sal. I've got a plan." Cannoli, a gray tabby, liked to hide out under the porch steps. Antony put on the heavy-duty, arm-length landscaping gloves that Francesco kept in a box in the garage. "Who names a cat Cannoli?" he asked, taking Sal by the hand and telling his brother that he was going to teach the old lady a lesson. At Salvano's porch, he crouched down and captured the cat, which was hissing like Linda Blair. Salvano, at the window, saw Antony holding her tabby by the neck and screamed *Bastardo*. He told Sal to flip her the finger, but Sal didn't know what that meant. They bolted before the old lady could reach the door. On the next block, there was a house with two rottweilers fenced in. Antony dangled the terrified animal over the fence. When the dogs ran over, he dropped it. As they fled, Sal remembers crying when he heard

Cannoli's screech. Antony stopped and grabbed him by the shoulders. "Grow some fucking balls, kid," he said, shaking his brother. When Sal told his father what Antony had done, Francesco pulled him close and whispered, "He's *onere familiare*, Sal. That's a Sicilian family burden. You're no *onere familiare*. You love him no matter what. He needs you. So, what he did is a family secret. A brother doesn't snitch. *Capisci.*"

Old lady Salvano told Francesco that she was going to the police this time, but somehow, he found a way to placate her. Years later Sal specu- lated that his father had sent his Mafia pals to threaten her. Or maybe he paid her off. Or maybe he charmed her the way Sal watched him beguile women during Sunday afternoon dinners in Little Italy. If Ida ever knew about Antony savaging the cat, she never said so.

The next week Francesco sent Antony to Sicily for the summer, and when he returned home, for a while he seemed reined in. In Palermo, he was taught to channel violence, to use brutality only to benefit *la famiglia*, which included the greater allegiance to the Mafia family. Back then, just six, Sal worried that Antony was sent away because he had snitched; he worried that when his brother returned home, Antony would no longer love him. What he couldn't know was that Antony would be indebted to his little brother because in Sicily he was being schooled in the arts of a Mafia soldier. At first Francesco was relieved that Antony seemed so changed. His boyhood friend, Salvatore Riina, whose name Francesco had given to his second son, sent him an encouraging letter. Riina, who at the time was the underboss of the Cinisi clan, deceived Francesco, saying he respected his old friend's wishes to encourage Antony to stay out of the family business. Riina said that he wouldn't be surprised if Antony became a cop someday. Imagine, *un poliziotto* in the family.

A few months after his summer in Sicily, Antony was back to his old ways. While the violence was less impulsive, he was still a wildcard, always *onere familiare*, with an instinctual and determined cruelty, and a zeal for vengeance. Antony spent most of his time with Bruno Cali and "cousins" from Staten Island. They had their own posse, Fresh Kills, named after the largest landfill in the world. He barely graduated from Our Lady Queen of Peace. Francesco had to bribe Father Giamatti with a donation to build a grotto in the schoolyard. Justin had moved in, and the boys never saw much of Antony, though sometimes he would take Sal aside and say, "You shouldn't get too close to the kid. You can't trust the Irish. You can only trust me, Sal. We're family. You know I love you, *mamaluke*, right? I'm your only brother." But by then, Justin and Sal were already inseparable.

In the two years before he entered the police academy, Antony managed to keep himself off the radar of police. Somehow, *a miracle*, Ida would tell Francesco, Antony never saw the inside of a NYC precinct house until he walked into the Ninth and put on his blues.

Under a Supermoon

The moon casts an immense swath of light across the Sound. Hart Island, rarely visible at night, lies in its path. There's a Coast Guard superstition that this swollen moon invites dangerous geophysical stresses, even earthquakes and tsunamis. Cadets are told to be on guard while sailing under it. Pay attention to tidal forces, because if there's going to be trouble, it usually happens under a supermoon.

Sal wonders why Antony isn't on the dock. He opens the gate and goes to the DOC trailer and flicks on the light. "Shit," he says, remembering that there isn't a flask in his locker. He's pissed at Antony for summoning him here for who knows what, and he thinks, *Where the fuck is he?* The "Blackbird" ringtone breaks out. It's Justin. Sal taps "decline" as he notices a van heading up Fordham Street to the gate. There's a boat hitched to it.

Antony steps out. "Jesus, Sal. Cut that friggin' trailer light. Can you kill the floods on the dock, too?"

"Why?"

"Because it's a fuckin' surprise party. Just do it."

Sal unlocks the circuit breaker box and pulls down the lever, cutting the three halide dock lights.

"Fuck this," Antony says.

"What?"

"The friggin' moon's so bright it might as well be a fuckin' spotlight."

"Why all of this covert shit?"

Antony grabs Sal's shirt neck. His breath smells like garlic and bourbon. "You're going to help me, and you're not going to ask a lot of questions."

"Antony, let me go, or I'm out of here."

"You're not going anywhere until we do this." He releases his brother. "You think you're, what did Dad say? Virtuous. *Nessuno mi unfungulo,* that's what I was taught in Sicily. You might like being fucked in the ass, but no one's fudgepacking me."

Sal worries his brother is on something. He has seen Antony worked up before, but never like this. He's mercurial, but he's never derided Sal like this. "What the fuck is wrong with you?"

"What's wrong with me? If you don't help me, I'm a dead man."

"What did you do?"

"What's wrong with me?" Antony repeats, ignoring Sal, his impatience intensifying. "I've got shit luck."

"You killed a Russian."

Antony gives him a look like are you crazy?

"I'm out until you tell me what's happening," Sal says.

Antony takes a deep breath in through his nose and lets it out slowly through his mouth. He puts his arm around Sal's shoulder. His shirtsleeve feels moist on Sal's neck. "You look scared."

Sal is silent.

"I didn't kill a fuckin' Russian. Francesco did something unforgivable and he paid for it. I'm not his avenging angel. Maybe you should ask Justin about our father. Francesco talked to him like he was his personal confessor."

Sal's so rattled he's a little dizzy. "That's not true."

Antony clenches his fist at his side. "Ha, you're fuckin' blind, Sal."

Sal can feel his heart rate accelerating.

"You still look scared. You think I'd hurt you. I couldn't, little brother. But I need you." Antony whispers in his ear, *"Famiglia."*

Sal nods.

"Look, we're going to Hart Island."

"What do you want on Hart?"

"You'll see."

"Jesus, Antony."

He embraces Sal. "I love you, brother."

Sal knows he should head down the street and leave Antony on the dock with whatever he's done and all the consequences that will follow. But he doesn't. Out of the blue, Sal goes: "Does Sherry O'Shea have anything to do with this?"

"Jesus, no. Did you tell her dipstick brother you were meeting me here."

Sal just looks at him.

Antony, his voice threatening, asks, "Did you?"

"Fuck, you're crazy."

He grabs Sal's arm. "Did you?"

"No."

"Good." He releases his grip and lightly slaps Sal's cheek. "Now let's do this."

They walk to the back of the old Chrysler minivan. Its wood trim on the sides is scuffed and torn off in spots. It has an Ohio license plate, LIFE'S A BEACH.

"Where did you get this?"

"Where you get cars you don't want traced. The boat, too. I know a guy. They look like total scrap, but they're indestructible."

Sal runs his hand across his head. "What kind of shit are you into, Antony?" His brother opens the rear door, which bounces back and hits Sal in the face.

"Jesus, Sal, you're bleeding." Antony takes out a penlight on his key chain and looks at the wound over Sal's eye. "Superficial." He kisses the spot and Sal flinches.

"What, your brother can't kiss you now." He wipes Sal's blood off his lips.

Sal is looking at a dead body, face down, in the back of the van. "Christ, Antony."

"Yes, this is the problem we're going to solve. We're taking him to your island of lost souls."

"Like hell we are."

"You've got no choice, little bro. If we don't, I'm going to end up looking just like him. He can't be found. Like Jimmy Hoffa."

"Who is he?"

"You don't want to know."

Sal's temple is pounding. "Jesus Christ, Antony."

"I want to wrap him. It's better you don't know. I'm only thinking of you, Sal. You got some tarp somewhere?"

"On *Vesuvius*."

"What the fuck is that?"

"The ferry."

Francesco shakes his head. "Go get it."

"Jesus fucking Christ," Sal says, fetching the tarpaulin and some rope from the ferry. Antony is taking a piss behind the trailer when he returns. He drops the tarp, turns the body around, and sees Bruno Cali. Hair slicked back and eyes wide open and still milky, staring past Sal. His white silk shirt blotched in blood.

Antony taps Sal's shoulder. "I told you not to peek, little brother."

"You killed Bruno?"

"Like they say in the movies, *this is a touchy thing*. Yeah, Sal, I killed a *made man*, no, worse, I killed the boss's son, no, worse yet, I killed a friend."

"Why?"

"It was an accident."

He finishes telling Sal about Rosa, and how Bruno dove into one of his uncontrollable rages. "I tried to take the gun and it fired into Bruno's gut."

Sal is unable to look away, staring at Bruno in the dim light of the van.

"You bastard."

"I said it was an accident."

"You want me to help you bury Bruno. When Carlo discovers what happened, we're both dead."

"He's not going to find out."

Sal's phone plays "Blackbird." "It's Justin again. He's wondering where I am."

"Fuck him." Antony grabs the phone, hits decline, and shuts it down. "Here." He tosses it back. "Now, let's get to this. We've got to be done before it's light."

As they wrap Bruno in the tarp, Antony pauses and makes the Sign of the Cross. Sal gives him a look and is about to say *Like that's going to do any good*, but he notices his brother is uncharacteristically shaken. "You stupid fool," Antony says as he folds the tarp across Bruno's head. "Where's the fucking rope?" he asks.

When they're finished putting Bruno into the boat, Sal says, "I can't do this."

"Shut the gate behind me." Antony climbs into the van. "You think you've got a choice?"

Sal stays behind at the gate and watches his brother unhitch the boat and walk it down the ramp to the water's edge. From a distance under the supermoon Antony looks more spectral than human. Sal turns on his phone and considers calling Justin, but his brother gestures, shouting, "Come on, *mamaluke*." Sal doesn't move, remembering how once there was nothing that he loved more than being summoned like this. "Come on, kid, I'm going to teach you something," Antony said, before taking him deep into Arden Woods to shoot cans. "Come on, *mamaluke*," before walking up to Giuseppe De Luca's concession at New Dorp Beach to lift a pack of candy cigarettes for his birthday. "Come on, kid," kissing him on his bloody cheek after he fell off the handlebars of a bike that Antony was weaving in and out of speed bumps in the Staten Island Yankees parking lot. How much he loved being called to action until the day Antony said, "Come on, *mamaluke*," taking Sal by the hand on his way to feed Cannoli to the dogs. And *now*, this.

Sal puts the phone in his pocket and closes the gate. He hears his father's voice in his head: *You gotta help your brother no matter what.* And then, heading to the boat, he says, "Fuck me."

"Sal, I knew you loved me."

Sal gives him a look. "Fuck you, Antony."

They haul the flat bottom into the water. Sal sits by the motor, staring at the tarp with Bruno's black Gucci loafers sticking out of it.

"We ain't got all night."

"Antony," he says.

In no mood for any more talk, Antony says, "Just shut the fuck up and go."

The engine coughs and Sal heads off, the luminous moon giving them a clear path to Hart Island.

Zip-a-Dee-Doo-Dah

BB is curled into the corner of the workhouse. Two field mice at his feet bolt across the floor when they hear him stir. The few Indian Poke leaves he ate before going to bed weren't lethal, as the sweet red root could have been. The devil itch leaves, though, were not without consequences, unleashing a swarm of hallucinations. He's still sweating. He looks out the empty window frame and makes the Sign of the Cross. His mind still not right. Not far away, the Holy Mother and what's left of Baby Jesus are visible in the sprawl of the supermoon. He thinks he sees a woman and goes to the statue. Unaware of BB's presence, the figure is wearing a white uniform and carrying an offering of peaches. She's the spectral body of Typhoid Mary, who died in quarantine on nearby North Brother Island in a cold and spider-infested bed. He watches her carried by the wind to the statue of the Holy Mother and her Child. She begs the Baby Jesus and Mary to take pity on her, to forgive her for the families she supposedly infected with typhoid, the wealthy bankers and industrialists who hired her to make beef Wellington and roasted duck and homemade peach ice cream that she served to guests in dining rooms overlooking Oyster Bay. She had no symptoms, so how could she have known she was a supercarrier, known that the germs on her unwashed hands would be preserved in fresh peaches she cut up and froze into ice cream the children loved. Have pity for me, she prays. She's paid her dues, she tells the Holy Mother, and still, why does God not forgive her? If only she could have remained simple Mary Malone from the obscure Irish village of Cookstown. The earth around her swirls like dirt devils, and she vanishes into the night.

From his grave the actor Billy Driscoll appears next to BB and leads him to the statue. "What happened to Jesus's head?" Billy asks. BB doesn't answer. Then Billy sings in the same voice he gave decades ago to Peter Pan: *Think of all the joy you'll find / When you leave the world behind / And bid your cares goodbye / You can fly! You can fly! You can fly!* He tells BB that's one of the Potter's Field children's favorites. Billy was buried in a Hart Island pine box in 1968 after two neighbor children found him dead on the floor of his roach-infested Avenue A apartment. He'd been stone cold for two days, the needle still in his arm. Andy Warhol called him pal.

Billy says: "I've had a hard life. It wasn't easy being a child actor. But I'm trying now. I've taught the children 'Zip-a-Dee-Doo-Dah.' Remember, I sang it with Jimmy Baskett in *Song of the South*. He was one of my only friends when I was a kid. Jimmy won an honorary Academy Award for playing Uncle Remus, but years later, he told me, 'There's only one damn good thing about the movie. That catchy tune we sang.'"

Billy gestures to Mary. "Why not let them sing it? Sing it for Jimmy Baskett."

So, the island fills with the sound of the dead children's voices: *Zip-a-dee-doo-dah, zip-a-dee-ay / My, oh my, what a wonderful day / Plenty of sunshine headin' my way / Zip-a-dee-doo-dah, zip-a-dee-ay.* When they're finished, Billy Driscoll vanishes.

It's almost midnight. BB waits until the voices and visions of the dead have stopped. He picks himself up from the ground. The island looks so peaceful washed in the light of the supermoon. He hears something coming from the shore, not the phantasmagoria that had been haunting his head. His stomach growls. He sees through the opening in sawgrass a small boat docking near the head of Baby Jesus. These men aren't phantoms, and he recognizes Captain Sal. Worried that they will discover him, he creeps back to the workhouse, where he sits by the window, watching.

Heart of Darkness

Sal cuts the motor, and with a stake-out pole he guides the boat over the shallows to Mussel Cove, where he drives an anchor spike into the packed sand and hitches the boat. The cove is covered in shells and carved into the reeds, remote enough a Coast Guard patrol wouldn't notice them. Antony shines a flashlight on the shore.

"*Che cazzo*," he says, "what's this? *Apocalypse Now?*"

"What are you talking about?"

"That." Antony focuses the light on the human bones and stone head of Baby Jesus.

Sal almost trips over Bruno's corpse, nearly landing in the water. "What the fuck."

"Exactly."

"I knocked it off a statue of Mary and Jesus today."

Antony gives his brother a look. They pull the boat farther ashore. "Frickin' freak show," Antony says. "Let's get this done."

Sal is picking up the head, and Antony asks, "What are you doing?"

"I'm going to take it back to the statue where it belongs."

"Like hell you are. We've got to bury Bruno. Fuck this voodoo shit. What's with these bones?"

"Storm erosion. These got away."

"A fuckin' hell," Antony mutters. "How far is the trench?"

"About a quarter mile."

"All this shore and you dock here?"

"It's the one spot patrol boats can't see."

"So, you've got Sicilian blood in you after all."

Sal lowers his head. "We can't do this."

"Bruno is going in the dirt." Antony lifts his end of the body. "He's all dead weight."

"This is crazy," Sal says, pressing his thumb so hard against his palm that it hurts. "Let's take him out to sea. What if he's discovered, for Christ's sake?"

"I'm not going to have Bruno's eyes eaten by fish and washing up on some shore. He deserves a proper burial, and since we can't give him one in Moravian where he belongs, we're putting him in the earth here, with a view of the Sound."

"Jesus, Antony. What the fuck is wrong with you." Sal puts the stone head back down with the bones and looks out at whitecaps under the moonlight whisking across the water. He sees how complicit in his brother's ruthlessness he's always been. Justin has told him that he doesn't have to make excuses for Antony's actions. Someday, Justin warned, Antony is going to rope him into something he can't get out of. Ashamed of his inertia, Sal nodded, unable to explain why he'd do almost anything Antony wanted.

"What the fuck, Sal. I said let's do this. I've got his shoulders; you take his legs." Antony moves back, dragging the corpse. "Hey, *gagootz*, get off the pot. Lift your fucking end."

Sal climbs into the stern. There's an opening in the tarp, and in the moonlight he can see Bruno's hand curled, as if, in his last moments, he had tried to claw away death. Sal grabs hold of his end and lifts until the body levels out. He can feel the tips of Bruno's shoes press against his hip.

"I should have wrapped him in plastic. I wasn't thinking right." Antony trips over Jesus's head. "Fuck this shithole." He kicks it, and the head strikes a tibia, splitting the bone apart.

"Keep going straight back," Sal says, as if he were reluctantly in charge. When they clear the mussel bed, they let Bruno down.

"Be careful," Sal says. "There's poison ivy everywhere."

Antony gives him a look like *now you tell me*. He goes to the boat and takes out a couple of shovels.

"We don't need those," Sal says.

"Why not?"

"The grave's open."

"No shit, isn't that convenient."

From the workhouse BB sees them carry Bruno's body. When they pass the Mother of God and headless Baby Jesus, Sal stops.

"What's the matter?" Antony asks.

"That's the statue."

"Like I give a fuck. Let's go. We gotta get back before daybreak."

BB follows them through the cover of the reeds. There's a screech nearby and a red-tailed hawk is circling.

Sal stops again.

"Shit, what's wrong," Antony says.

Sal sits on the ground, Bruno's legs in his lap. "I can't do this."

"Fuck, you can't."

Antony drops his end of the corpse and, crouching beside his brother, with one hand, he squeezes Sal's cheeks so hard this time that Sal can't breathe.

"You're hurting me," says Sal.

Antony gives Sal an aggrieved look. "Remember, I'm your brother. You know the family's cursed if you turn against your brother."

"Fuck the family curses."

"Lemme tell you something," Antony is surprisingly reflective. "You couldn't know because Francesco left you out of dirty work. He thought you might become a doctor. Respectable. No thug like me. Maybe a priest like Justin until he found out you were fucking our own adopted brother all these years. You were his great American hope. He celebrated when you became a hotshot Coast Guard officer, Homeland Security no less, but you screwed that up. He never believed you'd be hauling the dead in some fucking harbor ferry. What happened to you, Sal." And then, in a quiet accusation that strikes at his brother's heart, he says, "You could say you were a disappointment, Sal."

Sal's silent as Antony goes on.

"Francesco gave up on me a long time ago even though I was the one son most like him. Maybe that's it. Maybe he hated himself, so he couldn't see my accomplishments, how I outdistanced him in all the ways that a member of the Gambino family should. And you, like I said, he respected you until he didn't. That's when he turned to Justin. Go figure, putting his faith in a priest, adopted, the perfect son, at last. Fuck Justin, fuck Francesco."

Sal runs his hands through his hair, wishing Antony would stop talking.

"And what did he leave us? The Sicilian curse. You betray the oath, you, and everyone you're close to, suffers. He was up to something with the Russians. Fuckin' A. He put all of us in jeopardy. And now there's this test of *your* honor, *your* family obligation. You've got to stand with me, Sal. If you don't, the whole family suffers. No telling what Carlo's wrath will make him do if he finds out I killed Bruno. There's no controlling the consequences."

Sal looks out at the markers on the mass graves. Under the moonlight and sweeping thin clouds the white stones look like flickering votives. "I don't think we should desecrate this ground with Bruno's corpse," he says. "*That's* bad karma, Antony. Let's take him out to sea."

"*Basta!*" Antony is tired of waiting any longer. "We're burying Bruno in one of the pine boxes. End of story."

"You've murdered others, haven't you?"

"All these years you pretend you don't see what's before your eyes."

"Our father never killed anyone."

"You're sure of that?"

"Fuck you, Antony."

"I didn't tell you something about Rosa. She's pregnant."

"It's yours?"

"Whose else's? Part of me cares for her."

"Ha."

"You don't believe your big brother can love anyone else but you?" He flicks a finger on Sal's cheek. "Rosa Cali. Bruno didn't respect her. He beat her. He might have beaten the kid right out of her, which would, I suppose, be the best thing."

"How did you turn out like this?"

Antony ignores him. "If there really is a kid, I'm going to ask Rosa to make you and Justin the godparents. She'll do what I tell her. I can't be involved with some brat for all the obvious reasons. Besides, I don't know what to do with the ones I've got in California."

Sal's speechless. Antony picks up Bruno and nods to Sal. "Your turn."

His resistance spent, Sal whispers, too low for his brother to hear, "We're done after this, Antony." He lifts his end of the stinking, leaking rolled-up tarp. Together they haul Bruno to the trench.

~

Trench 189, which was opened two weeks ago, is about a quarter full. There are pieces of plywood, five feet by ten feet, covering the coffins. The human rot is palpable.

"Fuck, a mass grave. Where are we, in Nazi-occupied Poland?"

Sal doesn't say anything.

"Jesus, what's with this stench?"

Almost as soon as a person dies, a corpse begins releasing gases and chemicals that vent distinctive odors: a ubiquitous smell of hydrogen and sulfide, the rotten egg scent of decomposition, and then putrescent flesh. Always the same ensemble of putrid odors. Sal is used to them.

The brothers lay Bruno down along the edge of the trench. Antony covers his mouth. "You're in charge."

"What do you mean?"

"You've watched the burials, right. You know what to do. I want to put Bruno in a box with good company, but one that will never be exhumed. You choose."

Sal shakes his head and fetches a ladder propped up against the trailer and lowers it along the wall of the trench. He's decided to get this over with. "Let's go down and move the plywood." He descends into the trench and Antony follows.

"Jesus, maybe the sea would have been more hospitable," Antony says. "But Bruno couldn't even swim. Did you know that?"

"I thought you were in a hurry."

Uncharacteristically deferential, Antony does what he's told. They lift a board off, uncovering a row of coffins. Antony stops and reaches into his pocket for a bandana and ties it over his mouth and nose. He looks like a desperado. He's murdered more than a dozen men, cut them up, carried their bloody corpses, but he's never been in a hole with so many decaying bodies. The earth is still wet from the afternoon downpour, and the muck is oozing up his socks. Worms are burrowing into the mud, while scavenging insects climb inside his pant legs.

The odor in the trench is worse than Sal's used to above ground. He takes off his parka and T-shirt, which he wraps around his face under his eyes. He slips back into the parka and flips up the hood. Under the waning moonlight the two brothers look like the walking dead.

"This one," Sal says.

Antony shines the spot on it and reads, Ronald McDonald 042406. "Fuck, that's a joke."

Sal doesn't answer.

"Why not this one?" He points to Male Unknown 042402. "Who's going to be looking for an unknown piece of shit."

"If a body gets dug up, it's usually an unknown. Someone discovers a lost relative ended up here and brings the remains back home."

Antony's too sickened by the smell of the corpses to second-guess Sal anymore. Sal climbs back up the ladder and leans the tarp over the trench edge while Antony wraps his arms around Bruno's shoulders. By the time they get him into the grave, rearrange his limbs so that he can be stuffed on top of the clown, and put the trench back in order, it's almost three in the morning. Before he climbs out of the grave, Antony leans into the coffin and places his hand on Bruno's head. "Fuck us," he says. "I'm going to miss you, *compa*."

"You weren't this broken up at Francesco's funeral."

"Fuck off, Sal."

"If I broke Dad's heart, you destroyed it."

"Francesco was no angel, little bro. He did a lot to break his own heart."

"I think he was afraid of you."

Antony pauses, as if he were about to let himself reflect on what Sal has said. But he lets it pass, and says, "Don't worry, Sal. Someday you won't even think about the rotten things you've done."

"Like Cannoli?"

"What?"

"Salvano's cat you tortured."

Antony hasn't thought about that cat or old lady Salvano since he was a kid. "Yeah, like Cannoli. You do what you gotta do."

～

BB has heard enough to know that Antony scares him. Captain Sal, well, BB can't figure him out. He seems like a good man, but how could he help his brother like this? BB feels a sharp pain in his stomach, a vestige of the Indian Poke. He moans.

Sal puts back the ladder while Antony is wiping as much of the trench off his clothes as he can. "Did you hear that?" he says.

"What?"

"Over there in the reeds."

"No one's here. It's probably a bullfrog."

BB gets up and bolts.

"Look, the reeds are swaying," Antony says. He trips over a piece of plywood, but not before he's seen a silhouette of something running. Sal catches a better glimpse: BB carrying his flag and disappearing in the reeds.

Antony has twisted his ankle and sliced open his thigh on a rock. "Fuck, go after him."

"Calm down. It was a deer. I saw it bolt."

Sal helps Antony up. "That's a bad cut." He takes his T-shirt and wraps it around the wound. "It's pretty deep." He thinks, *What is BB doing here?*

"It didn't look like a deer. Fuckin' voodoo shit all over here. You sure it was a deer? We can't have a witness, Sal."

"Yeah, a deer. I saw it."

They are silent on the way back to City Island.

That was no deer, Antony thinks. But he knows right now it's important that they get back and leave City Island before anyone sees them together. *No witnesses*, he tells himself. *I'll find him, that guy's a dead man.*

Sal hasn't turned around to face his brother since they left Hart Island. *Jesus*, he thinks, *BB saw everything.*

~

Back at the workhouse, BB is lying under the window. He watched Sal and his brother leave Mussel Cove. He doesn't want to, but he closes his eyes. He wonders if it all was a hallucination. The blue weather flag is leaning out of the open window frame and flapping in the breeze. He's too tired to make the Sign of the Cross, and he thinks, *What good would it do?*

The Tarantella

Ida's sitting in the recliner. The chair's plastic cover has yellowed, and there's a tear on the side. Since Francesco was killed, she's been digging into it with her fingernails. Her feet barely reach the footrest, and her toes, which Justin painted ruby red for her, are sticking out of fuzzy slippers. Ida's still wearing the snap-button housedress that Sal laid out for her in the morning. The top three snaps are undone, showing her wrinkled breasts. On her lap is a small plate of *giuggiulena* cookies she hasn't touched. Her eyes, half lidded, twitch and then go still. A Judy Garland special from the sixties is playing on PBS. The screen might as well be black because Ida's retreated into herself, though her thoughts are hurtling helter-skelter.

She thinks she hears Justin saying, "Fuck, Sal, where are you?" But the words disappear before she can latch onto them. He doesn't swear often, she thinks, and then forgets that's what she was thinking. Everything she hears and sees flits and dashes, scurries and skims. She can't keep up with anything. Sometimes a memory more like a story than an image appears, and she hunkers in it as if it were a favorite movie. Her breathing softens, her eyes stop twitching, and if she had the ability to judge the twists and turns her mind is taking, she'd rather stay there in that fragmented past than be anywhere else.

Tonight, the movie playing in her head begins on the eve of her wedding in Cinisi. May 1969, just days before the Feast of the Visitation of the Blessed Virgin Mary. She's lying in her bed for the last time, nervous and expectant. Her window overlooks a lemon grove bursting with blossoms. She's lulled by the smell, not zesty like lemon peel but sweet and floral like hundreds of new gardenias. It's warm, so she has left the window open and feels the breeze on her hair and sees stars pulsing in a cloudless sky. There's a rustling below her window, a guitar playing, and Francesco's sweet voice singing: *E quannu s'affaccia la vurria vasai.* He sings the line again, this time decades later, under moonlight in the backyard on Staten Island, in English, a cappella: *When she shows herself at the window, I want to kiss her.* Ida smiles. She sees *confeitti*, pastel candy-coated almonds, on the wedding table. She's looking in a mirror at herself in her wedding dress and gasps, worried she's cursed, until she sees that she had removed a shoe, an earring, a glove to ward off bad luck. Everything is jumbled, in no linear course, but she loves cherishing that day and doesn't notice. She's walking to the Chiesa Madre Santa Fara. Surrounded on the road by her friends and family, she's the only one wearing white; her *testimone* follows behind, keeping her gown clear of the dirt. Francesco finds the garter, a wisp of lace for good luck, just above her knee; he brushes his fingers across her thigh before tossing it behind him. Attached to streamers held by wedding guests, she and Francesco dance the first dance. When they finish, guests circle around the newlyweds and do the *tarantella*, turning one way and then the other. Carlo Cali, back home in Sicily from New York City for the celebration, takes her hand and dances with her while Francesco looks on. He whispers in her ear in English, "Ida, like my dear godson Francesco, you are family, too. In America, you'll prosper. *Con amore, bellissima Ida.*" She smiles shyly, then trembles barely noticeably, already nostalgic for the sea and hills of Cinisi and worrying that Carlo Cali and the Cosa Nostra, which Francesco has avoided so far, will be part of their lives in America.

Still flitting through her wedding day, she watches Francesco smashing a glass vase on the floor. The groom's *testimone* counts the pieces. *Settantacinque*, he shouts. Everyone claps and cheers the prediction of a long and happy marriage. She's holding Francesco's hand as they leave the church to greet revelers gathered on the square. Her newlywed husband takes a small piece of silver from his pocket and gives it to Ida; she bows and shows him the tear in her veil. Shared gestures of their promised sacrifices. She looks back at Mount Pecoraro rising behind the church and thinks she can smell olive trees on the hillside and the scent of the nearby sea. Suddenly the images of her wedding day disappear. Ida twitches. She is cradling Francesco on the stoop, her love, the snow around them splattered with his blood, the stone lion grinning under the glare of tiny twinkling Christmas lights.

She screams.

Justin rushes to her. "Ida, what's wrong?"

She stiffens, then is blank again. She's trapped in everything she has forgotten, Francesco not even a shadow memory now, while she sits in glacial silence.

"You had another bad dream?" Justin watches her eyes close and kisses her forehead. She doesn't feel a thing. He tries to get her out of the recliner, but she won't budge. Sometimes on a night like this she insists on sleeping there.

Justin calls Anna and asks her to come over, explaining that Ida's had a scare and Sal might be in trouble.

When she arrives, Anna checks on Ida. Taking Ida's hand, she asks, "What's the matter, honey?"

Justin tells her that he doesn't know how they would cope without her. Outside the Cusumano family and the file buried in Sal's Coast Guard records, only Anna knows that Sal and Justin are lovers. Ida and Anna have been like sisters since they met at a Knights of Columbus supper not long after Ida arrived on Staten Island. Childless, Anna became the keeper of Our Lady Queen of Peace, working for two parish priests, including a monsignor, before Justin returned to the neighborhood to lead parishioners. For decades she's cleaned the rectory, cooked, prepared the altar and sacristy for daily services, managed the books, and, since Justin moved back, covered for him and Sal. If she were *connected*, Anna would be their most trusted and loyal lieutenant. Sal and Justin are sons to her.

"Sal's probably at Mother Pug's," he tells her, as he leaves the house. Ida hears his voice but doesn't know who's talking. It's as if she isn't anywhere.

Anna pulls over a chair and sits next to Ida. She surfs the channels and stops on TMC. "Look, honey, it's *One More Tomorrow*. I love Ann Sheridan. My mother said I look just like her." She takes Ida's hand again. "Don't worry, it has a happy ending."

$\sim$

O'Shea is at his perch at the end of the bar when Justin arrives. The karaoke DJ, packing up equipment, waves to Justin. A couple is sitting in the corner, holding hands, leaning in, and whispering. The man is wearing a pink Lacoste polo shirt and a leather bomber jacket; the woman has Morticia Addams hair that drapes halfway down her chair. They're not locals. They don't even look Italian. A guy who's a spitting image of Richard Castellano is playing ghost ball. *"Fanculo,"* he says, pocketing the eight ball with just one stripe left to run the table.

Nina comes over. "Sal's not here."

"I can see that."

"He left in a hurry a while ago."

"Any idea where?"

"I'm not my brother's keeper, Father. That's more your style."

Justin gives her a look.

"I didn't mean it as an insult. You know, a priest taking care of his flock. Brother watching out for brother."

"Sal isn't answering his phone. Did he leave it here again?"

"Nope. I haven't seen it."

"Was he drunk?"

"Nah, he didn't have time to get juiced. It takes a lot."

"Anything unusual?"

"He spent most of the time talking to O'Shea. They've become inseparable. Go figure, O'Shea's usually a lone wolf."

Justin looks over at Aidan, who's running his hand in circles and crisscrosses over his head. "What's with him?"

"He's basted. Always ends the night with a joint outside, and then another whiskey or two."

Justin walks over to him. "Aidan, I hear you were talking to Sal earlier."

O'Shea grins. "Well, bless me, Father. What are you drinking?"

"I'm looking for Sal."

"Nina, bring the man of the cloth a Jameson."

"Nina said he left in a hurry."

She sets down the whiskey. O'Shea proposes a toast. "Bless the Cusumanos and end the curse."

They clink glasses. "What curse?" Justin kills the shot.

"Sometimes you find you get what you need," Aidan mumbles, ignoring him.

He sees O'Shea isn't going to make much sense. "Do you know where Sal went?"

"I told him I loved Francesco. Sal was surprised. I explained that he broke my mother's heart. But you know all this, don't you, Father? A priest knows all. Omniscient."

"No, Aidan, that's God, not me."

"She would have done anything for him. She even asked if he wanted her to have an abortion. 'Fuck no,' he told her. Sherry doesn't know this, so don't tell her. It would break her heart. My mother should never have married a Black Irish piece of shit. She should have married Francesco. I usually don't like Guidos, even though my mother's all *Napoletano*. Francesco's an exception. Did I say I loved him? Did you know, Sherry is in the FBI?"

"Aidan, are you so high you can't answer me? It's important. Do you know where Sal is?"

"With Antony."

"You're sure."

"Sure, I'm sure."

"You know where?"

"City Island, maybe. Sal's not like you. He's never in the library. Does he read at all? Yet he has a good heart. It's rare for someone who doesn't read to have a good heart."

Justin pats him on the shoulder. "You sure he said City Island?"

"Sure? You can't be sure about anything, right? Maybe it was Titty Highland? How the fuck do I know?"

"Okay, calm down, Aidan."

"Uber."

"What?"

"Sal said Uber. He left in one. I saw it pull up."

Justin is thinking that he isn't going to get much else from Aidan, and if Sal is with Antony, there's not much he can do about it now. "Aidan, Sal told me that he went to AA with you."

"Fuck 'em."

"Have you both gone back?"

"Do you want another whiskey, Father? We've got time."

"If you and Sal have become pals, why not keep the meetings up?"

"Sherry tells me you're the only sensible Cusumano? And I remind her you're a Flynn."

Then Justin thinks, *Jesus, it doesn't make sense that Sal would meet Antony on City Island.* "Aidan, did Sal tell you why he was meeting Antony?"

Aidan gets up and staggers to the bathroom, muttering what he'd just said, "She says you're the only sensible one."

Justin's phone rings. It's Anna.

"Ida's walking in circles again. She won't sit down."

"I'm coming home."

~

Justin finds Ida still marching around the dining room table. Tonight, her heart doesn't seem in it; she's silent, no gibberish. Anna's worried, pleading with Ida to come back to the couch. "She doesn't hear a thing I say."

Justin pulls out a dining room chair to block her. When he says, *"Bella-mamma, rest a bit,"* he takes her hand and guides her out of the endless circling. He helps her to the bedroom, removes her slippers, and pulls up the sheet and blanket. He leans over and kisses her soft hair, more like a teenager's than an old woman's. "What's happened to us, Ida?" he whispers. "What's Antony doing now with Sal?"

When he returns to the living room, Anna is in the recliner, sipping Marsala. "I've never seen something so strange. She bolted up. She'd been sound asleep. She started circling. I couldn't get her to sit back down."

He gets a whiskey. "She's not our only worry, Anna. I'm scared. Antony is up to something terrible."

"He's so different than Sal."

"Like Cain and Abel."

"Ida has known Antony is dangerous ever since he was a boy. Once long ago she was so upset, she walked me back to Our Lady Queen of Peace. She wouldn't tell me what he had done. We lit novena candles and prayed that he would change. Ida cried the entire time."

"Sal would do almost anything for Antony." Justin sighs.

"It's a Sicilian curse."

Remembering that's what O'Shea had said, he asks, "What is?"

"Standing by your family, no matter what. I never believed in that kind of loyalty. There's such a thing as bad blood. You can't stand by bad blood without getting destroyed. Antony's bad blood." She puts on her coat. "Call me if you need me to come back."

Justin gives her a kiss and paces around the room. Trying again and again to reach Sal, he leaves the same message, "Where are you? I'm worried."

Malevolent

The road to the DOC dock is empty. While Antony hitches the boat to the back of the minivan, still too early for fishermen and most birds, he hears wailing nearby. "Jesus, what's that?"

"Loons. They're waking up."

"Like I need loons in the morning. Why are you lying to me, Sal? You saw someone in the reeds."

"I saw a deer."

"Like fuck you did."

"No one was in the reeds. You're paranoid."

Antony pulls him close. "You find him and bring him to me. *Capisci!*"

Sal breaks away. "I can't bring you someone who wasn't there. From now on, keep me out of your shit."

"Bring the asshole to me. Afterward, the *la famiglia* oath, we'll talk about it. Maybe enough is enough."

Sal's silent. He knows his brother is going to kill BB.

Antony gets into the minivan and rolls down the window. He's eerily calm. "Maybe there's no magic family bond." He pauses like what he's going to say is so important it needs its own air. "The tie that binds is *fear*. It's the same in all things. Politics. Families. The Mafia. If you can make someone afraid, you have power. Not love, not loyalty. *Fear.*" He gestures to his brother to come over. Grasping Sal's arm, he says, "Find him. Even brothers do bad things to brothers, when they have to."

Sal watches the minivan and boat disappear down Fordham Street. He's worn out. Cries of Canada geese awakening join the racket of the loons. "Christ," Sal says to himself. "He's threatening me." The scent of the trench on him is making him sick, so he removes his parka and tosses it into the trash barrel. Inside the trailer, he puts on an old Coast Guard sweatshirt—with *Semper Paratus, Always Ready*, printed across the front.

The DOC flag outside the trailer is flapping and Sal remembers wrapping Bruno in the tarp, his milky eyes staring up at nothing just before the canvas curtained them. He sees BB running through the reeds. Sal's dizzy and feels like he could vomit but nothing comes up. He powers on his phone and calls Justin, who mutes Yo-Yo Ma and asks, "Sal, what's going on? I've been up all night waiting for you."

"Antony killed Bruno Cali."

"Jesus!"

"BB was there."

"Who's BB?"

"A homeless guy. He was on Hart when we buried Bruno."

"You went to the island and buried Bruno? You're not making sense."

Sal walks outside and goes over the night with Justin. Crouched against an old buoy on the dock, his hand trembling, he wishes he could down a Jameson. He explains everything he knows about Antony and Bruno and says he doesn't know how or why BB ended up there. "Antony can't get to him," he tells Sal. "He'll kill him. And Antony threatened me, too. I think he'd kill me if he felt he had to."

"We have to call the police."

"Are you crazy? They'll think I was mixed up with killing Bruno. Imagine what Carlo would do. Besides, Antony is the police. You've got to help me hide BB."

"What are you talking about. Hide him where?"

"You can take him up to your priest friend in Maine. Give him sanctuary. He's on the island still. I'll bring him back after today's burials. Francesco, Bruno, I've had it with murders. I'm not going to let Antony kill him."

"Jesus, Sal."

Ida walks into the living room, and just before Sal ends the call, he hears her ask, "Where's Al Roker today?"

Ida hugs Justin. "You're a good son, Sal."

He shakes his head as if he can't take much more. "I'm *Justin*, Ida."

"Justin. The sweetest boy I've ever seen."

"Let's get you back to sleep."

"Is Antony dead? He was gunned down."

Justin rubs the back of his neck and winces. "What?"

"I saw him. It was Antony." She's shivering.

"You're cold." He takes her into his arms. "It's okay."

"You're the sweetest boy who ever lived."

"If you say so."

"What did I say?"

"You said you're sleepy."

"I did. I must be sleepy."

After he gets Ida back in bed, he clicks the remote to unmute Yo-Yo Ma performing Ennio Morricone's "Playing Love." Before closing his eyes and losing himself in the music, he calls Sal but it goes to voice mail.

Ida can hear the music and thinks it's coming from outside her bedroom window in Cinisi. She hears Francesco singing: *"When she shows herself at the window, I want to kiss her."*

~

Sal watches the Moretti brothers ready their fishing boat. He remembers what Antony said before driving off: *Even brothers do bad things to brothers, when they have to.* He searches for a word that must be buried within him, one to define Antony, truer than anything he's allowed himself to think. A word he's been hiding from. He's worried there will be no disowning it when he finds it. He thinks *malevolent*. That can't be it. He closes his eyes and says to himself, *disturbed . . . wild . . . redeemable*. Sal gets up and goes to *Vesuvius*. From the wheelhouse he watches the sun crawl over the water. Hart Island emerges in the early light, the nascent sun loitering behind it. Not *malevolent*, he thinks, but the word keeps resurfacing like a swell at sea. Still, he won't say it, and then he remembers old lady Salvano's tabby, and he thinks, *I'm not going to let BB die.*

The Moretti brothers wave as they pass *Vesuvius* and head out in their fishing boat. The crushing sound of a garbage compacter is crawling down Fordham Street. Sal's head hurts. A lone seagull settles on a piling and sizes him up, before squawking and flying off. Soon, Booker, Hemins, and the burial crew will arrive, and he'll have to act as if nothing has happened.

Floyd's on Fire Island

They met at Floyd's, a breakfast joint on Fire Island. Sherry had chosen it because it's probably the least likely place in the tristate where they'd run into a wiseguy, though you never can be sure; in Chicago, she knew a couple of gay gangsters. They're easy to turn. But in December before Christmas here on Fire Island? It's a long shot.

She came back to Staten Island because the agency had made her an *offer she couldn't refuse*. That's what her boss annoyingly called it. Not only had she proven herself to be smart, resourceful, and fearless in the fight against Chicago gangs, but she was the daughter of the enigmatic Staten Island bookie and Carlo Cali confidante, Francesco Cusumano. So, the Special Agent in Charge of the Manhattan field office had an idea that he ran up the chain to the deputy director in D.C. Maybe Sherry would agree to try to turn her father and get information about the remnants of the Five Families and their alliances with the Russian mob. Carlo Cali was a key player in deals with Bratva (the Russian Brotherhood, House of Putin) in Brighton Beach's Little Odessa. The Russians needed peace to carry out their stock market scams, gasoline bootlegging schemes, and drug and money laundering empire. Money laundering that included multimillion-dollar Trump Tower condos bought by Russian oligarchs for ten times their value. They needed Carlo Cali to provide the peace, not only with the Italians but with street gangs, too. Francesco could be their ticket in.

"Who said you can't go home again," Sherry said when the SAC explained the investigation, dubbed *Operation Friendship*, a nod to the 1933 nonaggression pact between Italy and the Soviet Union. She'd be the special agent in charge of the probe. It was risky; after all, Bratva was nothing like the American Cosa Nostra. Targeting a cop, G-man, judge was rare for New York's Italian gangsters. Not so for Russian thugs.

"Any qualms about trying to turn your father?" the Manhattan SAC had asked.

"What father?" she said.

"That close, hey."

"You know I haven't seen him since I was two, right? And I don't remember anything about him."

"No time like the present for a family reunion," he said.

She gave him a look and thought, *What the fuck am I doing?*

~

After just a few minutes at Floyd's, Sherry was surprised that she wasn't repulsed by Francesco. Her father had waved awkwardly when he entered the restaurant and saw her in the back at a table by a window overlooking the bay. He was sixty-seven years old and had thick speckled gray-and-black hair that he combed back naturally, no gel. Even when he was young, he didn't layer on the grease like a lot of other soldiers. He was a little overweight, but she thought he was handsome in the way some older men avoid showing their age. Sherry didn't get up when he arrived at the table. Her silence intensified Francesco's anxiety.

After what seemed like minutes but were probably just moments, Sherry asked, "Are you going to sit down? Or do you just want a quick look before you take off again?"

Before he could get into the chair, he said, more earnestly than Sherry could have expected: "I wanted to see you, Aidan, and your mother every day."

"But you *didn't*," she said brusquely. After all, she needed to be in control of the meet.

"It's complicated. You don't know Ida."

"You don't look like a man who's tied to a wife's skirt."

"Can we talk about you, honey?"

"You call me *honey* again and I'm out of here."

"Your mother liked it."

"I'm not my mother."

Francesco smiled, timidly. "I can see that."

They ordered lunch and sat a long time in that corner, occasionally turning from conversation to watching the view outside the window: a rainbow flag flapping on the dock, the sky cloudless, a blue bowl over the sea. Some fishing boats passing by now and again, and there were seagulls everywhere on pilings and benches along the docks. Sherry decided that she'd let Francesco reminisce to win his trust, and she was intrigued. The whole time together, he didn't touch his Buffalo chicken wrap and barely drank a quarter of his coffee. He picked at a few soggy wedge fries during a lull in conversation. When she asked him why he wasn't eating, he said, "I didn't notice." Sherry couldn't help being softened by his presence, though she wouldn't see it exactly that way until later at home when she went over everything that had happened, moment by moment, in her head.

Looking out at the rainbow flag and watching two men holding hands pass by, Francesco said, "I wonder if Sal and Justin have ever been here. Did Aidan tell you, they're gay."

"Adopted-brother-slash-priest hooks up with adopted brother. Your family's fucked up."

"It's your family, too."

Sherry gave a slightly chastised look.

Francesco told her that he was in the waiting room at Brooklyn Birthing when she was born. There had been a pregnancy complication. He couldn't remember what it was, but it was safer, the doctor said, to deliver her there than on Staten Island. He told her Brooklyn was better anyway because it meant Ida would be less likely to discover his "secret love, and you, Sherry." (Sherry, still suspicious, thought, *Like you really cared about love*.) He told her that when Ida discovered that he cherished her like the daughter he and Ida had never borne, she couldn't accept it (*Doesn't he know I don't give a shit about Ida*, Sherry thought). He didn't tell her that Ida called her "the cursed fruit of the womb." Instead, he said, "You can love two women, but their love will only bring trouble and suffering to everyone."

So, the time passed as she listened to her father's litany of remembrances: The day at the Saratoga Racetrack that had entered her dreams. How he helped Caterina bathe her—rubber ducks, manatees, and dolphins bobbing as he squeezed bathwater from a sponge that trickled down her tiny back. How she threw a handful of spaghetti and clams across the table and laughed when he took a *spachetto* that had landed on his nose and tilted back his head, slowly lowering it into his mouth. How she cried once when he left the house and forgot to kiss her. "*Mi dispiace*," he told her. "*Mi dispiace*, my little petunia." Sherry didn't remember any of it (*He's practiced in the art of lying*, she thought, *a gangster*). Francesco told her that he and Aidan would take turns tossing her onto a mountain of pillows on the couch, and she'd cry out, *Mo, mo, mo!* Caterina would say, don't be so rough, and Sherry would give her mother a toddler's shut-the-fuck-up look long before she'd learned those words. He understood even then, he told her, that she was stronger than anyone he's ever known.

By the time it seemed Francesco was running out of stories, Sherry was confused. There was no sea change like one that occurs in a television melodrama. She didn't feel like the abandoned daughter who pounds her fists on her absent father's chest, screaming about all the damage he has caused before inexplicably forgiving him and collapsing in his arms. She didn't tear up once through all the time Francesco was reliving a past that she was too young to remember. Still, the stone-cold idea of him that she'd created all these years was unmistakably warming. Francesco paused awhile, and Sherry finally said, "Francesco, I've got a proposition for you that I hope you don't refuse." She didn't mean for it to sound like the line from *The Godfather*. Perplexed, he looked at her expectantly and thought, *Whatever you want, Sherry, whatever you want.*

~

Driving home from Fire Island, Francesco was buoyant, dreaming up scenarios where Sal, Justin, even Ida in her forgetfulness would bring Sherry into the family. *Antony*, he thought, *he won't be easy.* He was so keyed up that he needed to piss, so he pulled off the Southern State at Valley Stream Park. His prostate burned as he watched the shallow snow cover melt, revealing steaming dead leaves and twisted twigs. And then he remembered this was where his godfather had taken him a week after arriving in New York from Cinisi. Two of Carlo's soldiers were in the back seat of a black El Dorado convertible with silver-streaked pinions like eagle wings. When they got to the park, the men hauled a canvas sheet that sagged like a hammock and dropped it on the ground, close to a ditch. "Come over here, Francesco," Carlo said. Francesco, worried about what he was going to see, was reluctant but he understood he had no choice. When Carlo opened the canvas, Francesco gagged. The corpse's face had been eaten away by acid. Pieces of teeth and jawbone were the only recognizable features. Carlo placed his hand on his godson's crotch. Francesco had pissed his pants. Carlo whispered in his ear, "Like I thought, Francesco. You're not cut out for rough stuff. You're so much like your father, and you're smart, too. I need someone like you, someone loyal with a brain bigger than his balls."

Francesco sat on a tree stump and considered Sherry's proposition. He would work with the FBI against the Russians even if it meant betraying Carlo and the other families. Sherry had promised that if Francesco could pull this off, there would be a get-out-of-jail card for the Cusumanos, and she would send them into witness protection. If Francesco rejected the offer, she told him that the FBI had enough on Antony to put him in prison for life. They had enough to put Francesco away, too. For old Italian gangsters in the twenty-first century, she said, a deal like this one was manna from heaven. What choice, really, did Francesco have?

When he returned to Staten Island, it was nearly seven, and he knew that Justin would be finishing evening confessions. Right before he was about to flick off the switch on the confessional light, Francesco kneeled in the compartment. Justin slid opened the shutter on the screen.

Francesco said, "I've got news."

Justin stopped him. "This isn't the place for news, Francesco. You can, if you'd like, make a confession, but you have to start over. Remember, *Bless me, Father, for I have sinned.*"

"I'm not confessing. It's news, and I couldn't wait. Good news, I think."

"Okay, what's so important that you have to tell me in the darkness of a confessional."

"Remember I explained a few weeks ago that I'm not the man you think I am. Well, now I've got a chance to make up for the past. A way we can start all over again."

"Are you drunk?"

"Ha, I've never been more clear-headed. And here's a secret, you can't tell anyone, not even Sal, not yet anyway: I've got a daughter."

"What daughter?"

"All I can say right now is that she's going to give us the chance for a new life, you, Sal, Ida, me, and even Antony, if he doesn't fuck it up. Now don't ask me any questions. It won't be long that you'll know everything. It's risky, though, so give me a blessing, Justin. It can't hurt."

Justin was speechless.

"Well, what about that blessing," Francesco said.

"I don't know what I'm blessing."

Insistent, Francesco said, "Just say it. I don't ask you for much."

"Okay, bless you, Francesco, in the name of the Father, and of the Son, and of the Holy Ghost."

"That's it, that's what I needed, and remember, even though this isn't a confession, and I haven't been in a church since Sal was baptized, you're bound by secrecy at whatever goes down in this booth. Don't tell Sal."

"Let's go to the rectory and talk. You're scaring me." Justin opened the confessional door, but Francesco was halfway down the aisle when Justin shouted, "Francesco, come back here."

Francesco turned and smiled. He was singing, *But I know I'm going to change that tune / When I'm back on top, back on top in June.*

~

Francesco wanted to find Aidan O'Shea and stopped at Mother Pug's. Before he could sit at the bar, Nina had already poured him a Crown Royal and soda.

"You okay?" she asked. "You're sweating."

"I'm fine, honey."

"None of these *cavones* here call me *honey.*"

Francesco smiled and put a fifty-dollar bill on the bar.

"Call me *honey* anytime, Francesco," she said, pocketing the money.

"O'Shea's not here?"

"If he were, you'd be sitting on his lap. That's his stool. He's in the can."

Aidan came back. "You're in my seat, Pops."

"You know I met Sherry today, right," Francesco said.

"Yeah, she told me she was going to see you."

"I'll do it."

"Do what?"

"You don't know?"

O'Shea told Francesco that she doesn't tell him everything. "She's a lot like you and Sal. Secretive until she isn't. And whatever you're going to do, I don't want to know it."

Francesco, tearing up, waited awhile, and said, "I don't think she hates me anymore."

"Never thought she did. She didn't know you. And that's on you." He lifted his whiskey and toasted, "Come on, Francesco, let's celebrate this."

Francesco kissed Aidan on the cheek.

"I'm one of your soldiers now?"

"Ha, you know you've been like another son."

"Like you need another son to disappoint you."

Francesco gave him a look.

"I'm kidding, Pops. Just so you know, even though I had a father, I never needed him. My motto: *Hey, Dad, I did it without you.* When your father's a piece of shit, you have to believe in yourself."

Francesco leaned in again. "Not another kiss," Aidan said.

"Caterina would be proud of you, Aidan."

Francesco, old school, didn't have a cell phone. He had asked Nina if he could use the landline in the office. Beside him was a *Chinatown* movie poster, Jack Nicholson, a bandage across his nose and blood dripping down his chin. He fetched Sherry's card from his wallet and tapped out her number. When she answered, he said, "I'm gonna do it."

"I could have told you that."

"I don't like Ohio or Iowa," he said. "Maybe Arizona, or some place on a lake in Michigan."

She laughed.

"Antony's going to be a problem."

"I figured. We'll talk about how to convince him. I need him in on this. Sal can help."

"You said Antony gets immunity, too."

"After he does a little time, if he plays . . ."

Francesco interrupted her. "He's bad, but not stupid." Before she might say anything about the bodies Antony is suspected of piling up, he said, "You've got to promise to visit. I want Sal and Jason to get to know you. We'll have to lie about you to Ida."

"You're jumping way ahead, Francesco."

He didn't respond, wondering if she would ever call him Dad.

"Be patient. This is going to take time."

Two days later, Francesco was gunned down.

~

At Francesco's funeral Mass at Our Lady Queen of Peace, Sherry was in the back standing by the holy water font and wearing her bug-eye sunglasses and scarf over her head. Carlo and Bruno Cali looked at her suspiciously as they walked past. They took seats behind Ida and Sal. Antony, who promised long ago he would never set foot again in a church, stayed outside in the hearse. Sherry noticed Carlo lean forward and kiss Ida. Bruno looked around, antsy, wondering where the fuck Antony was. Justin stood in front of the coffin, opening his hands to the mourners, inviting everyone to say farewell. Sal put his arm around Ida, who leaned her head on his shoulder.

Later that evening, in her office, looking at the sun setting behind the Empire State Building, Sherry couldn't get Francesco out of her mind. She didn't want to. The agency's logo was embossed on her academy diploma hanging next to her, with the words highlighted: *Fidelity, Bravery, Integrity.* Watching the reddening sky, she closed her eyes and saw Francesco's corpse in the morgue. His face was looking up at her as if he were going to say, *You know, honey, I'd do anything for you. All you have to do is forgive me.*

History of Violence

Antony drives deep into Pelham Bay Park and finds the dirt road through the woods that ends at an isolated stretch of craggy shoreline. He backs up the minivan close to the water, the boat trailer rutted in the sand. It's four in the morning. Barely time enough to do what he must and get out of the park before sunrise. He fetches gallon tanks of gasoline from the back of the minivan where Bruno bled into the carpet. The sweet, metallic scent of dried blood would cause most people to recoil, but Antony is used to it.

Antony knows the park's derelict backwoods, his go-to dumping ground. Even before Murder Inc., when he wanted to drive home a point to a loan delinquent, he'd drag some poor bastard into the woods, tell him to kneel, hold the cold suppressor of the gun to his head, and wait for the *sacco di merda* to piss his pants. Antony would say, "Next time, don't expect to be so lucky you just piss yourself." Some enforcers prefer to dump stiffs in the Meadowlands. But Antony hates the New Jersey swamps. He hates all of New Jersey. Pelham Bay Park is his killing field. His baptism in murder was a *sensitive* job, a risky one that if he proved himself, he would be the five families' golden boy: a hit on a brother of one of the bosses. Antony didn't know what the guy had done, but it had to be unforgivable. He and another soldier tied the mark to a tree and shot him in the chest, leg, and groin. After they threw him in the hole and started to shovel dirt on him, the wiseguy with him said, "Hey, Antony, the shithead is still breathing. I'll smash his head with a shovel." Antony grabbed his arm and said, "No, you fuckin' won't. Let the fuckface suck dirt." Details of the job got back to the Commission, as Antony knew they would. Next time, when the bosses ordered another hit, he told them he didn't need any help.

In Pelham Bay Park, Antony feels part of a history of violence. The terrain was shaped fifty thousand years ago after glaciers crawled in from the west and ruptured the land's huge slabs of granite. The site, it seems, was made for a killing field. At Split Rock in 1643, Siwanoy Indians massacred Ann Hutchinson and most of her family. Her daughter, who survived, was atop the rock and watched the slaughter. Later, she gathered leaves and scrub, covered herself, and hid for days like a fox in the rock's crevasse. The thing that struck Antony about the story is this: The Indians left a witness, something he'd never do. Something he isn't going to do with the fuckwit who saw him burying Bruno. Bet the fuckin' farm on that, he told himself.

Waving a flashlight into the scrub, he sees a few condoms and used tissues. Twenty years ago, when Antony walked deadbeats to mock executions, he'd have to step over a sea of wrinkled cock socks and crumpled Kleenex. *Jesus*, he used to think, *what if I come across Sal and Justin here*, and then he'd laugh. He's never been disgusted by fags like most other wiseguys. He's even a little wistful, if that is possible, thinking that at least Sal and Justin have each other. He remembers when Ida and Francesco brought Sal home from the hospital; his brother was wrapped in a blanket and all Antony could see was a scrunchy red face under a blue beanie. He couldn't believe the tiny eyes and nose, the mouth small and round as a penny.

"Do you want to hold him?" Ida asked.

"Sure," he said, surprising himself. Sal felt warm and helpless. He didn't cry or look nervous.

"He likes you," Ida said.

"He isn't smiling."

"Newborns can't smile."

Francesco looked relieved. "Brothers for life. *La famiglia per sempre*," their father said, proudly.

"What's *per sempre*?" Antony asked.

"Forever, family forever."

It won't be long before the sun rises over the Sound. "What the fuck," Antony says, as Bruno's leftover death scent brings gulls to the boat. "I've got to light this up." He looks out at the million-dollar homes between the parkway and Hutchinson River. All these years he's never torched anything on the shore. The minivan's gas tank is nearly full. He starts singing *Watch out you might get what you're after* and considers taking the Ohio license plate LIFE'S A BEACH, but the better part of caution tells him the memento isn't worth the risk.

∼

Antony remembers Bruno saying in the kitchen: "You were my brother. How could you?" The look in Bruno's eyes had lost momentarily the searing rage driving him. In that moment Antony thought of coming clean, but the flash of remorse disappeared as instantly as it had broken out.

And Antony, looking out at the somber river, says, "You stupid fool. You fuckin' stupid fool."

He remembers earlier in the day asking Bruno to meet him at La Mela's for a plate of bucatini. He wanted to explain a job that he needed help on.

"I'm gettin' acupuncture," Bruno said. "This chick is putting needles in my ass."

Antony told him it could wait until the next day. "Put it on your calendar, *cazzone*."

"Ah," he said.

"What?"

"She hit a sweet spot."

Did Rosa tell him when he got home? Antony thinks. "Fuckin' *gagootz*, a few hours after your needle fuck you come to me loaded to kill."

Antony douses the minivan and boat with gasoline. He fetches two Molotov cocktails, lights the cloth wick on one, and tosses it into the back seat. He lights the second and lobs it into the boat. The first explosion, the minivan's fuel tank, is deafening. The second from the boat's outboard motor just makes a pop. The fire reminds him of a nightmare he's been having ever since Francesco was killed. He's on the terrace of an apartment. Shoots of bamboo shelter him on each side. Across the street is an art deco building, its penthouse tower topped with terraced copper streaked in green patina. In the center of the apartment is a floor-to-ceiling window. It's night, and the penthouse is lit inside. Standing at the window, Ida and Francesco are kissing. They turn and notice Antony on the terrace across from them. As they wave, the tower bursts into flames. Below, other residents, terrified, appear at windows. Some are standing beside men Antony has killed. Bruno is the first to climb out a window. He's clutching the ledge, trying to hang on, and then drops. Francesco and Ida leap out. Others follow from every window on the high floors. Not only residents and the men he's murdered, but also nearly everyone he's ever known. When the last terrified person leaps, Sal and Justin appear on the penthouse tower roof. Flames race like tornadic winds. Justin makes the Sign of the Cross as if he's blessing everyone who's fallen, while Sal fixes a childlike gaze on Antony, and then, holding hands, they jump.

Antony rubs his eyes with the palms of his hands. When he opens them, he sees BB. "Fuck this," Antony tells himself. "Fuckin' asshole in the reeds. You're a dead man, too."

He hears fire trucks racing closer. So, he runs into the woods on a path that takes him to Split Rock Road, where he hops into his car and drives off.

Black Death

Sal's remembering Bruno atop the clown when Booker comes into the trailer and trips on a backpack. Sal's eyes are half-closed, and he hears "In-A-Gadda-Da-Vida" playing from the morgue truck. His head aches, and he's got to piss.

"You never went home," Booker says.

Sal nods on the way to the bathroom. "I stopped at Man Overboard and didn't leave until lights out." He hates lying to Book.

"A bender?"

"More like a slow drown." He looks in the mirror and notices caked dirt and what seems like a piece of dead worm in his ear. He picks everything out and drops it in the sink. *Shit*, he thinks, *I still stink of the trench.*

"You've got to see someone, Sal. You need to talk about your father."

If he cares about a person, Booker doesn't hesitate to sound like an armchair therapist. He's the only one, besides Justin and O'Shea, who can talk about Francesco. And usually, Sal tries to put a quick end to it. But this morning, he's content to let Booker think whatever he sees on Sal's face is all about drowning in whiskey and grief.

"You need to date. Find yourself someone to love."

Sal says what he immediately regrets: "Like I'd listen to Miss Lonely-hearts. You never remarried."

Booker doesn't seem offended. Losing a wife and infant son is an afflic-tion impossible to shake. It's foolish measuring grief, especially when you're in the thick of it like Sal. After all, Sal has a point. It's hard to get unstuck when you allow loss to remain so raw for so long.

Sal didn't intend to sound belligerent, and he would have apologized if suddenly the thought of BB hadn't pushed its way through his aching head. "Fuck, what am I going to do?" he says aloud, forgetting Booker is there.

"It takes time. You're going to wait until you make a truce with it. That's what you must do." Booker heads out to the morgue truck, where his impatience sneaks up on him. "Shut that fuckin' garbage off," he tells the

Russian kid. "What's wrong with you? Is half your brain tied around your neck? That's no music to play with those coffins in the ice box."

Hemins and the Rikers' inmates are gathered by the truck, waiting for Kalchick to back it to the landing.

Jesús says, "Yo, Sarge ain't happy today. Maybe it's because they thinkin' of closin' Hart."

"Who told you that?" Hemins asks.

"Can't say."

She's pointing her baton when she talks, out of habit, not menace. "You're like an old lady gossip."

Jesús decides to play with her. "Officer Hemins, lots of COs lookin' for woman like you."

"Yeah, Jesús is a prison wolf," says Zookie. "He tracks the good ones who aren't crazy."

Hemins knows she shouldn't do it, but she gives them the finger. Booker sees it and says, "What I miss?"

"These clowns say they've heard Hart could be closing."

"How's that? What's the city going to do with all the dead nobody wants?" Zookie asks.

"I've heard the rumor. They're thinking of making it into a memorial park," Booker says.

"What we need is a good plague." Franklin laughs. "That'll keep burial duty going."

"What's a plague?" Jesús asks.

"Like the Black Death," Jason says.

Jesús gives him a mock evil eye.

"Look it up," Jason says, oddly assertive. "The Black Death remade the world in the Middle Ages."

Jesús shakes his head. "That the shit you learn in college?"

"You heard of AIDS, right," says Franklin. "That was a plague until they got the cocktail."

Al, who's been on HIV meds for a decade, is looking like he's getting interested. "Ain't happening here," he says. "We've got the best drugs for any plague."

Booker says, "My great grandfather died of the Spanish Flu."

"You Latino, Sarge?" Jesús asks.

"My great-grandfather wasn't Latino, knucklehead. It's the name of the pandemic in 1918 that came here from Spain."

Jason knows the Spanish Flu probably didn't come from Spain, but he isn't going to correct the sergeant. And Jesús doesn't mind when Booker teases him. He thinks *knucklehead* is a kind of a compliment.

"So, what's the next one going to be?" Zookie asks.

"You gotta wait and find out," Franklin says.

Jesús doesn't want to hear any more about a plague. "How many in the truck?" he asks.

"Fifteen, three babies," Booker says.

Jason winces.

"Shit, that many," Jesús says. "It's gonna be a bad juju day."

~

The Coast Guard sweatshirt smells like the trench that's lingered on Sal's chest. He finds a T-shirt in a drawer. It's burgundy, and screen-printed on it are a photo of Ray Charles playing the piano and lettering mixed in with drawings of saxophones and drums. It says: *Newport Jazz Festival 2001.* He smells it and puts it on.

When he comes out, Booker says, "That's my shirt."

"Mine stinks of beer and whiskey. Some other shit, too."

He pats Sal on the shoulder. "You okay?"

Sal shrugs.

It's warmer than yesterday, but still too cool to wear just a T-shirt. "Where's your parka?" Booker asks.

He remembers tossing it into the trash barrel outside the trailer. "I must have left it at Man Overboard."

"You're a piece of work."

"Yeah." Sal walks past the crew on his way to *Vesuvius.*

"You like jazz, Cappy?" Jesús asks.

Sal ignores him.

"You don't look good."

Sal's wondering how he's going to find BB and hide him from everyone.

"You need java, Cappy."

Sal turns away, unlocks the gate, and heads down the dock.

The crew loads the fifteen coffins onto the ferry, all numbered and identified with black marker: three unknown males, two unknown females, three little people shoeboxes, and seven males and females with names but nobody to give them the kind of memorial anyone anywhere would want. It's a big one-day haul. The only saving grace: there's no oversized box among them. Morning fog has lifted, and the sun is dodging in and out of clouds. It's windy and *Vesuvius* is rocking against the dock. Swells and whitecaps on the Sound are visible from shore. Franklin trips and just misses splitting his head open on a dock cleat. Al helps him up, and they unhitch the ties and give Sal the thumbs-up to shove off.

"Choppy," says Jesús.

"Hope I don't hurl," Zookie says.

"You puke and I'll toss you overboard," Hemins says.

Zookie hunches over and puts his head in his hands. "You're too small to lift me, mean girl," he whispers into his palms.

Lined up on a bench, the inmates are quiet as *Vesuvius* sails to Hart Island. Jesús is humming some Haitian tune no one recognizes. Jason's sitting close to the three shoeboxes as if he were the babies' guardian. Booker and Hemins are standing at the rail. They're talking in barely audible voices about how strange Sal has been this week, moodier than they've seen him since his father was murdered. Sal is in the wheelhouse and puts the ferry on autopilot. He looks out to the island with binoculars, waiting for the moment Hart comes into clearer range, hoping to catch sight of BB.

Once *Vesuvius* docks, the crew transfers the coffins to the island truck. Zookie is a little woozy from the sail and vexed by all the talk of plagues and Hart shutting down. Nobody knew he was the anxious type who gets a fear in his head that can't find its way out easily. He taps Jason on the shoulder and says, "If they shut Hart, we gotta spend all day in the hole. And what about the poor dead suckers who come here and get some peace."

"They're just talking about it because that's what politicians do. It doesn't mean it's going to happen, Zookie."

"What else you know about Black Death?"

"Not much more than it killed about two hundred million people way back when there weren't nearly as many people in the world as now."

Zookie's the same age as Jason, barely out of their teenage years. "I don't know. I guess I don't want to die until a long time from now. You know, fifty or sixty years. I don't want to end up in one of those pine boxes and die alone."

"You have a family, right?"

"I have a mom somewhere in Africa. My old man's in prison. A lifer. No bro, no sis. I lived with a priest until he died. He was a good guy. Not one of those *chomos*."

"Who says you're going to be alone all your life?"

"College boy?"

"Yeah?"

"Why're you always so interested in the shoeboxes?"

"I don't know." Jason pauses. "I feel sorry for the babies. Most of them haven't lived even a day."

Zookie considers what Jason's said, and after a few moments, he lightly punches Jason in the arm. "I bet you're going to be a friggin' good father someday. I wouldn't mind being one, too."

Hemins has been listening. "Hey, tagger and frat boy, you don't want to see me cry, do you? Get on the bus, we've got fifteen stiffs to deal with." She goes to the truck loaded with the day's haul.

Sal's sitting by a window, and Booker is at the wheel reading the *New York Times*. He had folded the front section down the middle and tucked the bottom half under the top. Old school. He's reading a story about women who could be president someday.

He nudges Sal. "I'd vote for a woman if she wasn't Hillary Clinton. How about you?"

Sal looks at the newspaper. "I don't think it matters who's president. This country is fucked."

"Elizabeth Warren, I'd vote for her," Booker says.

Sal doesn't say anything and turns back to the window. Booker puts down the paper and starts the bus. Sal is thinking of combing the island for BB. They pass the dilapidated chapel and a patch of pin oak trees. He's keeping an eye on the brush, thinking that BB might be hiding there until it hits him: more likely, BB's squatting in one of the buildings, in one of their abandoned recesses. When the bus nears the workhouse, he's stunned. "Christ," he says, noticing BB's blue weather flag sticking out a window.

"What?" Booker asks.

"I didn't say anything."

"You said, *Christ*, like you were surprised by something."

"I pulled a muscle in my leg. I move a certain way and a pain shoots down it."

"Sciatica. You gotta take care of it. It's a bitch."

The bus pulls up to Trench 189. Hemins and the truck with the coffins arrive behind them.

"Hey, why don't you get some ZZZs," Booker says.

"I think I'll walk around the island. Clear my head."

"You still look like shit."

Sal turns to leave.

"Wait, Sal, I've got a sweater in the bus."

Sal stops. "Fuck," he says to himself.

"Here you go. It's like I'm your personal tailor. Don't go knocking any heads off statues."

Sal laughs distractedly.

Jason, as usual, is the first crew member to start unloading. He fetches the three shoeboxes, and Booker surprises him, giving him the okay to head out by himself to the baby graveyard. When Jason passes the trench, he stops and sets down the little ones. The plywood cover on the pine boxes that they buried yesterday is leaning up against the dirt wall and the lid on Ronald McDonald's box has been torn off and tossed on the mud floor. Jason is speechless looking at Bruno, contorted on top of the clown.

"Sarge," he croaks, and then yelling, "Sarge!"

Nobody's heard Jason raise his voice before. Booker races over and everyone follows. Sal notices the commotion at the trench. Everyone is staring at Bruno on top of Ronald McDonald. Jesús is the first to break the silence: "Said so, clown is bad juju."

Sal walks up. He puts his hands on his head. "Jesus."

Franklin says, "The guy looks familiar."

"How can you tell?" Al asks.

"He looks like somebody I saw somewhere," Zookie says.

"That's Bruno Cali," Sal says.

"Like the mob boss?" Franklin asks.

"His son."

"The Mafia, fuck. Don't touch anything. Everyone back away," Hemins says.

Booker, who's been silent, says, "Why dump the son of a mafia boss here? It doesn't make sense."

"Maybe there are others," Al says. "Maybe Jimmy Hoffa's somewhere on Hart."

"Who's Jimmy Hoffa?" Jesús asks.

Everyone ignores him.

Booker looks at Sal. "You knew him?"

Sal thinks Booker sounds disappointed. He's never revealed that Carlo Cali was his father's godfather. "Yeah, Bruno grew up with my brother."

Booker raises an eyebrow. Then he looks at the corpse and mutters, "Fuckin' animals."

Sal doesn't hear Booker. He's thinking BB must have opened the trench and coffin and that he needs to find a way to break loose and get to him. Sal walks over to the scrub, puts his finger in his mouth, and vomits.

"He knew the guy so well he chucks?" Hemins says.

"He's hungover," Booker says.

Sal's still in the scrub, pretending to need to puke more. He estimates that he might have a half hour to get BB stowed away on the boat before the police arrive. Booker is calling the DOC when Sal returns. He tells Booker that he has Pepto-Bismol on the ferry. "My stomach is on fire. You got this?"

"Yeah," Booker says just as the commander gets on the line.

Sal gives him a thumbs-up and walks off.

"Cappy knows a gangster," Jesús says. "Ain't he a riddle, college boy."

Jason nods, remembering the hit on Francesco. He saw it on NY1 before Christmas while he was waiting for his trial. He was having breakfast with his father, a public defender. He remembers the shot of Sal holding up his mother in the driveway and Jason's father saying, "That's mob justice."

Hemins and the crew gather around the bus. Booker stays on the phone by the trench talking to DOC and NYPD. "Usually, you might think someone would rob a grave," he says, "not donate to it." Hemins is leaning against the back of the bus. She's not in any mood to talk. The inmates, except Jason, who's gone to the baby graveyard, are nearby, speculating on how a gangster ended up on top of the clown. Sometimes they're shaking their heads, sometimes they're laughing, sometimes they look worried like they've been implicated in a crime. "Bad juju," says Jesús, a few times more until Hemins tells him to shove his voodoo shit up his ass. Everyone is stunned. That's more vitriolic than she's ever been.

~

Sal approaches the workhouse and crouches behind tall sedge grass, a patch of poison ivy an arm's length away. He hasn't a clue how he's going to handle BB and convince him that if he doesn't let Sal take him back, some fisherman one day would be trawling BB's cement-footed carcass out of the Sound. He gets up into plain sight and enters the workhouse, stepping over hundreds of faded and mildew-covered work shoes, the wicked-witch kind nuns wore before they ditched habits. There's white and gray mold crawling up the walls. The stench of animal feces permeates the air. BB is asleep in the corner, the stone head of Jesus in the crook of his arm. On the ground Sal sees a pinky ring, dark-blue lapis lazuli on silver, that must have been on Bruno's finger when they put him in the trench. *How did they miss it last night*, Sal thinks? The exact ring that Francesco had worn and was buried with. One of only three rings like it that he has seen. The third on the hand of Carlo Cali.

Sal squats and pats BB's shoulder. "I'm not going to hurt you. We've got to talk. You're in danger."

BB stirs and rubs his eyes as if he were waking on his own. "I thought you'd come."

"You don't know the kind of trouble you're in."

"I know more than you think. I talked with Mary after you left."

"The body you trawled up, with the Virgin tattoo. It's buried on Hart. So, that's why you're here."

"I saw you knock off the head of Baby Jesus."

Sal nods and knows he must act fast. "You can't stay here, BB."

"I know, she told me."

"You're in a lot of danger."

"I saw what you and your brother did."

"That's why you've got to let me help. Antony is going to kill you if you don't."

BB pauses, taking in the threat, and says, "I'm not sure I can trust you, captain; I thought you were a good man, but I don't know now. You can't trust some good people either. I learned that on my own. Mary didn't have to tell me. Yeah, good people aren't good all the time."

Sal gets an idea. He takes Justin's card from his wallet, and without BB seeing him, he rubs it on his muddy boot and hands it to him. "I found this card in the dirt around Mary."

BB reads it: Our Lady Queen of Peace, the Rev. Justin Flynn. It's got a drawing of Mary holding out her hands like she is welcoming you.

"The priest, Father Flynn, he's my adopted brother. Imagine the coincidence of it being here. It was meant for you to find."

"She talked to him?"

"Yes, and he told me that she wanted him to give you sanctuary."

"She didn't say anything to me."

"She meant for you to find this card and go to the church."

"She could have told me."

Sal remembers his scapular and takes it off and shows it to BB. "I forgot. Mary also wanted Justin to give this to you."

"What?"

"Her Brown Scapular, see, it's got her image on the cloth."

"Never saw one before."

"They're rare," Sal lies. He puts it around BB's neck. "It saves you from untimely death."

BB looks skeptical but tucks the scapular under his shirt.

"Why did you break into the coffin?" Sal asks.

"Mary told me to. I found this." BB picks up the ring. "I pried it off. It was tough because his whole hand was swollen. The dead puff up."

"Can I have it?"

"No, it's mine now."

"It's a gangster's ring, BB. Bruno Cali's. He's the son of a mob boss, the body we buried last night. You don't want to be seen with it. They'll think you killed him. You're in enough trouble just seeing what you've seen."

"I'm keeping it."

Sal realizes he doesn't have a lot of time. "Okay, it's yours. We've got to find a place in the ferry to hide you before detectives get here."

"Sometimes I wish I never snagged that corpse."

"This isn't easy, I know."

"What did I ever do to deserve this? I'm not a bad man like your brother. I didn't stuff a gangster into a coffin with some poor lost soul who probably had a hard-enough life before he ended up dead and didn't deserve to be defiled like that. So, why'd *you* do it?"

"I don't know."

"You do something like *that*, and you don't know why?"

Sal thinks about it awhile. "Do you have a brother, BB?"

"I've just got me."

"Stand by your brother no matter what, my father told me when I was a kid. I'm learning the *no-matter-what* is bad advice, even for a brother you love."

BB puts the stone head in his sack and gathers whatever else he's taken out or collected on the island. "Didn't look like much love was happening last night."

Sal nods. "And that's why I have to make sure you're safe."

"Okay," BB says.

"What?"

"The engine room. You can hide me there. That's how I got here, that's how I'm leaving. I guess I've got to trust you."

~

After Sal secures BB, he returns to the trench and joins the crew, where Booker is talking to the police, who had already cordoned off the crime scene. The head of the Department of Corrections shows up. A media drone is still filming the trench and island. After everyone is interviewed, they are given the go-ahead to put the coffins in the ground at the other end of the trench, which forensics had cleared. There is none of the usual banter among the crew. Even Jesús is quiet. Occasionally the inmates break and watch Booker, Sal, and detectives, with the coroner crew taking pictures and gathering evidence. Later in the day, the inmates will feel relieved because another NYPD boat will have hauled the pillaged coffin to the morgue, saving them from sailing back with Bruno and the clown. "Don't need mo bad juju," Jesús will say.

Sherry O'Shea walks up to the trench with other FBI agents. She expected to find Sal there, and pulling him aside, she tells him not to talk to anyone about Antony. She says she knows Sal helped his brother put Bruno in the box, but she's on his side. They'd meet later that night. Eight o'clock at Mother Pug's.

He asks, "What are you up to?"

She leans in. "Not here, Sal. Here, you don't know me."

"That's true. I don't, here or anywhere."

She surprises him with a sympathetic look before walking over to the cops and coroner team.

Booker had seen her taking Sal aside. "What she want?"

Sal shrugs. Sherry is calling them over.

Booker grabs his arm. "She's FBI. Are you in trouble?"

"She knows I'm my father's son. It happens. Law enforcement thinks we're all connected."

"You're not mixed up with this?"

Sal, startled by Booker's suspicions, after giving him a look, says, "It's complicated."

"Jesus, Sal."

"Look, I didn't kill Bruno."

"I believe you. Don't let them fuck you over."

Sal rubs his eyes. "She's calling us. Let's go."

The Ninth Precinct

Antony had hoped that he could ditch the Ninth Precinct and concentrate on finding whoever was on Hart. He's pissed that the new commander, an asshole with a law degree from Yale, ordered him in for a group bullshit session on policing tolerance. In the detective squad room, everyone is gathered at the back before an enormous flat screen to watch the NY1 drone video from Trench 189. The anchor says something about a throwback to the grisly Cosa Nostra days in New York and warns viewers that the video contains graphic images. The shot begins with a long view of Hart Island surrounded by Long Island Sound, and then moves to *Vesuvius* at the dock, patches of trees, Hart's ruinous red brick buildings, grassy fields flecked with white grave markers, the open trench lined with police emerging like video game figures as the camera pans from side to side and zooms in for closer looks and cutaways. The breaking news ticker at the bottom of the screen reads: SON OF MAFIA CRIME BOSS BURIED ATOP HART ISLAND CORPSE.

"Jesus, Antony. Come see this," his partner yells to him.

Fuck me, he thinks as he goes over to her, hoping that he doesn't see a frame of the guy who was hiding in the reeds. He's hoping his dumb-fuck brother has hidden the shithead. *No witnesses*, he thinks, *no witnesses*. Antony isn't used to being worried. Earlier, he was certain he'd make the dipshit disappear, but now, he doesn't feel like he's in control of what's going to happen next. The whirring of the drone in the video is fucking with his brain.

"Isn't that your brother?" his partner asks.

He'd just seen it himself, Sal in a Newport Jazz Festival T-shirt.

"Your brother runs the ferry to Hart, right?"

Antony nods. It didn't take long, not more than a week, before Antony knew he hated Sarah Jenkins. A day doesn't go by that he doesn't curse his old partner, Jimmy DeLillo. They were on their way back from Brooklyn after running down a murder case lead when the call came in that an armed assailant was holding a liquor store clerk hostage on Avenue A and First Street. They were about two minutes away. Jimmy said, "Let's take it." But

Antony told him it's Code 3, cops elbow to elbow. Leave it. Usually, Jimmy did whatever Antony wanted, but this time his partner insisted that they were answering the call. The perp ran out brandishing something that in the heat of the moment looked like a gun but was a bottle of Sam Adams. Jimmy fired just as the guy was ducking and yelling that he didn't have a gun. The bullet struck him in the head and the drunk bastard never had time to see stars. The review board cleared Jimmy, but he wasn't the kind of cop who, once he kills a guy who didn't have a weapon, can stomach carrying a gun again. Ironic, since he was the kind of cop who could look away from the worst that he suspected Antony was up to. Now, with Sarah Jenkins beside him on the job, Antony is cautious all the time, limiting his mob enforcer opportunities. Jenkins is nothing like Jimmy. She can't be bought. He could make her disappear, but what good would that do? He'd have to groom a new partner, and grooming takes time, and there's no assurance it can work in the long run. Take Jimmy. How'd that investment go?

"You knew Bruno growing up, didn't you," Jenkins says.

He gave her a look. "You know I'm the *Mafia cop*, right?"

"Did you like him?"

"Yeah, but he could be a gagootz sometimes."

"*Gagootz?*"

"A low-hanging squash shaped like a baseball bat. Fuckin' batshit crazy."

"Any theories about who'd want to risk killing him?"

"That's a conundrum. Got to be someone outside the five families, though."

"It's weird. You know, Bruno ends up on Hart Island where your brother ferries the coffins. You all being *connected*."

"Where you going with this, Jenkins?"

"Your father massacred on the stoop of his house? A lot of happenstances."

"Fuck off."

"Hey, I'm just brainstorming. We're detectives."

Antony stares at her for a few moments, then says, "You're not going to work out."

"That's what I tell my boyfriends."

Antony turns away and walks into the handicapped bathroom, the only place in the squad room he can be alone. He calls Sal and gets his friggin' message: *I'm not picking up for a good reason. Don't call me back unless you have to. Just kidding. Leave a message.* Antony says, "Fuckin' Sal, call me *now*."

It took about an hour for the precinct to settle back into its normal routine: detectives on the phones; cops coming and going with information from the streets; cops arguing about the mayor, everyone hates de Blasio; grousing over restrictions and paperwork; chatter about cases and their families; and that morning, with all that's already happened, dozens of Dunkin Donuts and congratulations for an old fuck who should have retired five years ago. The Ninth won't have any role in Bruno Cali's murder. That will be run by the FBI and a special NYPD organized crime team that Antony would be on if anyone else except a Cali had been whacked. He'll be called in for advice, which he's hoping won't happen until tomorrow.

"You knew Bruno Cali, didn't you, Antony?" a detective asks him. "Any idea who wanted him dead?"

"Like I told pretty pants over there," he says, pointing to his partner, "*fuck off.*" Antony flips him the finger. The group masturbation session on policing tolerance gets postponed.

"Where you going?" Jenkins asks.

He takes his gun from the desk drawer. "Like I'd tell you."

"Asshole," she whispers before diving into a case the desk sergeant had tossed on her desk.

On his way out of the precinct, Sal calls him.

"Tell me you found the bastard," Antony says.

"No, I looked all over the island, in every building, in every patch of reeds. No one's here. I told you, Antony, it was a deer."

"You're lying. No deer digs up Bruno Cali."

Sal doesn't know what to say.

"You're hiding something." Antony, frustrated, says, "If you're fuckin' lying, you could end up in Fresh Kills with the asshole."

"Nice, Antony. Look, whoever broke into the coffin, he's gone."

In a far more menacing tone, Antony says, "Remember what I said about brothers doing bad things to brothers."

"Fuck you. It's up to you to find him. I'm done."

"I'll be outside Pug's at nine. Be there. We're going back to Hart." Antony taps off just before he could hear Sal say, "I told you, I'm done."

Go Start a Novena

Sal races ahead to *Vesuvius* while Booker and the crew gather their stuff from the bus. Hemins is pulling up the truck.

"Cappy haulin' ass," Jesús says.

Booker gives him a look.

While the crew is dumping their burial clothes into a wash bin, Sal checks on BB. He's curled into a corner and covered in a blanket so that you can't tell if he's breathing. Sal crouches and puts his finger under BB's nose and feels his breath. It tickles, and BB is startled awake. He swallows a few times. "Hey, Captain Sal, you're back."

"You okay?"

"Did you know if you hush up a ghost, it grows bigger? This island is full of ghosts. They've been talking to me in my sleep."

"No ghosts where we're going. I'll be starting the engines, BB. Put these earmuffs on and stay clear of the gears and hot metal. This room heats up fast."

"I know. I was a captain, too."

Sal musters a weak smile. "You're going to be okay. "

BB looks up. "That's what I've been telling myself."

"You've got to be *real* quiet."

"Quiet as a church mouse."

"I think the phrase is poor as a church mouse."

"I've seen mice. They don't make a peep when they're hiding."

"When we dock, I can't come and get you until the bus leaves for Rikers."

"Right."

"Then we'll go to Staten Island."

"The sanctuary."

"That's right," Sal says. "Stay put."

After Sal leaves, BB takes the stone head out of the bag and holds it up. "You gonna look after me? Or you gonna just watch while I get fucked?"

Booker catches Sal on the deck before he goes to the wheelhouse. "You were in a hurry."

"I remembered a noise in the engine room when we docked. I wanted to check it out before we go. Engine's okay."

"Let's get out of here."

"Yeah, before someone digs up another gangster," Sal jokes, trying to allay Booker's suspicions.

He doesn't laugh. "You got the sweater I gave you?"

"Fuck, I left it outside the trailer. You pissed?"

"No. Worried."

"Why?"

"You're not yourself."

"I'm okay, Book."

"Tell me, is it a coincidence Bruno ended up in that box?"

Sal ignores him.

"You never spent a night in the trailer before."

"I'd never stayed at Man Overboard for last call before."

"Can't imagine what it was like growing up with the mob around you, and your father in it."

"He kept me in the dark. My brother, well, Antony is another story."

"And Bruno. You're not involved, right?"

Annoyed to be going over this again, Sal says, "What do you think?"

"You can tell me anything. You've got a lot on your shoulders."

"We're loaded," Hemins says.

Al and Zookie unhitch the ferry. "Ready!" Franklin shouts.

The crossing is uneventful. Booker reads the sports section of the *Times*. Hemins twirls the baton between her legs and thinks about her vacation coming up: a week in Costa Rica with her girlfriends, a posse of lesbian corrections officers, cops, EMTs, and firefighters. With everyone else outside her secret klatch, she's still on the down-low, though it's not because she's afraid of being harassed. Years ago, she heard two guys in the academy call her *bed death*. She went up to the biggest asshole and kicked him breathless in the balls. She's not ashamed; she insists on respect and privacy.

The inmates are dozing or remembering a time when they weren't tossing the dead into mass graves. The only one who looks attentive is Jason. He's reading *The Heart of the Buddha's Teaching: Transforming Suffering into*

Peace, Joy, and Liberation. When he had taken it out, Hemins said: "Good luck with that, college boy."

Sherry O'Shea calls Sal. She's back in the Manhattan bureau. "Remember, Pug's at eight. I want to talk about Francesco. It's about time you know what he wanted for your family."

He was going to say, *your family, too*, but she ended the call. *What the fuck is she up to?* he thinks.

As *Vesuvius* approaches City Island, Booker gives Sal a CD.

"What's this?"

"It's Robert Johnson's *Kindhearted Woman's Blues*. Take a couple days off and listen to it good and hard. Then when you get back, we're going to Man Overboard to talk." He pats Sal on the shoulder and says, "You do what I say."

"Yeah," Sal says, slipping the CD into his backpack. After the ferry docks, he watches Hemins and the crew board the bus.

Booker calls up to the wheelhouse. "You coming?"

"I've got boat checks to make."

"You take those couple days off."

"Maybe, Book. Maybe."

"Robert Johnson. Listen to him."

Sal waves, squeezes his forehead, and calls Justin. "I've got him." He hears NY1 playing in the background; a reporter is talking about Bruno's body. "Turn that shit off."

"Ida won't let me. She's been watching it all day and talking to the TV. She's swearing like crazy at Bruno."

Sal takes a deep breath in and lets it out. "I'm going to get an Uber. Meet us at the church at six."

"Take him to the back door to the sacristy and wait for me there. I've got confessions."

"What about Ida?"

"She'll be with Anna."

"Good, in case we have to split with BB."

"I've been thinking, we really should call the police."

"Not necessary. Sherry's involved."

"You've talked to the FBI?"

"I talked to Sherry, barely."

"Be careful, Sal."

"Yeah, go start a novena."

Target Practice

Antony decides he isn't going to wait to meet Sal at Pug's and heads out to City Island, where he's guessing that he'll find Sal with the phantom witness when the ferry docks. On his way, he gets caught in a pileup on the Hutchinson River Parkway. He snaps the light and siren on the hood, but there's no place to move. For miles, a cacophony of blaring horns and frozen road rage. A lane across the median is cleared so that police and rescues can race to the wreckage, but the guardrail makes it impossible for him to enter the open pass. Antony tries to reach Sal, and the call to his brother goes straight to mailbox. He redials the number incessantly, as if the phone were on automatic, firing call after call to drive Sal crazy with the ringtone *black bird singing in the dead of night.* "Sal's off the rez," he shouts, tossing his phone on the passenger seat, where it bounces onto the floor; he punches the dash so hard that it shatters a plastic vent. His knuckles bleed.

He thinks about the drone footage that morning at the trench. When he finds the guy who opened the coffin, he'll cut out his balls and stuff them down his throat and watch him choke to death, he tells himself. It's all Sal's fault. His brother isn't dependable, never has been, no matter what his father used to say. Sal's soft. Antony remembers the summer he spent luring dogs into the backyard. He'd stuff Ida's leftover meatballs and ribs into a freezer bag. When he saw one that didn't look threatening, he'd let the dog smell the meat and walk it back to the house. He'd shut the gate and give the dumb animal the meatballs and ribs, then he'd go inside and fetch the BB gun. The dog, thinking Antony brought more meat, waited with an expectant look. From a distance, he'd fire the first pellet, which pinged its butt. At first, the dumb dog didn't know what had happened. After the second or third strike, the dog figured out Antony was the source of its pain and ran to the gate. One afternoon, before Cannoli, Sal saw Charlie, the Picarazzis' blonde Lab, doing circles in the grass. He ran outside, and Antony turned the gun from the dog and aimed it at his brother. *Can I do it,* he thought, *can I?* He shot, deliberately far right, hitting a birdhouse hanging from a tree. *Maybe next time.* Francesco had come home from the track and saw it all. He tore the gun away from Antony and slapped him so hard it felt like a Linda Blair head spin. Francesco told Ida to take Sal for a walk. He grabbed Antony by the collar and dragged him into the attic, removed his belt, and told him to drop his pants and bend over. The buckle, a racehorse head carved in it, made his skin bleed. But Antony didn't cry. Even that young, he didn't see a beating as punishment. It was something inevitable. Something he had to take for being the kind of boy he was. Once he knew it was coming, he wiped it out of his mind so that he believed he no longer felt the pain. When the thrashing was over, welts were a badge of endurance. "You're not like your brother," Antony once heard his father tell Sal. "Fuckin' right he isn't," Antony shouted before throwing a baseball, signed by Joe DiMaggio, into the mantel mirror. "He's *buono a nulla*, a fuckin' wimp."

Antony sees an opening that will let him out of the parkway jam. By the time he gets to a side road, which takes him to 95, it's already six o'clock, three hours lost. Sal would have left the dock by now. He pulls over, grabs the phone from the car floor, and leaves one last message: "Don't make me go crazy, Sal. You show up outside Pug's tonight."

The Sacristy

The church tower bell at Our Lady Queen of Peace tolls six o'clock. It's the start of Thursday evening confessions. An old woman with a skin condition, her face red and scaly, laboriously climbs the steps. Presumably, she's on her way to tell Father Justin the sins she's committed since her last confession. The chance that her transgressions will include anything serious is slim. Or maybe, who knows, the Forgotten Borough's Sicilian women have dark secrets, too.

There's a statue of Mary on a marble pedestal in the center of the churchyard. She's beautiful. Young. Her head is slightly bowed to the right. There is no crown. No adornments on her robe. No jeweled beaded rosary. Not even an olive branch. Simply a kind countenance. Her eyes, nearly closed in a sign of divine modesty, look down at her hand reaching toward the bed of daylilies beneath her, while her other hand rests on a shawl over her heart. It looks like she was about to smile before the sculptor halted his work in a pose more melancholy than joyful. At the base of the statue an inscription reads: *Our sweetness and our hope; to you we cry.* On the side of the church is the grotto that Francesco's donation built. The rocks were imported from a chapel by the ocean in Rhode Island that had been dismantled to make room for a resort and spa. There's another statue of Mary tucked into a niche in the rock, with a cascade of coral bell behind her. Her hands are folded and she's looking to the sky. A rosary is draped on an arm. A Marian blue sash hangs from her waist to her knees. Small flames from hundreds of votives flicker nervously across the rockface. A woman is kneeling before a rack of candles, while her son beside her, bored, walks off to the schoolyard, where he hears friends shooting baskets. There's about a half hour of light left, enough for one more Around the World.

The Uber pulls up to the front of the church, and BB is the first out. He walks up to the statue of Our Lady Queen of Peace, kneels, and makes the Sign of the Cross. "You're everywhere," he says, consoled that he might just be spared more trouble because this Virgin Mary looks so kind and attainable. When he sees the grotto, he shouts, "You're kidding me!" at yet another Mother of God, and races to her. He hasn't washed in weeks, and the woman praying covers her nose when BB kneels beside her. He touches her arm and asks, "Is Mary helping?"

She waves for her son on the basketball court. "God bless," she says, and rushes off.

Sal steps up, carrying the weather flag and BB's sack. BB says, thinking of Mary, "Sometimes I wonder if she's mocking me."

"Didn't you tell me something about God's mysterious ways?"

BB, feeling less bedeviled than he was on the island, smiles at the statue in the rocks. "I guess."

"Remember, Mary brought you here."

∿

Ida and Anna are entering the rectory for their "girls' night out." Ida, suddenly agitated, whispers *Basilisco*, pointing to BB across the churchyard. Anna doesn't know all that's going on, but she figures the dirty bearded man with Sal must be the person who Justin said would be seeking sanctuary in the church for the day. It's confusing to her because Our Lady Queen of Peace has never been a sanctuary for anyone before, and she imagined its first refugee would be an immigrant, someone from Guatemala or El Salvador, not a homeless man with a Rasputin beard.

"*Basilisco*? What's that?" she asks Ida.

"Evil."

"You're in some mood. Let's go inside, honey."

Ida takes her arm, and they climb the few steps into the rectory.

∿

Sal and BB head to the back of the church and the sacristy. A man in a SI Firefighter jacket passes by with a pit bull mix. The dog growls at BB.

"It's not you. She's afraid of poles." He points to the flag. "She must have been beaten with one. She's a rescue. She wouldn't hurt a fly."

BB sets down the flag and squats. The dog comes to him, wagging its tail, and licks his face. "Good boy," BB says.

"She's a girl," the guy says, walking on.

"Why'd you do that?" Sal asks.

"It was a test."

"For what?"

"I wanted to see if Mary was still protecting me."

"Jesus, BB. A pit bull. It could have torn off your face."

He squints like he can't believe Sal. "You don't know what faith is, do you?"

"I know about stupid risks. Come on, you can talk all night with Justin about God and belief."

The stained-glass window on the sacristy door depicts Mary draped in lapis lazuli. She's kneeling while an angel with turquoise wings watches over her. Behind them is a dove, the color of birchwood, the Holy Spirit perched on a cross, ready to take flight.

BB says, "Maybe if Jesus was born to an ordinary Mary and not some immaculate being, maybe instead of wandering around, ridiculed and tortured, Jesus would have been someone else. A quiet fisherman, maybe."

"But no one would have heard about him."

"You think? He'd drop a net every day like I did. He'd wait and wait for a big haul. Some days better than others, and depending on what you pull up, you might catch a surprise."

BB, who hasn't been in a sacristy since he was an altar boy, walks over to the piscina and puts his face close to the sacrarium, the drain for baptismal water and washed linens that flows into the ground, bypassing the public sewer. He yells into it: "Mayday! Mayday! Who's there?"

"What are you doing?" Sal asks.

"A priest told me the drain is piped to heaven."

Sal gives him a look and checks the time. "I'm going to see if Justin's finished. You've got to stay here, you know that, right. No excursion to Mary outside." He points to a chair, an enormous, throne-like piece of polished mahogany with red velvet cushions. "Here, this looks comfortable." Sal smiles. "Be good." He bolts the upper lock of the door to the yard and pockets the key in case the fisherman gets the idea to explore.

Once Sal has left for the church nave, BB picks up the chalice from the top of the credens; a square of stiff linen—its pall—falls to the floor. He crosses himself and fetches it, blows off specks of dirt, and puts it back atop the chalice. He opens a drawer, which is packed with linens for the Eucharist. In another drawer he finds the priest's vestments. Before a mirror, he holds up an amice neck cloth with an amber cross stitched on the front. One drawer contains a mound of hand-knotted cinctures. He tosses around chasubles in flamboyant colors and stitching that mark different liturgical services. Out of the piles he picks out what he wants and puts the vestments on over his stinking clothes.

~

Sal waits in a pew next to the confessional for the last penitent to leave, a boy, maybe seven years old. He's saddened to see that someone so young feels the need to ask for life-or-death forgiveness. He remembers his own confessions at that age: *Bless me, Father, for I have sinned. I swore, I was disobedient, I had dirty thoughts.* He wanted to say that he liked to watch Antony play with his penis in the shower until his brother moaned. Sal wanted to say he thought he liked boys more than girls and Ida told him *that* was bad, and this was long before he started loving Justin. He wanted to say he suspected his father was a gangster and he had heard the sins of the father were the son's, too. But he never did. Always, *I swore, I was disobedient, I had dirty thoughts.* The penance never changed: three Hail Mary's, one Our Father, and a brief Glory Be. He shakes his head as the boy walks by to join his mother in a pew. Sal thinks, *What a waste of time, kid.*

Before Justin can turn off the confessional's green light, Sal opens the curtain and kneels before the screen. "I've got BB. He's in the sacristy."

Justin clicks off the light. The sound of it in the dark startles Sal. As they walk through the sanctuary, Sal asks, "What were the boy's sins?"

Justin gives him a look. "You know I can't tell you that."

"I was thinking of myself back when I was his age. Why should a kid feel guilty about anything? Sure, he can be taught right and wrong, but why guilt?"

"Confession isn't about shame, Sal. It's about forgiveness, and it starts with forgiving yourself."

"Come on. *Pray for us sinners now and at the hour of our death.* You really think a seven-year-old kid should be thinking about sin and death?"

"Okay, the kid murdered his parents and set fire to his house. Is that enough to feel remorse?"

"Why so touchy?"

"It's forgiveness, Sal, that's what counts, not guilt."

"I guess, if you say so, you're the priest," Sal says, dismissively.

Justin shakes his head.

When they enter the sacristy, BB, smiling in all his priestly regalia, waves.

"What the fuck," Sal says.

Justin laughs and extends his hand. "Father BB, it's a pleasure."

"These are *some* vestments, Father." BB takes the stone head of Baby Jesus from his sack. "Look," he says. "This is what your brother did. He knocked it right off the Baby Jesus's shoulders."

Sal looks sheepish, and Justin turns to him. "Why?"

"It's a story for another day."

"He's made his amends," BB says, "and now the head is mine to keep, at least until Mary tells me what to do with it."

Justin carries it to the piscina, pours Holy Water over the stone, and recites the blessing, "In the name of the Father, and of the Son, and of the Holy Ghost."

BB is visibly moved, taking a lavabo towel from a drawer, and drying the head in Justin's hands. "It's pretty beat up. Not by your brother. The island's storms and time's ravages." BB places it on the credens. "Can't hurt to have His eyes on us."

Justin smiles and turns to Sal. "Can't hurt."

"Your other brother wants to kill me," BB says.

Justin and Sal look at each other. "He's not going to find you," Sal says.

"Mary isn't so sure."

Sal explains all that happened last night and at the trench today. Justin, impatient, says he doesn't understand why Sal took Antony to Hart Island. "Didn't you know it had to be trouble? When you saw Bruno? What were you thinking?"

"I was thinking, *family*."

"A lot of good Antony brings to *this family*," Justin says.

"You believe he's a lost cause? You're a priest."

"I believe he's not going to change in this life."

"He's never been so threatening to me. He warned that *brothers can do bad things to brothers*."

"Antony was more explicit with me years ago. He said that if I ever betrayed the family, he'd cut my balls off. Remember? He said he'd make sure we *never fucked again*, his words."

"He was drunk."

Justin gives him a look.

BB, who's been listening patiently, says, "Complicated family."

The observation leaves Sal and Justin speechless for some moments, and then, realizing how late it is, Sal tells Justin that Sherry wants to meet.

"I'm going with you."

"No, you have to stay with BB."

BB nods.

"She knows why the Russians killed Francesco," Sal says. "She knows Antony killed Bruno. She knows I helped bury him. I don't trust her."

"Hey, don't go jumping to conclusions. You don't know what you don't know. She's not the enemy. I think she's trying to help us."

Sal looks at BB, who's pouring altar wine into a chalice. "I need a drink," BB says.

"You need a shower," Sal says.

"My last was at the YMCA in Yonkers. I snuck in. I would've had a swim, too, in my boxers, but the lifeguard wouldn't let me."

"I'll take him to the rectory," Justin says. "If you're going to be a priest, BB, you can't smell like Fresh Kills." He turns to Sal. "I've got a feeling your sister is going to give you answers you've been looking for."

"I've got a feeling she's trouble," Sal says.

"I know one thing for sure, Francesco loved her."

"How do you know that?"

Justin looks surprised, like he's divulged something he didn't intend to. "Intuition," he says.

"Fuck it," Sal says, on his way out to see Sherry at Mother Pug's.

Basilisco

Antony's grip on the steering wheel is so tight, the veins on the back of his hand throb. He's caught in another tie-up, this time on the Throggs Neck Bridge. Every call to Sal still goes to mailbox. He sends a text: ASSHOLE, ANSWER YOUR FUCKING PHONE. He tries Ida, but she isn't answering. He remembers that Sal had given her an Apple Watch instead of one of those I've-fallen-and-I-can't-get-up pendants. If she collapses and stays flat for about a minute, the watch alerts 911. Antony scours his contacts and finally finds the number near the end of the alphabet: *W. Watch Ida*. "What the fuck. At W," he says.

~

Ida's got her eyes closed, sitting with Anna, who's watching *The Real Housewives of New York City*, when Dean Martin starts singing: *Volare, oh oh / Cantore, oh, oh, oh, oh.* Her eyes open and, jolted out of her evening fog like someone having a eureka moment, Ida scans the room. Anna sees that the music is coming from Ida's watch, which is lit up with "ANTONY" calling.

"Ida, it's your watch."

She's not paying attention to Anna and gets out of the chair determined to find her Italian idol. Anna grabs her arm and taps the handset icon on the touch screen. The music stops and Antony says, "Ma." Ida, disoriented, falls back into the chair. Somehow the watch had gone to speaker, and they can hear Antony shouting, "Ma, are you there? Where's Sal?"

Anna leans in. "Antony, it's Anna. Your mom's confused. The Dean Martin ring has freaked her out."

Horns and shouts of road rage around Antony make it hard to hear what he's saying.

"Where are you?" Anna asks.

Antony ignores her. "Ma, have you seen Sal?"

Anna looks at Ida, shakes her head, and mouths, "No."

"*Basilisco*," Ida says in a tremulous voice.

"What the fuck is that?" Antony asks.

Ida realizes that Antony's voice is coming from the watch, so she tries to shake it off, as if it were venomous, and all the while she's repeating, "*Basilisco, Basilisco, Basilisco!*" He's shouting, asking over and over if they know where Sal is. Running her fingers along Ida's arm, Anna says, "Calm down, it's Antony." The phone connection snaps, and Anna stuffs the watch under the chair cushion; muffled sounds of "Volare," barely audible, as Antony calls again and again until he gives up.

Anna hasn't seen Ida this shaken and fetches a Valium from her purse. "Here, take this, honey. Drink some water." Ida leans back on the couch, fixing her attention on *The Housewives of New York City*. Sonja, drunk, had jumped naked into the pool. Now the other housewives are trying to put panties on her while she's squirming on a lounge chair and babbling. Someone says, "It's like trying to put a bikini on a piece of spaghetti. I haven't seen this much of *my* vagina." Ida's forgotten about Antony. "Who are these *puttane*?" she asks.

"Borough trash who married up," Anna says, relieved that she's settling down. "Come on, Ida, let's have some tea and *giugiulena*."

"Gi-gi-li gi-gi-li," Ida says.

~

Antony bangs his hand so hard against the steering wheel the horn sticks. He snaps the light and siren back on the hood. "Fuckin' Sal," he says. The car ahead moves slightly to the right to give him room, and when he tries to squeeze into the open space, the Jersey barrier scrapes and slices the length of the doors, a chimpanzee cry, the screech piercing like a full-body laceration. Antony, trapped, isn't going anywhere anytime soon.

~

After BB is finished showering, he opens the door, standing in his dirty boxers.

Justin shakes his head. "I'll be right back."

When he returns, he gives BB a clean pair, which BB unfolds and holds out, saying, "Perfect."

Justin hadn't noticed that he'd brought the boxers with dolphins surfacing on the aqua blue shorts. Sal had given them to him for Christmas, with plane tickets to Key West. They never got to Florida. What was there to celebrate after Francesco was gunned down.

"And here's a set of clergy clothes, BB."

"All black. I prefer the vestments."

"A sign of seriousness, and black hides coffee stains." Justin closes the door while BB dresses.

He comes out again, holding the collar. "I can't get this."

"Give it to me. Here, it snaps around the back."

BB smiles.

Seeing him transformed into a tidy imposter of a priest, Justin says, "You clean up nice."

BB looks in the mirror. "I wasn't so weathered years ago."

On their way back to the sacristy, they run into Ida and Anna. Ida stops dead in her tracks, vaguely remembering BB. She grabs Anna's arm.

"So, ladies, we have a guest," Justin says, "This is Father BB. He's visiting from Arizona."

Anna doesn't know why they're creating this elaborate ruse. "BB?" she asks.

Before he can say anything, Justin answers. "Benedict Bartholomew, BB for short."

BB knows enough to play along. "Are you sisters?"

"Not even related," Anna says.

"I meant holy sisters of the Church."

"You're crazy," Ida says, warming up to him.

BB smiles. "Maybe."

"Ida," Justin says. "Be nice."

"We're on our way to the kitchen for tea and cookies. Want to join us?" Anna asks.

"Gi-gi-li gi-gi-li," Ida mutters.

"Gi-gi-li gi-gi-li," BB repeats.

Ida laughs.

"Rain check. Father BB wants a tour of the church," Justin says.

"Antony called," Anna says. "He was looking for Sal."

Justin tries not to seem worried. "What did you tell him?"

"Just that we haven't seen Sal today."

Ida, grabbing BB's hand, says, "Antony is il diavolo."

Anna pulls her away. "You don't mean that, Ida. Come with me. Justin and his friend need to go."

"Don't worry, Ida. Mary, the Mother of God, is watching over us," BB says.

"You're funny," she says, walking off.

~

On the way to the church BB stops at the grotto to visit Mary. "We're in a world of trouble, Mary."

Suddenly exhausted, and thinking about Sal, Justin kneels beside BB and whispers the beginning of the poem "Dark Night." *In an obscure night / Fevered with love's anxiety.* Some nights, before entering Sal, Justin whispers those words. And on those nights, all that matters are his breaths on Sal's shoulder and the sense that he's disappearing inside the one he loves. *St. John of the Cross understood love*, he thinks.

BB sees Justin tearing up. "What's wrong, Father."

"Faith and love are hard."

"If you say so."

"I wanted to believe it could be easier."

BB doesn't understand and says, "I'm sorry."

"For what?"

"You're not as happy as you seem."

Justin nods. "You missed your calling, fisherman."

"You think?"

"You'd be a better priest than some I know."

"No doubt."

In the sacristy, BB asks if he can "go whole hog again."

"What's that mean?"

"Get back into those church clothes. I don't like this black uniform."

Justin says, "Why not."

BB makes another mess of the vestments. When he's dressed in all his liturgical splendor, he grabs the Processional Crucifix from the corner. "Can I carry this?"

"Why?"

"It reminds me of a pilgrimage I made after hauling up the corpse. I was in Assisi, a guy carried a cross on his shoulders. He thought he was Judas."

"That's stretching devotion, BB."

"That's what I thought until Mary started talking to me. Anyway, I wouldn't mind carrying one around. See what it's like. Maybe, for good luck."

"You know we're going to keep you safe, right."

"Sure, miracle worker."

156

Justin smiles.

"So, what about the crucifix on the pole?"

"Go for it."

When they get to the nave, BB leans the cross against a statue of Archangel Michael. He looks at Jesus staring down at him. "You would think a mother would do anything not to see her son being tortured and dying," he says. "Father Justin, will you hear my confession?"

Justin gives him a look but says, "If that's what you want." They go to the confessional and Justin flicks on the dim amber lamp in his compartment, folds down his seat, and turns his head to the lattice screen. BB kneels in his darkened nook and waits. The shutter opens, and Justin says, "Yes, my son."

BB is surprised that he remembers how to respond. "Bless me, Father, for I have sinned. My last confession was, let me count." He pauses. "Thirty-eight years ago."

"Where've you been?"

"Everywhere and nowhere, Father."

"And why are you asking for penance?"

"I told you. I've sinned."

"Of course, you have. Go on."

"We're all sinners, right?"

"Without a doubt."

"Is the confession of a priest to a priest the same as any other?"

"It is."

"Okay."

"When a penitent has waited as long as you between confessions, I advise him to speak about sins in global terms. You don't have to list them all, BB."

"For years, I didn't believe in God, until I pulled up the corpse. Mary is teaching me a lot about faith and grace. At least, that's one of the things I think she's doing. She's hard to read. I have my doubts."

"Like I told you earlier, believing isn't easy. God understands. Besides, not believing isn't a sin, and doubt is ubiquitous."

"I never killed anyone, but I thought about it a few times. My father was a go-to victim."

"Do you want to talk about that?"

"Not really. He's dead now anyway."

"I'm sorry."

"Yeah." He pauses. "I'm not sorry."

"So, you want to be forgiven for not feeling sorry your father is dead."

"No. I just wanted you to know I thought about killing him."

"Do you want to talk about *that*?"

"Not really. My other sins are petty ones. Little things. Not believing in God and desiring to kill my father, those are the biggies."

Losing interest in what seems more like role play than a confession, Justin asks, "Are you sorry for all these transgressions you've confessed tonight?"

BB says he is.

"Okay, I'm going to give you your penance, unless there's something else you want to tell God."

"I'm done."

Justin forgives BB's sins in the name of the Father, and of the Son, and of the Holy Ghost. He asks BB to repeat after him the Act of Contrition and then metes out the standard penance: the three prayers he gives everyone.

Before BB leaves, he says, "Now it's your turn, Father Justin."

"My turn?"

"Yeah. I'm a priest."

"You're not a priest."

"You can pretend. It might do you some good."

Justin considers this, and then out of the blue says, "I've lied to God ever since I became a priest."

"That's a big one."

"I've told God that I believe it is possible to love Christ wholeheartedly, devote my life to Him, while all the time I've loved Sal at least as much. Maybe Sal is right. Maybe that's not possible."

"I forgive you," BB says, not wanting to go there. "Any others."

Justin ignores him. "But I'd still choose Sal, if God demanded it."

"You want your penance?"

"Why not?" Justin says, oddly pleased by his admission.

"Well, here it is. Don't beat yourself up."

Justin smiles. "You know, you're really warming to this role, BB."

Pizza Strips and Peanuts

When Sal arrives at Mother Pug's, Sherry is sitting at the bar next to her brother. She's turned away and doesn't notice him. Sal is struck by how much she resembles his *nonni* in a photo that he keeps in his wallet. Sal had met his grandmother when he was a boy on a trip to Sicily. At that time, Clorinda was much older than Sherry now, but she had the exact slate blue eyes and the same I-can-do-anything-better expression. One morning, she took Sal to a shed behind the house, sat him down on a stool across from her, and slaughtered a chicken between her legs. She had stretched the neck as if she were pulling taffy and slit its throat with an effortless scissor snap, blood shooting into a rusted pot. Later that day, Clorinda gave Sal the wallet-size photo of herself taken when she was younger, and said, "Now don't forget me, in America, *nipotino*." "You speak English," Sal said. "You'd be surprised what I can do," she said as she made a clipping gesture in the space between them.

As Sal walks up to the bar, he overhears Aidan talking to Sherry.

"Why would he want to kill Bruno Cali?" Aidan asks her.

Sal, worried, asks Sherry if she should be talking to her brother about this, and O'Shea feigns a wounded look.

"Isn't this a family matter, Sal," Sherry says. "Aidan's my confidant. I guess in your world, you'd call him my *consigliere*."

"That's not my world."

"Sensitive boy."

"Sal and Justin are pretty good at keeping secrets," O'Shea says. "I'm not judging their lifestyle. I'm just saying they know how to keep a secret."

"And where is Father Justin? I told you this is a family affair."

"He's busy."

"Well, I'm going to have to talk to him, too."

Nina sets down a Jameson for Sal.

Fixing on Sherry, Sal says, "You know why the Russians killed Francesco."

"Don't get ahead of your skis, Sal," she says.

He's decided he's going to let Sherry control the pace of the meeting but to surprise her, maybe soften her, he says, "You know, Sherry, you look like my Sicilian *nonni*." He hands her the photo, and she studies it awhile, seemingly intrigued by the resemblance. "I'll keep this," she says, taking another look before pocketing it and calling out to the bartender: "Another round. Make them doubles." Sherry is suspicious of Nina and doesn't like her lingering around their side of the bar. When Nina delivers the whiskeys, Sherry sends her an icy stare and says, "Let's get a table."

They sit under a sign with an outline of a neon purple pug and below it in flickering neon script: *Beware of pugs*.

"I'm hungry. Any food here?" Sherry asks.

"Soggy hot dogs, pizza strips, peanuts," O'Shea says. No one responds. "I'll get the strips and nuts."

As he walks away, Sherry says, "He's different these days, happier. Maybe it has something to do with us."

"Us?"

"Yeah, my coming home and meeting Francesco, and now you."

Surprised, Sal doesn't know what to say.

"You know he reads everything. A human RAM of literature. I sweated Freshman Comp. What about you?"

"What?"

"Do you like to read?"

"Sure. History more than novels." Sal looks at his watch.

"You've got somewhere to go?" she asks.

He doesn't answer. Sal is thinking how much Sherry's self-confidence reminds him of Antony, except for being opposites in what's most important to them. She's got the crusader gene and Antony's inherited the fuck-everyone-but-me marker. Both judge-and-jury bruisers, though.

"Anyway, tonight it's all about you and Antony," Sherry says. "We can save the *As the World Turns* brother-sister reunion melodrama for another night. You looked at your watch again."

He doesn't tell her that he's meeting Antony.

"Do you know where your brother is?"

"No idea."

He doesn't tell her about BB hiding in the church with Justin. He doesn't know if he can trust her.

O'Shea comes back with a stack of pizza strips and a dog dish of peanuts in the shells.

"A dog dish," Sherry says.

"Nina ran out of paper bowls. I watched her wash it. Clean as a whistle." Aidan dangles a sagging pizza strip before his mouth and bites off a third.

Sherry cracks open a peanut shell. "Sal, your father told me a lot about you. I suspect you're not a willing accomplice. But I know you had something to do with Bruno ending up in the box on Hart Island."

"*Our* father. It's the second time today you didn't call him yours."

"I'm working on it."

"When did you talk to him?"

"We met a few times before he was killed. He was going to help me get to the Russians."

Sherry tells Sal about Francesco agreeing to pass on information on the Russian mob. She explains that she offered him a way out and witness protection for his family, including Sal and Justin, even his psycho son, Antony, in exchange for helping to bring down the Russians. He knew it was dangerous, but he freely accepted the risk, she says, with what Sal thinks is a tinge of remorse.

O'Shea gathers the empty glasses, and before going to the bar for refills, he whispers, "I'm living in a Mario Puzo narrative." He knocks the peanuts off the table and takes the bowl to the bar for a refill.

"An FBI agent sold out to the Russians," Sherry says. "We fucked up. The asshole discovered that we were recruiting Francesco to be a mole against the Little Odessa mob. He's in the Alcatraz of the Rockies now. He's fucked for life."

More worn down than angry, Sal looks at her. "And like that, because of you our father is dead."

After letting that sink in, Sal goes, "So, you ask Francesco to get shit on the Russians. You promise him witness protection. Francesco agrees and the Russians find out and gun him down."

"That's about it."

"And now what? You're asking for fuckin' forgiveness."

"I'm not asking for anything; I'm offering you the same deal. You and Antony continue the job Francesco signed up for, and I'll make sure Carlo Cali doesn't find out you wasted Bruno and buried him in the mass grave."

"I didn't waste Bruno."

"An accomplice in crime, Sal."

"Fuck you," he says.

"You don't have to love me. You just have to see this is a way out. Otherwise, it's lights out for you and Antony, and knowing the Mafia thirst for vengeance, I wouldn't be surprised if Justin and Ida die, too."

She lets Sal take it all in before asking, "Now, why the fuck did *you* help your brother bury Bruno? And why did he off the son of Carlo Cali, for Christ's sake?"

Sal is stone silent.

O'Shea comes back with the whiskeys and more peanuts.

"You know why, don't you?" she asks.

"It was personal."

"Maybe it's better I don't know Antony's motive, but why the fuck did you help him?"

"He's my brother. *Family.* You wouldn't understand."

In her most sarcastic deadpan voice, she sings, *"He ain't heavy, he's my brother.* Jesus. Didn't you hear the one about the brother who follows his brother off the cliff. Christ, what are you, a lemming? But back to the reason for this meet, you better think hard about the offer, Sal."

"How the fuck do you think I can give you shit on the Russians?"

"You can convince Antony. We know he's the hookup between Bratva and Cali and the other families. Francesco said he could get him to agree, and now it's your job, and mine, to follow up."

"You can't keep Carlo from finding out about Antony and Bruno."

"We've got that covered. Trust me."

"Ha. Trust you? Like Francesco trusted you? And what about the Russians? Nobody can hide from them," Sal says.

"Not true. Deserts. Mountains. Wide open plains. It's a big, beautiful country outside Staten Island. Hey, you look like it's a tough choice, Sal. I wish you would have brought Justin along. He's sensible."

Sal kills his whiskey and stares at Sherry. "Haven't you done enough damage? Francesco was your father, for Christ's sake."

"Don't be so fast to judge, Sal. You don't know what kind of father Francesco was to me."

Sal turns to Aidan. "Don't look at me, pal, I'm just listening."

"Antony said he wanted to see me tonight," Sal says.

"Why?"

"He's looking for BB."

"Who?"

"A homeless guy who saw us bury Bruno that he wants dead. I'm supposed to meet Antony outside Pug's in an hour."

"Jesus, what a clusterfuck. You think he'd come inside? I don't want him to see me with you until you get the chance to talk to him."

"He won't put one foot in here. He despises Pug's and *shit-ass losers*, his words, who waste time here."

"Talk about losers," Aidan says. "Son-of-a-bitch doesn't deserve this deal."

Sherry gives Sal a look. "We don't need another body, especially an innocent sucker."

"I'm not going to let that happen," Sal says.

She looks away, pauses, and then fishes through her bag for her sunglasses and headscarf in case Antony is outside. "Is there a back door?"

"Over there." O'Shea points to the dartboard.

"Don't mess this up, Sal," she says on the way out like the good ghost her training made her.

O'Shea lifts his glass. "She likes you. She's got a lot of Cusumano in her, that's for sure."

Sal wants to get back to Justin and BB before he decides anything. He looks for his phone and realizes he's left it in the church. "Give me your phone, Aidan. I've got to call Antony." He gets his brother's voicemail and leaves a message that he can't meet him until midnight. He passes back the phone and gets up.

"Hey, wait a minute, Sal," Aidan says. "The way I see it, you've got a lot to live for. Just today I was reading *Fight Club*. You know it? *It's only after we've lost everything that we're free to do anything.* Leave the Staten Island shitshow behind, Sal."

Sal downs what's left of the whiskey Sherry left on the table. "I didn't read the book, but I saw the movie. The way I remember *Fight Club*, there wasn't much to live for in the end."

Maybe Taos

BB is standing before the Sixth Station of the Cross, *Jesus Is Scourged at the Pillar and Crowned with Thorns*. The Son of God is handed a purple cloth the color of the chasuble BB's wearing. "I'll have to ask Mary if this is a sign or coincidence," he whispers, respecting the solemnity of the Stations. Not far away, Justin is reciting pieces of prayers that the faithful burdened by tortuous choices say: *Help me to understand myself in my actions . . . bless me with insight . . . Though it cost all I have, help me understand.* Sal, exhausted, steps in from the other side of the aisle and kneels beside him.

"You're crying," Sal says.

"I can't do this anymore."

Sal isn't sure what he means.

"I can't be a priest anymore. God understands, why can't you? I don't know what I'd do without you," Justin says.

Sal stiffens, and knowing there's no time for this talk, he says, more thoughtless than he intends, "You'd live."

BB proceeds to the next Station: *Jesus Bears the Cross*. Mary, hand on her breasts, watches without tears her son's anguished countenance. In a voice more beseeching than he's used with her before, BB says, "So, what is it you want, Mary?" No surprise to him the Mother of God is silent. He rises and joins Sal and Justin in the front pew. "Can you walk in the footprints of silence?" BB asks, a line from the hymnal he read at the last station.

Justin and Sal give each other a look. Sal says, "Let's go back to the sacristy."

"Can I keep these on?"

"If that's what you want, BB," Justin says.

In the sacristy BB settles into the chair, placing the Crucifix pole across the armrests. Sal explains the FBI proposal. BB, taking it all in, thinks about witness protection and says, "Maybe the desert would be a good change from the sea."

"We don't have much of a choice, Sal," Justin says. "I've wanted to leave ever since Francesco was killed."

"Maybe Taos," BB says, "a little adobe for me, and next door, a bigger one for you guys and Ida. Depending on how this turns out, a Mary-in-the-half-shell in the front yard."

They ignore him.

"They're going to leave me behind," he whispers.

"I don't think Antony will go for it," Sal says.

"A few years, instead of life. Afterward, a new identity and relocation. It's as good as absolution," Justin says.

"You're the expert on forgiveness, not me, but I've learned that Antony isn't a forgiven or forgiving type."

BB says, "I'm a dead man."

"He won't get anywhere near you," Sal says.

"Count on that," Justin tells him.

BB, remembering Mary's indifference, says, "Maybe there isn't a ticket out of this."

Family Shitshow

Antony hasn't noticed the tail on him. A cop in the Throggs Neck pileup spotted his car and called it in to the FBI. It's Antony's first time back to Staten Island and the Cusumano house since Francesco's funeral. The FBI agent, who took over the tail once Antony crossed into the Forgotten Borough, pulls in along the street behind a Pipe Monkeys Sewer and Drain van. Painted on its side are a monkey in a superhero costume snaking a hose down a pipe and another hanging from its tail and doing chin-ups on a monkey wrench. The road curves, which gives him a good view of the driveway. Through a thermal-vision scope, he watches Antony's fluorescent white image go to the front door. Once Antony is inside, the agent creeps up to the house and crouches beside a laurel hedge, giving him a view of a bay window. It's too dark inside to see if anyone else is home.

Antony yells in the empty foyer: "Are you hiding the asshole here, Sal?" He passes through the kitchen and living room and flicks on a light. The agent gets a glimpse of him at the bottom of the stairs, as Antony climbs the steps and goes out of sight. He pauses at photographs that Ida has displayed along the way. The *family shitshow*, she calls them, affectionately. She and Francesco are wearing straw hats in a Sicilian church square. In another, Antony is carving his hair into a Mohawk. Family milestones: Sal's Coast Guard commission, Justin's ordination, Antony's NYPD swearing-in, and Francesco, the Grand Marshal, draped in the Italian flag, riding in a Mustang convertible during the Staten Island Columbus Day Parade. He stops before fat Uncle Stefano lifting Antony over his head in one hand and grinning like a pig in a mound of muck. Every *goombah* in Francesco's circle was *family*: Uncle Luigi, Uncle Flavio, Uncle Angelo, and on and on. Once Sal remarked to his father, "We have a lot of uncles." Antony slapped Sal's head lightly as he liked to do, and teased, "*Stupido*, they're Dad's gangsters, not brothers." He mimicked Stefano, saying, *Only two slices of lasagna, five meatballs, and three bowls of pasta?* Francesco, annoyed by Antony's disrespect, knuckled him across the chin. Antony remembers giving Francesco an icy stare back. When he saw his little brother's eyes well up in solidarity with him, he imagined showing the kid the virtue of payback by beating their father senseless before his eyes. Antony was strong enough then, but a hair shy of the fearlessness he'd acquire. As he ascends the stairs, he passes Sal and Justin, maybe ten, shooting baskets, happier in the unremarkable driveway moment than Antony believes he's ever felt anywhere. His ex-wife, Donna, and their son and daughter, lounging under an umbrella at Midland Beach. It's Fourth of July, and Antony is standing nearby in American flag trunks. Everyone is smiling except Antony, who looks like he wishes he were anywhere else but there. Near the top landing is Francesco's godfather, Carlo Cali, wearing a Santa hat and cradling Sal in his arms. Antony raises his arm and a photo tumbles down the steps, landing face up: in it, Sal is five, and under the glass, shattered like a boyhood dream, he's looking up at Antony as if in a moment of unconditional sibling love he could save his big brother from whatever is eating his soul.

Antony checks Ida's room, thinking that she might have gone to bed, so estranged from what's been happening at home that he doesn't know she can't be left alone in her dementia. "Where the fuck is everyone," he says. On the nightstand is a photograph of his father. In it, Francesco isn't much older than Antony is now, and the resemblance is so striking that it startles him. The same slate eyes, the Roman nose and chiseled cheekbones, enough hair for two heads. Like father like son. He lifts the photo and studies it. He tries to find subtle differences. Nothing stands out, except for Francesco's slight smile, a sideways drift of his mouth. Antony's, it seems, is always frozen in a hard line. "Fuck you, Francesco," Antony says. "I'm the man you couldn't be, the wild one you pretended to be ashamed of, even when you envied me." He tosses it onto the bed.

The door to Sal's and Justin's room is open. Above the bed, next to the wooden crucifix, is a religious icon, in shimmering shades of gold, depicting a phalanx of monks ascending a ladder to Jesus, who is holding out his hand to lift each supplicant through an opening that looks like a half moon. On a night table is a signed photograph of Notre Dame's Father Hesburgh embracing Martin Luther King Jr. The inscription: *To Father Justin, be kind, be strong. Love conquers all. Salut, Father Ted.* All their clothes are tucked neatly away in drawers and the closet, not even a shirt hanging from a chair or a stray sock on the floor. Their bed is so tightly made in the Coast Guard art of manliness that you could bounce a quarter off it. On the other night table is a tube of Adam and Eve anal gel. Antony remembers spying on them fucking there when they were boys, moving so slowly in an embrace, so involved in themselves that Antony, for a moment, felt their tenderness. "Who would have thought?" he said back then, and as he did those many years ago, he quietly closes the door. His anger waning, and with a hint of something like sadness, he understands that he's never known such love.

Across the hall is Antony's room. It's unchanged since he was a teenager. There are no banners of New York sports teams. No classic rock or metal posters. No neon beer sign. No Playboy pinup. The walls are covered with movie bills that Antony stole from cases he had busted open at theaters throughout Manhattan: Al Pacino, in *Scarface*. The born-to-kill helmet, lined with M 14 ammo and suspended in air, in *Full Metal Jacket*. "Fuck this," he says. "Where are you, Sal?"

The agent's been tracking him each time he switches on a light. Antony takes a beer from the refrigerator, turns on the lamp beside Ida's recliner, and sits. Finally, the agent has a good view through the window and sees Antony swilling the beer, rubbing his eyes with the fingers of both hands, sliding them slowly down his face. Exhausted, he whispers, "Fucking Sal. Where the fuck are you and dipshit?" He returns to the kitchen for another beer and plops back into the chair.

On the end table is a diary covered with a cutout of the Sicilian flag: diagonally divided in red and yellow halves and, in the center, a three-legged Medusa with wings and three ears of wheat. He opens it. On the first page in letters snipped from magazine headlines and pasted on is the title: IDA CUSUMANO. Below it, a line written in his mother's rickety script, barely legible: *I have become stupid.* There are no entry dates. Huge spaces on the pages separate Ida's random thoughts: *I shouldn't tell people I hate them. . . . I think I used to like chestnuts. . . . I don't remember what I just thought. . . . I do things. . . . Antony is bad. . . . Someone took my wedding ring. . . . Thieves are everywhere, you don't see them.*

Antony puts down the diary. His jaw slackens and he's tearing up. *Antony is bad*, he thinks, *that's the shit in her head when she thinks of me.* He hasn't slept in two days. He shuts off the lamp and closes his eyes, but it isn't long before he remembers the figure in the reeds on Hart Island. He switches the lamp back on. Whatever melancholy that he was feeling passes. His cell rings. It's the precinct sergeant calling with information about Sal. An Uber dropped him off at Our Lady Queen of Peace.

"Fuck, the church," he says, ending the call before the sergeant, a compatriot, one of the city's dirtiest finest, could ask why the FBI is looking for him.

Cocksucker. Corkscrew. Cock-a-Doodle-Doo

Antony notices the car behind him was parked near the house. He's learned to be suspicious of coincidence, ever since the one night he got careless and barely ducked a drive-by. So, he makes quick turns on streets he knows like a human GPS, and when he's left the suspicious car behind, he turns onto Hyman Boulevard and races into Last Chance Park. He leaves the unmarked cruiser in an isolated corner and takes a zig-zag route on foot to Our Lady Queen of Peace.

The church is dark, and the dim light in the sacristy is out of his view. *They must be in the rectory*, he thinks. Antony's never been inside the residence before. He slides a credit card between the lock and the door frame, jiggles it until the latch releases. Next to him on the table is a bowl of holy cards—Mary in two poses. He picks one out and scratches the back of his neck with a corner of the card and tosses it back in. Antony has never held a faith beyond himself, never felt the anguish of God's benevolence diminishing in his heart as so much boyhood faith evaporates for others. He doesn't care about a funeral Mass and burial like other wiseguys who believe God will forgive their sins, like the made men who march down Mulberry Street behind a statue of Mary draped in dollar bills, waving like benefactors to families of fathers, sons, and husbands they've gunned down. He's never imagined a priest spreading incense over his casket. He's a realist. On his police DNR form he wrote: "BURN ME."

Once past the foyer, he sees his mother sitting on a sofa in a room at the end of the hall. Anna has left her alone to take Lola for a walk. Ida's asleep, her head bowed, and her chin tucked into her chest. For a moment, from the doorway, Antony thinks she could be dead. When he sits beside her, she doesn't budge. Her breathing is heavy, and with every few breaths, she sounds like she's sighing.

He whispers, "Ida."

She doesn't hear him. A decades-old issue of *TV Guide* with Dean Martin on the cover is on her lap. She twitches when Antony strokes her arthritic knuckles. He takes the magazine and drops it on the floor.

"Ida," he says, louder this time. "It's Antony, Ma."

She raises her head and struggles to open her eyes as if the lids were fighting back. She recognizes Antony but then forgets what she recognized. He strokes her hand again. It pleases her. Surprised by the intimacy, Antony runs her palm across his cheek. "Remember me. I'm your bad son." Her lids open wider this time and he's struck by how forlorn she looks.

"Antony," she says.

"Bad Antony." He smiles.

Ida nods, though she isn't sure why. Unexpectedly, fragments of what she was dreaming in her sleep fly by: glimpses of a sea, an octopus, lemon trees, Antony holding a gun. She says, "You had a gun."

"I have a gun. I'm a detective, Ma."

"Water," she says. Ida in her dementia sometimes doesn't recognize her thirst until it becomes insistent. If it weren't for Justin, Sal, and Anna, she'd probably forget to eat.

Antony follows her into the kitchen. He's subdued, forgetting for the moment about Bruno and the witness Sal is hiding. Ida opens the refrigerator and pulls out a plate of pizza slices and hands him one, a piece of sausage falling on the floor. She says, "Good," and fetches a quart of milk and fills a glass. She takes a sip and spits it out.

"You only like milk in cereal, Ma." Antony is surprised he remembers this. "You said you wanted water."

Ida turns to him, accidentally knocking the carton on the floor.

"What do you know," she says, stepping on the puddle in her slipper socks with snowflake grips, the kind a hospital patient wears. The cold milk seeps through a sock and she lifts her foot and scrunches her face like a toddler. She takes another glass, fills it with water from the faucet, and guzzles it. With his sleeve, Antony wipes milk from her chin and neck.

The water has made her a little more lucid. "Antony," she says.

He takes her arm. "Let's go back to the other room, Ma."

After she is settled on the couch, Ida searches nervously for something, though she can't remember what it is. "Cold," she says, rocking back and forth.

Antony sees an afghan on the floor. "Is this what you're looking for?"

She smiles, and he places it on her lap. "You're nice, Sal."

"I'm Antony."

"I know. You're bad."

He pulls up a chair and sits so close he can feel her breathing. Once she has focused on him, Antony asks if she remembers when they went to Sicily together. He was fourteen, Sal was six. It was 1990, and Francesco and Ida had decided to celebrate their wedding anniversary in Cinisi, the first time back to the old country. There was a stopover in London, and he told her that she used to like telling the story of the pilot who announced on the speaker that he had a piece of twisted history-making for them. A butcher from Cumberland, his hometown, had just beaten the Guinness record for creating the longest sausage in the world, 20,921 meters, or for the Yankees onboard, 13 miles long. And what did Antony say, according to Ida, loud enough for others around him to hear? "My cock's bigger."

"You remember? You know you made that up, Ida."

She doesn't understand and says, "Cocksucker. Corkscrew. Cock-a-doodle-doo." But after a few moments, she pictures Salvatore's seaside villa: White with basil green shutters. The front door carved in holm oak from Mount Etna with a serpentine face of a lion in the center of knotty vines and laurel leaves. The door was heavy as stone. She hears seagulls and the sea lapping on shore. She forgets that on the roof Salvatore's soldiers guarded against threats while everyone else ate dried sausages, olives, cheese, and *fragole*, *peche*, and *fichi* sweeter than any fruit anywhere. And wine, there was Marsala from Salvatore's vineyard on the hillside.

"Remember Monte Pecoraro?"

But the remembrance of that day disappears like a flash of a firefly among the hundreds of flashes Ida doesn't remember igniting the Sicilian meadow.

Antony leans into her ear and whispers, "Where's Sal?" He repeats, whispering, "Where's Sal? Where's Sal? Where's Sal, Ida?" until he surrenders to the vacancy she's entered.

He wonders where Justin is and then notices a light in the church that wasn't on when he arrived. Antony lays Ida across the couch and places a pillow under her head. Her arm is twitching. He spreads the afghan over her chest and legs, her socks sticking out its end. If she feels his kiss on her forehead, she doesn't react. Before going to check out the church, he sits a while longer with his mother, wondering if she's thinking, *Even a kiss can't make Antony good.*

Brothers

Sal is trying to figure out how he can convince Antony to take the FBI deal and wishes he had a Jameson; he's talking to Justin, who is storing the vestments BB had piled up. In the church nave, finishing the Stations in the dark, BB hears "Blackbird" playing on Sal's phone, which had slipped out of Sal's pocket onto the pew earlier. He answers it. It's Sherry O'Shea.

"Sal?"

"I'm Father BB. So, you were playing 'Blackbird.'"

Sherry doesn't know what he's talking about. "Give the phone to Sal."

"Who's this?"

She raises her voice. "I'm his sister."

"His sister?"

"Give him the fuckin' phone."

"I'll find him." On his way to the sacristy, he passes Mary and whispers, "Sal's sister is some piece of work."

Sal puts the phone on speaker. Sherry tells them that an agent had followed Antony to their home but lost him when he left. She wants to know if Sal's met with his brother, and he tells her that he left Antony a message that he wouldn't be at Pug's until midnight.

"Where the fuck are you?" she asks.

"I don't think I like her," BB says.

Justin gestures for him to be quiet.

"I'm in Our Lady Queen of Peace."

"And the guy you said Antony wants to kill?"

BB shouts, "That's me, we talked, and you were rude."

"Christ, what a circus show." Sherry says she's sending a car to sit outside. She suggests moving BB to a motel until Antony knows he isn't a threat.

"Antony wouldn't set foot in the church," Sal says.

Sherry tells him that she's sending the car anyway and heading over herself. She wants this all settled tonight.

∼

172

BB, becoming visibly agitated, says he wants to go back into the nave.

"Why?" Justin asks.

"That's where Mary is. I've got to talk to her."

They sit in a circle before the altar. Security lights outside illuminate a stained-glass window nearby. Beside it is a statue of Our Lady Queen of Peace. BB, exhausted, turns to Mary and asks, "What have you done?"

Antony and Justin look on. BB goes, "I'm sorry."

"For what?" Sal asks.

He's tying and unknotting his fingers on his lap. "I'm sorry I pulled up the corpse from the Sound. I'm sorry I left the *Mary Lee*. I'm sorry I stowed away on *Vesuvius*. I'm sorry Mary got me involved in this mess, and I'm sorry I carry the head of Jesus around. I'm sorry I watched Sal and his brother bury Bruno in the box." He pauses and then, as if in a trance, he makes no sense: "Shark, rock, musk. Boat, crab, moat. No, no, no."

Justin pats his knee. "It's okay, BB. We're here."

BB mumbles something about Mary abandoning him. Sal catches the gist. "Well, BB, we're not going anywhere."

~

Antony, unseen, enters the vestibule, stopping at the baptismal font. Votive candles flicker, and as he crouches beside a metal case of newsletters and pamphlets, a hook snares his holster. Antony readjusts his gun belt, which had ridden up his back, and checks to make sure the safety strap is unsnapped. Nothing focuses him more than his gun. When his eyes adjust to the murky light, he sees Sal, Justin, and BB huddling in the sanctuary. He hugs the wall, and as he goes low, he steps on something that crackles.

Sal looks around. "Did you hear that?"

Justin says he didn't.

BB raises an eyebrow, and Sal settles back, while Antony, still unseen, sneaks into the confessional.

BB says, "Mary, I've got a feeling this is the day you said was coming."

"*Fuckin' right,*" Antony mouths the words.

Justin turns to BB. "Mary told me you'll be safe."

"I don't believe you, Father Justin."

"Why would I lie?"

"*Because you're a fuckin' asshole,*" Antony whispers.

BB says, "She's not reliable, Father."

Justin turns to Sal. "We're going to Maine tonight."

173

"Like fuck you are," Antony mouths the words.

BB turns to Mary and says, more plaintively than he's ever sounded, "I don't want to die."

~

Anna is back from walking Lola. She's cleaning up the spilt milk and pizza in the kitchen, while the dog rushes into the living room to see Ida. The dachshund jumps up beside her and burrows under the afghan, bundling herself against Ida's hip. Anna walks in and pulls over a chair. "You made a mess in the kitchen, honey."

Ida turns away, forgetting that Antony was ever there.

~

After Justin leaves for the sacristy to call the priest in Maine, Antony slips out of the confessional. "Fuckin' A, little brother, you've been ducking me."

BB turns to Mary and says, "Do something."

Antony gives BB a look as he moves closer. "You disappoint me, little brother."

"We need to talk," Sal says.

"That's what we're doing." He pats his gun.

"I've met with Sherry."

"Our FBI bastard sister, fuck her. You know she killed Francesco, right?"

"You know that's not true," Sal says.

Antony ignores him, and turning to BB, he asks, "Why do you want to protect this piece of shit."

Sal winces. "You don't have to worry about BB. He's not a risk."

BB nods while Antony is pulling on his cincture. "Aren't you a pretty priest?"

BB says, "A fisherman."

"What?"

"I was a fisherman before I found the Mother of God on a dead man's back."

"That's where I saw you. The miracle of Long Island Sound."

BB smiles.

"You still believe in miracles?"

He nods.

"Too bad."

Sal says, "There's a way out of this for all of us."

174

"Aren't you the thinker, little brother?"

"Sal's always thinking," BB says.

Sal notices Antony lifting his gun from the holster and gets up. "You fuckin' want to stay in the chair, Sal," Antony warns, shoving his brother back down. He presses the barrel against BB's forehead. "How's that feel, dumb fuck? Sal, want to see a head explode?"

BB's forehead furrows; he's shaking. "What the fuck, Antony!" Sal says. Antony, laughing, lowers the gun and steps back.

BB swallows, and says, "You're nothing like your brother."

"Hey, fuckwit, you think you're some fisherman prophet? Did you sense you were a dead man as soon as you set foot on that voodoo island?"

Sal signals BB to stop talking. "I'm telling you. BB won't be a problem."

"Damn right, he won't."

Justin, returning from the sacristy, stops at the door. No one notices him inching his way toward the altar. He picks up the sanctuary lamp.

"Mary told me to tell you Sal loves you," BB says.

The remark, out of the blue like this as BB is wont to do, makes Antony pause long enough to give Sal time to leap up and push BB away. But in that instant, in what surely must be the work of the Cusumano curse, as a bullet meant for BB hits Sal, Justin rushes Antony and strikes his head with the heavy clawed base of the lamp.

Sal is aware that he's mostly dead. He senses Justin kneeling beside him and then being pulled into Justin's arms. He struggles faintly to unseal his lips. Nothing else except this kiss is important now as death closes in, and when their lips touch, everything Sal knew of living disappears. Not far from him, Antony, his skull split open, is going where he's been heading all his life. Unaware even that he has killed his brother. No white light at the end of a tunnel. No thought of the pain and heartbreak he's wreaked on the family. No comfort.

BB crouches beside Sal and Justin and whispers something about riding a big wave deep in the Atlantic. Sherry arrives with the agents too late to do any good. "Jesus," she says, standing over this shattered family.

BB looks up. "Jesus doesn't have anything to do with this. It's all Mary's work." And more out of sorrow than confusion now, he tells Sherry: "Why the Mother of God let this happen, only she knows."

Final Crossing

They meet at the DOC dock on City Island. It's the last trip the Rikers angels are making to Potter's Field. Tomorrow, they will get early prison release for good behavior and the humanitarian aid they rendered survivors of the plane crash. The captain of *Vesuvius* is Billy Hopkins, who usually runs cargo to and from the boroughs' ports. His load today: five coffins, all containing dead Hart Island lifers. "No shoeboxes, thank God," Booker reports when he reads out the names: "Female Unknown 042325, Jennie Haskin 042326; Auggie Nunez 042327, Male Unknown 042328," and, his eyes tearing up, "Sal Cusumano 042329." Everyone on the crew is silent. Jesús makes the Sign of the Cross.

After the coffins are loaded on the ferry, the inmates stand together, like Guards of Honor, around Sal's pine box, which they have draped with a Rikers-issued blanket. On the center of the coffin, Zookie, the graffiti tagger, has spray-painted a portrait of Sal in the wheelhouse looking across the Sound to Hart Island. Hemins has a bundle of forsythia that she cut from the bush outside the DOC trailer; she scatters branches in dazzling yellow bloom over the blanket. According to the secret language of flowers, she tells everyone, forsythia is a harbinger of hope.

"Who knew you a shaman, Officer Hemins," Jesús says.

The Rikers angels give her a thumbs-up.

Booker, Justin, Ida and Anna, BB, and Sherry and Aidan O'Shea are sitting on the benches across from Sal. Booker says, "It's the kind of morning Sal loved: big puffy clouds, a good breeze, the sea alive."

Ida is watching him and asks, "Do I know you?" He walks over and whispers something in her ear. "You're funny," she says. He gives Anna a wink.

BB looks at the sky, thinking that he sees a patch of cloud sculpting the face of the Virgin Mary. He elbows Justin and whispers, "Look up, she's there."

"Who?"

"Mary."

By the time Justin looks, other clouds have coalesced with the image, and the likeness of the Mother of God that BB believes he saw has been absorbed into what looks to Justin like a head of cauliflower. "BB, you'd see the Holy Virgin in a potato chip."

Sherry overhears them. "Clouds are clouds."

Booker has brought coffee, worm juice for the inmates, frothy for Hemins, and a stash of sugar and cream for the others. As *Vesuvius* leaves the dock, he makes the rounds with a bottle of Jameson and says, "Sal liked his coffee this way," giving everyone a little pour. Jesús lifts his cup and says, "Cappy!" Billy Hopkins blows *Vesuvius*'s horn.

"Poor bastards," Franklin says.

"Who you talkin' about?" Jesús asks.

"The yardbirds going to take our place. Rikers, that shithole, should be burned down."

Jesús nods. "Hundo P."

Jason has been silent since he boarded the bus from Rikers. He hasn't touched his coffee.

"You gonna toast Cappy, college boy?" Jesús asks.

Jason rests his elbows on his knees and covers his face with his hands. He whispers, "Leave me alone."

Zookie is tapping nervously on Sal's pine box. "How did you do it, Sarge?"

"Father Justin got it started," Booker says.

Justin studied in the seminary with the mayor's nephew. He had convinced City Hall to talk to the DOC commissioner, who gave Booker the green light for Sal, the only corpse to make this crossing that didn't die indigent or unclaimed.

Jesús turns to Justin. "Your bro was gooch."

"That's right," Franklin says. He raises his cup again and says, "He's GOAT."

Justin smiles.

"When it's my time, throw me in the trench with the captain," says Zookie.

Al seems lost and says, "Only the good die young."

"What's that mean?" Jesús asks.

Al gives him a torn-down look and says, "You're so Pollyanna sometimes."

"Yo, what's that, bro?"

Al shakes his head.

Justin says, as if he were talking to himself, "I loved him more than I loved God."

No one knows what to say.

Booker gets up and takes everyone to the wheelhouse to give them a sense of what it felt like for Sal when he made the crossing, while BB stays behind with the crew.

"Hey, look over there," Billy shouts. "Bottlenose dolphins. They're breaching."

Jesús sees them, too, and points to the site. Anna helps Ida up. "Where's Francesco?" Ida asks.

"He's with Sal," Anna says.

"What did Antony do now?"

"Look, Ida, dolphins."

She sits. "Get away from me."

Justin comes over and embraces her. "Ida, it's okay. We're on Sal's boat. We're saying goodbye to Sal."

She smiles. "You're a good boy, Justin."

"What's happening?" Hemins asks.

"They here for Cappy," Jesús says.

Everyone goes to the starboard side, and as if on cue, the dolphins leap once more and swim away.

"A miracle," Jesús says.

"Not sure Sal believed in miracles," Aidan says from the wheelhouse. "I'll give you this, though, those dolphins are beautiful."

Sherry nods. "Ditto."

Justin puts his arms around Ida's shoulders. "They're saluting Sal."

She gives him a look like *you're crazy*.

Jason, his head still in his hands, isn't interested in the dolphins.

"I found your ID by the Mother of God," BB says.

Jason looks up, bewildered. BB tells him, "I've been there, too, kid."

Jason manages a half smile, while BB goes to the wheelhouse to join the others and see what Sal used to see whenever he left for Hart.

~

Sal's is the last pine box that the Rikers angels put in the trench. First, they lift out coffins from the back row to find a spot for Sal that won't be disturbed by the next days' burials. They lower him so carefully into the earth that you'd think the fate of the world depended on setting his coffin just right. Jesús and Zookie fold the blanket into a square and give it to Justin. Before they place two of the other pine boxes on top, Booker announces it's time that they say their last respects. Justin tosses in a photo from Ida's family shitshow wall. In it, he and Sal are kids. Sal's shooting a basket at the rim and Justin's arm is flush against Sal's. They're in the air, the ball in both their hands. "I love you, Sal," Justin says, his voice cracking. Sherry tosses in a photo, too. It's Francesco and her mother at the Saratoga Racetrack. BB takes off a scapular, which he lifted from a drawer in the sacristy. "Maybe Mary will finally do the right thing and protect you, Sal." He kisses the Virgin's image and drops it on the pine box. Hemins throws sunburst forsythia branches into the grave, and the Rikers angels toss in quarters, each making a wish they hope Sal will carry to the afterlife. Anna drops a necklace of Archangel Michael escorting souls to heaven, and Ida, tearing up in a rare moment of recognition, whispers, *"Sal."* Justin gives her the postcard of Cinisi that she kept on her night table: Mount Pecoraro and the sea below. "You always said you were happiest there. It would make Sal feel good."

She looks at the postcard and lets it fall into the trench. "Where's Sal?" she asks.

After a long silence, Jesús says, "I wish you alive, Cappy."

"That ain't happening," Al says. "Try another."

Jason doesn't know why but he tosses in his NYU ID card and says, "Good karma, that's what I hope you carry."

Booker climbs into the trench and flips on an old iPod that loops Eric Clapton's "Tears in Heaven." He places it and a small speaker into the space between Sal's pine box and the trench wall.

"That smokin', Sarge," Jesús says. He helps Booker out of the trench, and the sarge whispers to him, "Sal said you had a knack for making others happy, Jesús. You be good outside."

Aidan tosses in a Mother Pug's bar coaster and passes around the Jameson bottle. He invites everyone to take a swig. The only sound is the breeze rustling the reeds and surf washing up at Mussel Cove. "Hear that," Aidan says, and adds: *Half my friends are dead. / I will make you new ones, said earth. / No, give me them back as they were, instead, / with faults and all, I cried.*

~

No one says a word as they board the bus back to *Vesuvius* until Booker notices BB isn't with them.

"Where's the fisherman?" he asks.

"I think I know," Justin says. He finds BB making one last visit to Mary, placing the head of Baby Jesus at her feet on a bed of mussel shells he had gathered from the cove.

"What's done is done," he says, kneeling before her. Seeing Justin, he says, "She's stopped talking to me."

"That's because you did all she'd hoped for, and she's setting you free."

"You think so." And after a long pause, he says, "She won't tell me why Sal had to die."

Justin, worn out and looking more uncertain than he's ever been, doesn't know what to say.

Once everyone is on board, *Vesuvius* crawls back across the Sound to the DOC dock. Hart Island blurs as a light fog passes over from the east. BB takes Justin's arm and leads him to the stern, where they catch a last glimpse of where Sal now lies before an insistent, denser fog swells and Hart Island and all its dead melt away.

Neighborhood of Bones

When darkness falls on Potter's Field, the dead stir. They prefer Hart Island like this, empty of the living, free to listen to the night: wind whistling, sea tides sloshing, leaves and branches rustling, hawks sweeping low, deer lollygagging across fields, squirrels, mice, and rabbits scurrying everywhere, and their closest companions, beetles and worms, feeding sedulously in the earth. Revenants weaving in and out of grave markers are their only annoyance. These ghosts slink their way through bones and dirt to prowl the chapel and workhouse, ballfield and missile base, hoping for someone to haunt. Good riddance, the dead say, when revenants flee.

Once these dead lived in all your neighborhoods: In the Bronx and Queens. Walkups on Mott, Bleecker, and Christopher. On benches in Tompkins Park, Alphabet City, Harlem, and Washington Square. They died in Flatbush, Greenpoint, and Bedford-Stuy. The Rockaways and Ozone Park. On Mulberry Street. In Bensonhurst. Hell's Kitchen and the Bowery. The dead breathed their last breaths without ceremony. A heart stopped with no one to resuscitate it. A brain hemorrhaged. A malignancy swelled. No one here is a stranger to hopelessness. They were poor and slept restlessly. No one died in a plane crash. Overdose didn't take long. Just five minutes. Sometimes less. And sometimes someone would lie dead for days before a neighbor, catching the scent of decomposition, called 911 and said, "Something's wrong next door."

Many deaths didn't have to happen, but once you're dead, you say, hey, what death makes any sense? The dead don't judge anymore. They made choices; advantages came their way or didn't; some seized a moment, others let it slip by. The babies put into the ground, though, are tough, even for the dead. Who wouldn't weep? Their bones are so small, so inchoate. Still, what's done is done, and once the dead, young or old, are buried, depending on weight, sex, the nature of the dirt, a metamorphosis transpires day by day, and it isn't until the dead become bones and memory that they truly know the fellowship of the grave. This neighborhood of bones.

Captain Sal used to walk among the markers; sometimes, in a warm-hearted voice, he would recite what's written on the stone by the dock: *He must have loved them; He made so many of them.* When Sal talked to himself like this, the dead imagined he was talking to them. Lately, though, he seemed so unhappy, and then, suddenly, not too long ago, Sal returned at night, with two strangers and a freshly dead corpse, trespassers. The dead didn't know what to think. Why would he disturb the quiet of their night? And then the next day, the intruder corpse was unearthed and sent away. Order restored. And now today there's another surprise, though this one not at all unwanted. The dead don't know how or why Sal has ended up with them, but they welcome him into their earth, someone they know. They can almost taste the whiskey mourners pass around. They see how much the captain was cared for and wonder, if love like this is buried in this earth, can it spread through *their* graves, too.

Acknowledgments

I can't imagine having written this novel without the work of Melinda Hunt and the Hart Island Project that she founded. Her film, *Hart Island: An American Cemetery*, and the book *Hart Island* that she and photographer Joel Sternfeld published in 1998 were key sources of inspiration for me. I'm also grateful to the New York City Department of Corrections for allowing me to join a media tour of Hart Island in the spring of 2019, and especially to Rikers Island Press Secretary Jason Kerston and DOC Captain Martin Thompson, who were engaging guides and rich sources of information.

I first read about Hart Island in an Associated Press story that came on the wire some thirty-five years ago while I was working on the copy desk of the *Providence Journal*. New York City's Potter's Field remained implanted in my consciousness and surfaced prominently again about six months before COVID struck in the United States. Much of the novel was written during the time of "confinement" that so many of us experienced during the pandemic. Without the support of friends, the solitary work of writing would have been excruciatingly lonely. I am especially grateful to David Elliott, Marhsa Recknagel, Rita Rogers, Libby Cozza, Frank Barrett, Peter Phipps, Odile Mattiauda, Karen Ziner, Gary and Joan McGuire, Rick and Peggy Zebrun, Wendy Roberts, and Veronique Allard. Most of all I am indebted to longtime friends Jim and Karen Shepard, not only for their friendship but for their keen, invaluable editorial advice. And finally, thanks to all the people at the University of Wisconsin Press, including its director, Dennis Lloyd, for the advice and care they gave me and the novel.